A Fire In His Head

Loreto Todd can tell a story superbly well:
to her innate imaginative art she has added her knowledge
of myth and legend, her awareness of the Celtic inheritance,
expanded by her African and Pacific travels, where she has found
extra dimensions, further explorations of the magic that
blends fantasy and reality.
This book is truly a tour de force.

A. Norman Jeffares

Academic, lecturer and author of many books on Irish writers,
including WB Yeats, Swift, Goldsmith and Joyce.

A Fire In His Head *is a wonderfully engaging journey*
through the world of Irish myth and legend. Loreto Todd
effortlessly takes her reader into an apparently endless
sequence of narratives, exquisitely framed within the story of
Aengus's search for love, beauty and inspiration. It is the most
creative use imaginable of traditional Irish material, which here
serves as a starting point for Todd's engrossing and frequently
mischievous interpretations and inventions.
Intrigue, romance and magic are to be found here in abundance,
all of them contributing to a book which reminds us
of the richness of the Irish literary heritage
and of its infinite potential for rediscovery and renewal.

Robert Dunbar

Lecturer at St Patrick's College of Education
and Trinity College, Dublin.

Loreto Todd

Loreto Todd is Professor of English at the University of Ulster, Coleraine and a Visiting Fellow, Academy of Irish Cultural Heritage. Born in Northern Ireland, she attended Queen's University, Belfast, and, after graduating, went to West Africa as a volunteer. She worked for many years in Leeds University where she was Reader in International English. The author of thirty books, she has travelled extensively and lectured in Africa, America (North and South), Asia (India and Singapore), Australia (Brisbane and Sydney), the Caribbean, and the Pacific (Hawaii, the Solomon Islands, New Zealand, Papua New Guinea).

She has served as Chief Examiner for A-level English Language and been a Consultant to a number of major publishers, UNESCO, the BBC and Yorkshire Television (where she was the Language Advisor for the long-running *Countdown* programme).

She has also carried out sponsored research on literacy. Currently she is director of POWER (Programme of World English Research); is contributing to a Dictionary of World Languages; and is leading research on the *Surnames of Ireland*, an electronic project to appear on CD-Rom/DVD in 2005.

A Fire In His Head

Stories of Wandering Aengus

LORETO TODD

THE O'BRIEN PRESS
DUBLIN

First published 2002 by The O'Brien Press Ltd,
20 Victoria Road, Dublin 6, Ireland.
Tel: +353 1 4923333; Fax: +353 1 4922777
E-mail: books@obrien.ie
Website: www.obrien.ie

ISBN: 0-86278-757-2

British Library Cataloguing-in-Publication Data
Todd, Loreto
A fire in his head : stories of wandering Aengus
1.Folklore - Ireland 2.Mythology, Celtic
I.Title
398.2'09415

1 2 3 4 5 6
02 03 04 05 06 07

The O'Brien Press receives
assistance from

Layout and design: The O'Brien Press Ltd.

Cover painting: 'Rainy Shoreline, Mayo'
© Copyright Mary Lohan
Printing: Betaprint Ltd

The Song of Wandering Aengus by W B Yeats ,
from *The Wind Among The Reeds* (1899) is
reproduced by permission of A P Watt Ltd
on behalf of Michael B Yeats.

Contents

Acknowledgments

It is extremely difficult to list all the people, poems or books that have shaped my imagination and contributed directly or indirectly to *A Fire in His Head*. The most obvious is, of course, Yeats's poem, 'The Song of Wandering Aengus', but it is only one of the threads in the weave. I remember my Tyrone mother telling us stories and singing to us if we were good – and even when we were bad! I remember my Aunt Eileen, who was from Fenit in Kerry, moving effortlessly from a bit of local gossip to conjuring up the majesty of Deirdre and the Sons of Usna. They did not cite their sources and I got them at one remove, or maybe at a thousand removes. Later, I remember sitting – almost literally – at the feet of Sean O'Boyle as he explained how he thought Irish verse and music were linked. I have not done justice to any of these mentors but, even if I did not always comprehend the technicalities of their message, I absorbed their love of the subjects.

Some well-known poems appear in modified form in *A Fire in His Head*. Macha's song in Book Two is an approximation to *Is é saigte gona súain*, a beautiful medieval lament written by an unknown woman. The third year scholar's ideas on what would be lost if poetry was suppressed were voiced by Giolla Brighde Mhac Com Midhe in the thirteenth century; and many will recognise Liamor's song as an anglicised version of Cathal Buí Mac Giolla Gunna's poem, *An Bonnáin Buí* (The Yellow Bittern). These are the obvious borrowings, but my debt to past writers cannot be reduced to a few specific references. Much of the verse is what might be called loose approximations of poems I have read or learnt. Because they are not taken in their entirety from any collection, I should like to refer to texts that have informed my mind or sparked my imagination. Among these are R.K. Alspach's *Irish Poetry from the English Invasion to 1798* (Philadelphia, University of Pennsylvania Press, 1959), James Carney's *Medieval Irish Lyrics* (Dolmen Press, 1985), K. Hoagland's *1000 Years of Irish Poetry* (New York, Devin Adair: 1947), G. Murphy's *Early Irish Lyrics* (Oxford, Clarendon Press, 1956) and S. Mac Réamoinn's *The Pleasures of Gaelic Poetry* (London, Allen Lane, 1982). Not all my sources, however, have appeared in the written medium. I learnt a great deal about poetry from a Coalisland man, called Francis Quinn, who never published what he wrote, but shared his creations with all those who were willing to listen. In time-honoured fashion, of course, I should stress that none of the above can be held responsible for any error or infelicity that may occur in my versions.

Finally, I should thank the friends with whom I have discussed books and poems and plays and sport. Their thoughts and ideas have influenced mine. In particular, I would like to record my gratitude to my extended family. It can't be easy living with an enthusiast! I'd also like to offer my sincere thanks to two Marys: Mary Penrith, who commented on an earlier version of *A Fire in His Head*, and Mary Webb, who edited with skill, sensitivity and courage!

Introduction

We cannot know for certain when the pre-Christian stories of gods and goddesses began to circulate in Ireland. What we do know is that they were first written down by monks perhaps two centuries after St Patrick converted the country. Ireland's deities were not like the Hebrew God. They were not eternal, omnipotent, unknowable. Nor indeed were they either religious or the upholders of any obvious moral code. Rather, they were like those of Greece, human in all ways except two: they had supernatural powers and they lived almost for ever. Like humans, however, they took pleasure in good food; they knew the pangs of love and the anguish of jealousy; they delighted in music and poetry; and they found opportunities for lovemaking, often with someone else's spouse! They also had children, some of whom were envious of their parents' power. Just as Saturn could be deposed by Zeus in Greek mythology, Irish gods could plot against their relatives, and, on occasion, usurp their position.

Aengus, the god of love and poetry, is often referred to as Aengus Óg or Aengus Mac Óg and although these names are usually translated as 'Young Aengus' or 'Aengus Young Son', it has also been suggested that the second title could mean 'Aengus Son of a Virgin'. Whether or not we accept that interpretation, his birth was indeed unique. He was the son of Dagda, who was often described as Ollathir, 'Father of all', and of Boann, a mother goddess. When Dagda first met Boann, he fell instantly in love with her and was not put off by the fact that she was already married. He sent her husband Elcmar on a short journey, and although Elcmar was suspicious of Dagda's intentions, he agreed to the journey, knowing that it would take only a day. Dagda, however, caused the sun to stand still for nine months so that his son, Aengus, could be conceived in the morning and born in the evening of the same day.

Aengus was like his father in his love of music and beautiful women. One of the best-known stories tells of how the young god fell asleep. In his dream, he saw a beautiful maiden, called Caer. When he woke up, he knew that life would have no meaning for him without her and so he began his quest. He enlisted the help of Bodhb and eventually found her near the river Boyne. Caer was living on the lake with 149 other maidens. Having found Caer, Aengus was faced with two small problems. Caer and the other young women had been transformed into swans, and they were bound to each other by a silver chain. He knew that he would only be able to release his beloved from her spell if … but that's another story for another time!

The Aengus tale has appeared in many versions and is known throughout the world because of William Butler Yeats's poem, 'The Song of Wandering Aengus'. Like many people, I first read the poem as a young teenager and, like many teenagers before and since, I was captivated by the ideas of love and destiny and the promise of fulfilment. Yeats does not mention names in his poem and it is only because of the title that we can link it to Aengus.

A Fire in his Head is certainly based on the Yeats poem and it certainly leans heavily on Irish folktale traditions. I have not tried to follow straight lines, however, preferring to be true to the spirit, rather than the letter, of the tradition. This novel is, therefore, like an intricate Celtic design, blending, adapting, restructuring strands, and it is not bound by the strictures of time any more than our memories are.

Loreto Todd, Tyrone, 2002

The Song of Wandering Aengus

I went out to the hazel wood,
Because a fire was in my head,
And cut and peeled a hazel wand,
And hooked a berry to a thread;
And when white moths were on the wing,
And moth-like stars were flickering out,
I dropped the berry in a stream
And caught a little silver trout.

When I had laid it on the floor
I went to blow the fire aflame,
But something rustled on the floor
And some one called me by my name;
It had become a glimmering girl
With apple blossom in her hair
Who called me by my name and ran
And faded through the brightening air.

Though I am old with wandering
Through hollow lands and hilly lands,
I will find out where she has gone,
And kiss her lips and take her hands;
And walk among long dappled grass,
And pluck till time and times are done
The silver apples of the moon,
The golden apples of the sun.

W B Yeats

BOOK ONE

A Fire In His Head

1: Midlight

Midsummer night. A time when darkness lasted for less than half the day and even at midnight the sky was already touched with the omens of dawn. Aengus called this time midlight.

Aengus was, some would say, a young god. He could already ride as fast as the wind in *Faoide*, the month of winds. And he could strike a ball from one end of the land to the other. But feats of prowess were so easy to Aengus that they gave him little joy. What he wanted was to be a poet, a maker of lines and melodies that were so beautiful even the birds would come to listen to him and learn from him.

Sometimes words came easily to Aengus, sometimes even whole lines, but tonight he had created nothing. His brain was on fire with seething thoughts, but they stayed unrealised, unaired. 'What should I do? Where should I go?' he wondered. Sleep was out of the question. He felt he was being guided towards someone, towards something, but what? No answers came, only the cacophony of thoughts that never got to the point of words or even of mind pictures.

Aengus decided to do what he often did when he needed to sort out his mind. He would get a rod, sit by the river and let the quietness of fishing impose a semblance of order on his mind. There were coll trees all around him, trees associated with druids and their deeds of magic. Aengus gently cupped the oval, serrated leaves, each perfectly formed by Nature's unseen teeth, each like a perfect note in an unheard melody.

One day, I'll write a song that's as unique as a leaf, he thought. But perhaps I'm already touching a song. The leaf is singing silently in my hand of its uniqueness, of its transitoriness. Perhaps we can only admire a beauty that is touched by death. Even melodies die if people forget them.

He touched the spot where the tiny nuts were growing. In two months or three, near the end of *Lughnasa*, these little promises of nuts would be round and brown and ready to eat.

Aengus chose a thin branch, supple and strong. He broke it off gently, not tearing it. Then he stroked the wound in the wood, making it whole again. He sang quietly to himself, a tune that children often sang as they cut and peeled wattles they were turning into fishing rods:

> *May the maker of trees make my rod last for life!*
> *May the giver of life give me fish of the best!*
> *May the mother of all keep me safe from all strife*
> *And if strong winds must blow, let them blow from the west!*

They were foolish words really, but the rhythm of the words matched the rhythm of peeling and preparing. Soon the rod was ready, a rod that looked silver in the moonlight, a rod that only needed a berry on a string to coax any fish from any stream.

The river was close, a flowing ribbon of molten silver. It was called Owenmore, the big river, not for its size, but to remember Big Owen who had drowned himself in it. Owen had felt the need to journey to the other world and the easiest way to do that was through water. Aengus could have saved him, but there are times when the kindest act a god can perform is to let a woman or a man choose their own time to go. Even gods cannot will life on one who no longer wants it.

The end of the rod bent under the stress of the catch. Quickly, in one fluid movement, Aengus flicked his wrist and landed a silver trout on the grass. It jerked once or twice and then lay still.

'Don't worry, little trout,' whispered Aengus. 'Soon you will be in me and of me and while I live, you will live. Nothing ever dies totally. Nothing ever lives forever without joining with another.'

Aengus gathered twigs together. Then, his head bent, he lit a fire. Every flame was like life, like death – both sustainer and destroyer.

'Aengus!' A gentle voice broke into his dream. 'Aengus, I've been waiting for you. What took you so long?'

'What?' Aengus looked up and could see no one.

'Aengus, I'm here.'

And she was. The little trout had vanished. In its place lay a maiden whose eyes shone brighter than the moon or the fire. She wore a silver dress and her hair was wreathed in apple blossoms. Never had Aengus seen such beauty or known such joy. This was his destiny as sure as the river had been Owen's.

'I've been waiting for you for all eternity,' he breathed, and watched as she stood up.

There were no sandals on her feet. Nothing between her and the grass. Nothing but a short space between him and perfect fulfilment. As he stretched out his hand for her, she turned, rose onto her toes, and calling, 'Aengus, follow me, follow me,' she faded into the half light.

For a moment he stood, unable to move, unable to act. 'Aengus,' echoed the voice, now far off. 'Aengus, don't lose me.' And then even the sound was gone.

Aengus shook his head to clear his brain. 'Am I mad?' he said aloud. 'Maybe the moon can really make men mad and women beautiful?'

Perhaps it had all been a dream. But there on the ground was a single blossom, loosed from the maiden's hair as she stood up.

'She was here. She was mine and I've lost her.' He picked up the flower, silvery white and edged with pink, and he heard her voice in his head, 'Aengus, follow me.'

And he did.

2: I have a Ball of Yarns in My Head

Aengus walked in the midlight, following his lost love. Although his eyes could no longer see her or his ears hear her, his spirit felt her presence and echoed her call as though she was beside him. And his spirit knew her name: it was Caillte. On he walked through the woods, not worrying about distance or direction, but certain always that somehow, somewhere, Caillte waited for him.

Hours passed, but Aengus did not stop until the sun rode high in the sky and the pangs from his stomach reminded him that even gods get hungry. He looked around and saw that he was standing outside a long, elongated house with '*Teach a Phobail*' written on it in lovely, clear script – an inn where a wanderer could get rest and sustenance. 'What is a *Teach a Phobail* doing here?' he wondered. As if to answer his question, out stepped the owner.

'A hundred thousand welcomes, traveller!' said a voice with a hundred thousand smiles in it. 'By the looks of you, boy, you could be doing with a bite and a sup. You've stepped some this day, or your dusty clothes are the beginning and end of a lie. Come in and rest and wash and eat. While you eat, you can listen to my wife's music or, better still, you can hear my stories and tell me yours. And I'll make a bargain with you, stranger. When you have heard my story, if you can prove to me that you have ever before been so well entertained, then you will pay me nothing for your food and lodging. There's my hand on it.'

Aengus felt his hand being gripped by the owner of the smiling voice and gently but firmly he was led through the door. His host was tall, extremely tall, not quite a giant but not far short of one. And he had the blackest hair and the reddest beard and the whitest teeth that Aengus had ever seen.

'My name is Gáire Mór,' he introduced himself, 'and it is my pleasure to be serving ... ?' He waited, smiling.

'Aengus.'

'Yes,' said Gáire, 'that would be right. Well, young Aengus, sit yourself down and rest till my wife prepares a bath for you. And I, Aengus, I will ready your food and prepare my story. You look like a man who has a long journey ahead of him. Rest, and when you're at yourself again, I'll tell you a yarn that will have you biting your lip with the joy of anticipation.'

In an hour or so, Aengus was well washed and well rested. He was also very hungry, but the smells coming from the out-kitchen assured him that the wait would be worth it. Gáire appeared again, almost on cue, and set the food on the low table before Aengus.

'Eat, young Aengus, eat until you're as full as a stuffed trout and as fat as a ball of butter. Eat until you think you'll never eat again and then eat a little more, for you know where this bite is, but you don't know where the next bite's coming from.'

Aengus did as he was bid, and found the food delicious. Seeing him pause for a moment, Gáire took the opportunity to find out more about his guest.

'Where are you bound, Aengus? Are you journeying to a fixed destination or to where the great god pleases?'

'I'm searching for a girl.'

'A girl, is it? Well, that should be no hardship to an upstanding young man like you. Would it be any girl you're seeking, or a particular one? Oh, I can see it's a particular one. Is it a girl running with the speed of a deer? A girl with hair the colour of honey, with skin like soft moonlight and with eyes that neither star nor diamond could match?'

'You've seen her?' exclaimed Aengus.

'Ah, well now, not exactly. I haven't seen her but I've heard tell of her. And if she's the one you must find, well, eat up, eat up and gather your strength for it's not likely that you'll catch up with her tomorrow or tomorrow's morrow. But you will find her if you do not lack courage and perseverance. In the long run, Aengus lad, every achievement in life can be put down to courage and perseverance. Tell me, did you ever hear tell of Maeldun? Yes? I can see from your eyes that you did, but let me assure you, you may think you know Maeldun's story, but you don't know more than the half, or maybe the quarter of it. I have this story from a man that was there, and there is no greater authority than an eyewitness account. Eat now, Aengus, and I'll tell you how a man of courage and perseverance can conquer the world.'

3: The Story of Maeldun

It was long ago when the rivers and the sea were full of fish. There were deer and hare in the woods, berries on the trees and a drop of the water-o'-life, *uisce beatha*, to drown sorrows or greet joys. There were also young men and beautiful young women, and you'll always find one or other or both at the heart of a good narrative.

In that time lived a fine young man called Ailill Ochair Aga, a man with the courage of an eagle and the beauty of spring water. Like you, Aengus, he had an eye for a beautiful maiden, but the maiden he had his eye on was not for him. She was dedicated as a virgin and only a fool or a poet would break the laws of man and god. But that's not the story I want to tell you, although it's a grand story to be sure, full of passion and power. It is of his son I wish to speak. Ailill Ochair Aga mated with his maiden and the union produced a son who was given up to the queen. She called him Maeldun and brought him up as her own child.

Need I tell you that, in time, Maeldun had fire in his blood and strength in his arm? No one could conquer him in the mock battles the young princes played at. As you know, Aengus, to be the best is not always to be the happiest. People envy your prowess and seek to outdo you in guile. There was one young man in particular, a lad called Dúrú, who could not overcome Maeldun in any challenge. Dúrú worked at his skills until he was master of the court – master, that is, except for Maeldun. Whether they fought with fists or swords or lances or bat and ball, Maeldun always got the better of him. One day, while they wrestled, Dúrú felt sure he was winning, when suddenly his back was on the ground and Maeldun was claiming yet another victory.

'That was a great fight, Dúrú,' said Maeldun, 'a great fight indeed. Here's my hand on it.'

'I won't take the hand of a bastard,' snarled Dúrú. 'You're only good at fighting because your mother was a witch and your father was, well, that's anyone's guess.'

The fight and the breath were knocked out of Maeldun by Dúrú's venom. For a time he stood stunned. Then the honour of the queen, his mother, had to be defended:

'Dúrú, my mother is a queen and no witch. You have insulted her honour and I cannot let that go unpunished. I challenge you to a fight to the death. Choose your weapons. We fight at once.'

'But you *are* a bastard,' insisted Dúrú, 'a bastard and not fit to live with honourable men. Ask the queen about your pedigree and if I have spoken one word of a lie, you won't have to fight me. I'll fall on my own sword.'

Well, Aengus boy, eat up, eat up. You can guess what happened. Maeldun found his mother and soon she had the beginning and end of the narrative.

'Tell me it's not true, Mother,' Maeldun urged.

'Son,' answered the queen, 'I am your mother in every way that counts. You came to me when you were but one day old and I have loved you and taught you and cherished you like my other children.'

'But I am not your flesh and blood?'

'You and I share the same blood, for your mother was my kinswoman, but I did not carry you for nine months or know pain at your birth.'

'I'm a bastard, then?'

'You were born out of wedlock, yes, because your mother was dedicated as a virgin and so, for her, marriage was not possible. But your father loved her and would have married her.'

'Who was this father of mine? He was a coward to leave my mother and myself without his name and protection.'

'No coward he, Maeldun. To give up your life is easier than to give up your love. He had to sacrifice his desires so as not to call down on us the voice of an angry god. We pleaded with him to leave, and for all our sakes he did, but the name of Ailill Ochair Aga is the name of a hero and no coward. It is his blood running in your veins that gives you your courage and your strength and your prowess. What he and your mother did was wrong, but they paid a heavy price for their love. He had to leave his people and his heritage. She lost her son and died young.'

'Where is Ailill Ochair Aga now?' asked Maeldun.

'I do not know. No one knows, for part of his punishment was that he would never get in touch with his seed, breed or generation ever again. Leave things as they are, Maeldun. You are my son in name and in deed. Forget your father and think only of us.'

'I can't, Mother. I must find my father and learn who I am.'

Well, Aengus, knowledge is a strange thing. To have knowledge that you don't want can be a millstone around your neck, and the only way you can get rid of the weight is by getting more knowledge – knowledge that you do want. So it was with Maeldun. He visited every man and woman of the queen's age to ask about his father, but no one knew any more than she did. At last, he went to the oldest of the druids, a man who had talked so much to and with his gods that he was nearly as knowledgeable as a god himself. As Maeldun approached the hawthorn grove in which Seanfhear lived, he heard a voice:

'Maeldun, go home. Do not enter this hawthorn grove, because if you do your life will be changed, changed utterly. You will be at the mercy of the wind and sea and man and beast. Go home. Live as a prince and die in your bed.'

'I can't,' said Maeldun, as he put his foot within the boundaries of the grove. 'I can't and I won't.'

'Come then,' sighed Seanfhear. 'Come and I will tell you what you need to know, but you would have been a happier man, Maeldun, if you had not been goaded by Dúrú's jealous taunts.'

Maeldun found Seanfhear sitting by a fire, looking into the flames. He sat by the old man and watched as he cast a handful of leaves on the fire and read the pictures in the rising smoke.

'You seek Ailill Ochair Aga, but you seek in vain. He is long dead and already his body is part of the earth and the sky and his spirit roams with the wind and the waves. He did not die a hero's death, facing his enemy in honourable combat; no, he was murdered by a coward who killed him from behind. But death was no torment for him, rather a welcome release from the life he valued so little.'

'How will I find the man who killed my father?'

'You would be well advised not to try, Maeldun, but I can see no words of mine will dissuade you. The man you seek is alive and well. But you will find him and avenge your father only if you follow my instructions exactly. There must be no deviation, no additions, and no subtractions. I can tell you *how*, but only you can decide *if.*'

'Tell me how, wise man, and I will follow your instructions to the letter. May my body wither if I deviate ... '

'Don't bring bad luck on yourself, Maeldun. I can give you instructions, but you alone may decide how to carry them out. To find your father's murderer you will need a boat. This boat must be built within one moon's cycle of the day you start. You will begin on the morning following the first full moon in the Month of the Yellow Eye and finish on the evening before the first full moon in the Month of the Great God, Lugh. You must take with you young men to the number of two sevens and three. Not one man more or one man fewer, do you hear, Maeldun?'

'I hear you, wise man.'

'Well hear me and heed me. Now go, for the night of the full moon approaches.'

Gáire stopped long enough to drink deeply from the ale jug in front of Aengus.

'Well,' encouraged Aengus, 'and did he build his boat?'

'He did indeed,' replied Gáire, and picked up the threads of his story again.

Aengus built his boat, and a finer boat never floated on the waters. And he picked his seventeen companions with care and attention, making sure that his foster brothers were not among them. After all, it was enough for the queen to lose one son. When they were all on board and their vessel about to be thrown on the mercy of God and of the waves, Maeldun saw three of his brothers swimming out to join him.

'Go back,' shouted Maeldun, 'go back. You cannot come.'

'We're going with you,' yelled the brothers. 'This is our fight too. No man goes into battle without his brothers.'

And Maeldun, heedless of Seanfhear's warning, pulled his brothers on board, glad of their company and proud of their courage.

The sea was calm and the wind light, and they journeyed swiftly for one whole day and part of a night.

'Look, Maeldun,' called the navigator, Diuran, 'there are two small islands ahead of us. I can see lights and I think I hear people singing.'

'Make for the shore,' ordered Maeldun, 'but go quietly.'

Gently and silently, slowly but surely the boat edged towards the first of the two islands. Diuran was right. As they neared the shore they could hear clearly the sound of music and celebration. There were houses built close to the shore, and through the open door of the biggest house they could see a group of men. One stood up, a black-haired man with a cunning face:

'You are all boasting about your deeds of war, but I am the greatest warrior of all. I, I alone, killed Ailill Ochair Aga with one blow of my sword, and no relative of his has ever challenged me. None would dare!'

'I will dare. I, Maeldun, son of Ailill Ochair Aga, I will dare. Choose whatever weapon you wish and I will send you to the next world faster than you despatched my father.'

Maeldun shouted his challenge from the prow of his boat, but just as he attempted to put his foot on the shore, a sudden squall seized the vessel and hurled it back from the island. A mighty wind roared all round, whipping the waves into a frenzy. The boat was twisted one way by the wind and tossed back again by the waves. There was no sky to be seen and no daylight. It was as if the wind and the sea were having a contest to see which of them could hurl the little boat furthest.

Maeldun looked at his brothers: 'This is all your fault. Seanfhear warned me not to take extra men with me, but I didn't listen.'

The brothers would have replied that if that was the case, then it was really Maeldun's fault for not telling them, but there was no time to talk. The boat was caught up in a churning maelstrom and then spewed out into the mother and father of all storms.

Maeldun's adventures had begun.

4: Sweet and Low

Have you ever travelled on the wide mid-ocean, Aengus, where the sea and the sky are constantly at war? Have you heard winds that roar, not like lions but like a thousand claps of thunder rolled into a roar? Have you seen the waves towering mountain-high above your head so that you think every minute is your last? Well, if you haven't, Aengus, then you know nothing of what Maeldun and his twenty men faced. I wasn't there myself, mind you, but I know a man who was, and it is from the very mouth of that individual that my story flows.

For three long days and three long nights our men struggled to keep their boat on the top of the water. There was little time for cursing fate and no time at all for eating or sleeping. They were exhausted to the point of welcoming death when the smallest crack of blue appeared between the metal grey of the sky and the seething grey of the sea.

'Maeldun, Maeldun,' shouted Oigín, the youngest man on board.

Did I say 'man'? Ah well, he was hardly more than a boy before they left court, but now he had aged with the weight of experience that was exceeded only by Seanfhear, the Druid.

'Maeldun, Maeldun,' Oigín yelled again, cupping his hands around his mouth because the wind carried his words away faster than a seagull carries its fish. 'Maeldun, Maeldun, do you see that sliver of blue? Either there's good weather over there or we're coming to the edge of the sea.'

'Head for it anyway, whether it's the crack of light or the crack of doom,' instructed Maeldun. 'Better to fall over the edge and join my father than to spend another hour fighting the elements.'

Off they sailed towards the slit of blue and soon it widened into a rupture through which they could glimpse land.

'Land – dead ahead, Maeldun,' reported Oigín.

'Land!' echoed Maeldun. 'Land, boys, where we can rest and eat and get our bearings.'

'Shouldn't we be careful?' asked Diuran. 'We don't know where we are or what the people are like. Maybe we should sail round a bit, just in case.'

'Don't be such a baby,' Maeldun laughed. 'There's nothing in this whole world that could be worse than the storm we've just been through. Having survived that, there's nothing we can't survive.'

And everyone on the boat, barring Diuran, was of this mind and why shouldn't they be? The land that lay before them was green, with softly sloping hills and one conical mountain. The trees were tall and straight, mainly oak and yew, and their tops barely moved in the light wind that caressed them. And the flowers! No words of mine could describe them. Now, if you could imagine a very large lily and multiply by twenty or thirty times the height and width, then you might have some idea of the size and grandeur of the flowers. And as for colours! Rubies and sapphires and emeralds were poor, faded things in comparison. And there was one other thing about these flowers that made them remarkable: they grew down and not up. It was as if there was a roof over the land from which the flowers dangled like beautiful lanterns.

'Make for a cove, lads,' encouraged Maeldun. 'We'll camp under a tree, build a fire and with the help of the Mother of All, we'll find food and rest and somebody to tell us where we are.'

The boat made for a little inlet and Maeldun lifted his spear. He cast it ahead of them and it stuck, firm but quivering, a boat-length from the shore.

'That ground looks as solid to me as any I've trod on,' he declared. 'Follow me.'

They all got out, first Maeldun, then the others and lastly Diuran. Up the hill they walked, the last rays of the setting sun warm on their shoulders and the scent from the flowers more refreshing than any perfumed bath.

'I have to admit,' said Diuran, 'that it's like the fields of paradise. I would not be surprised to find that it is a land flowing with fresh water and honey. Not to mention fine deer and … '

'Don't start us thinking about food we mightn't find,' warned Maeldun. 'Tonight, we'll settle for fish cooked over a fire. Tomorrow, we'll find all that we could ask for and then some.'

Morning came unnoticed by the tired men. In spite of the fact that the sun had been up for two hours, they were still stretched out around the fire that had been built high by Diuran. The air warmed up, the light penetrated their eyelids and a buzzing noise gradually caused them to wake. They stretched and yawned and began to think of food.

'What's that droning noise, Maeldun?' asked Oigín. 'It's very loud, isn't it? Is it the wind, do you think, or is it people snoring?'

'Now, how would I know?' asked a hungry Maeldun. 'Am I a mind reader? I only know that it woke me up before I have had my fill of sleep, but, now that we are up, we should make good use of the day. Let us walk round the island in groups, four to the north, four to the south, four to the rising sun, four to its place of setting and the remaining four can make this site more comfortable for us and check the boat to see if it needs patching. We'll set out when we've had something to eat. Is there any fish left?'

While they were cooking the fish, young Oigín walked eastward towards where they had seen the flowers. Although the sun was in his eyes, the ever strengthening smell of the perfume and the swelling drone assured him that he was heading in the right direction. Suddenly, a cloud appeared over his head, big, dark and threatening – and very noisy.

'That's funny,' thought Oigín. 'It doesn't look like rain anywhere else and I never heard a cloud drone before.'

He looked up and the more his eyes grew accustomed to the dark, the more he saw; and the more he saw, the less he understood. The cloud was low, only twenty or so paces above his head. That's if you could take paces uproads as well as you can take them sideroads. Well, twenty paces or thereabouts above his head was the oddest cloud Oigín had ever seen. It had hairy edges. And it had two long, thin, hairy branch-like protuberances hanging from its middle, one to the left and one to the right. Coloured stripes encircled the cloud, some black, some orange, all of them hairy. And the noise – Oigín had never heard a noise like it, so he had nothing to compare it with. It was a bit like the snoring of a giant, with a wind yowling inside it and the rasp of sawing wood running through it. Only it was so much louder than all of these that it was like comparing a louse to a lion. As he looked up in wonder, the cloud began to move in an anti-clockwise direction, coming lower and lower and getting louder and louder.

'Look out, Oigín,' shouted Diuran. 'There's a giant bee flying over you.'

'A what?'

'A bee, a great big, buzzing bumble-bee! Run!'

It was too late. The bee – for that's what it was – caught Oigín up in its long legs – for that's what they were – and carried him off towards the flowers.

'Jump Oigín, jump,' called Diuran. 'Better to break your leg in the fall than risk what will happen if it takes you back to its hive.'

But Oigín could not jump. Indeed, if the truth is to be told, he could barely move, for the hairs on the legs of the bee were so sticky that each time Oigín moved, another part of his body became even more firmly stuck to the bee. Only his mouth was free and he used it: 'Help me, Diuran, help me. In the name of Lugh, get me down.'

Diuran could not hear him, for Oigín's calls were droned out by the noise made by this gigantical insect. And even if he had heard Oigín, he still could have done nothing. Diuran's legs were weak from the shock, but he managed to stumble unsteadily back to the camp. Maeldun saw him approaching and called out:

'Have you been drinking, or what? You're like a drunk man running on even drunker legs.'

'Didn't I tell you to be careful about this island?' gasped Diuran. 'I warned you, but none of you would listen. Now it's too late. It's got Oigín.'

'What's got Oigín?' the others chorused.

'The bee! That droning noise that woke us up – that came from a giant bee, and it's carried Oigín away to the hive.'

Maeldun looked at Diuran and then at his men: 'Don't anyone else put a foot outside this camp. There must be something in the air or on the land that makes men mad. Come now, Diuran. Lie down here and rest your mind. You'll soon be yourself again.'

Diuran was stunned. 'You think I'm mad, don't you, but I'm saner than any of you.'

'Of course you are, man,' coaxed Maeldun. 'All you need is a little rest and ... in the name of Lugh ... ' his voice broke into a shriek, 'in the name of Lugh, what is that?'

'That' was a sky full of enormous bees that were heading towards the camp.

'Head for the sea, men,' roared Maeldun. 'Cover yourselves up to the nose in water.'

Maeldun's roar and the sight and sound of the droning heavens galvanised the men and put firm muscle even into Diuran's legs. Before the bee clouds could reach them, every last man was in the sea, with the water up over his top lip. For an hour or maybe four, the bees circled, blotting out sky and sun, droning menacingly. No one moved. Fear rooted their feet to the seabed. Hunger and fatigue were forgotten. At last the bees began to leave, first one, then two, until finally the last one flew off in the direction of the glade.

'Let's get into the boat,' urged Finbar, the tallest of the crew and the one who could most easily raise his head out of the water. 'Let's leave this hellish place quickly before they come back. If I hadn't seen those monsters with my own eyes, I wouldn't have believed it and I still wouldn't believe it if we weren't all stuck here in the water like old shipwrecks. I'll take my chances with the waves any day.'

'Finbar's right,' came a chorus. 'Let's escape while we have the chance.'

Maeldun agreed with his crew, 'We don't know what other horrors are lurking here. If the bees are that size, what size must the birds be?'

'I haven't seen any birds,' replied Machaire, 'and I've been looking for them all morning.'

'It would have served you better if you'd looked for bees,' ssaid Finbar, testily.

'But what about Oigín?' asked Diuran. 'We can't leave without Oigín.'

'Oigín is dead, I'm sure of it,' insisted Finbar. 'You saw the size of those creatures. What chance would he have against them?'

'We just can't leave him, can we, Maeldun?'

'I think Finbar's right,' replied Maeldun. 'We can't risk everyone's life for the sake of a boy who's probably dead already.'

'Well, I don't think we should go without trying to find him,' persisted Diuran. 'After all, bees don't eat insects and they don't like to sting because if they sting you they die.'

'That's what everybody says, Diuran,' agreed Maeldun, 'but have you ever seen a bee die after stinging somebody? Well, have you? And even if it's true, how do we know that these bees are like the bees we have at home? For all we know, they're just as carnivorous as we are.'

The men argued and debated, but eventually they agreed with Diuran that if they turned their back on the youngest of their party, they could not expect luck for the rest of their journey. They made their way cautiously to the shore, each man keeping his toes in good running shape just in case the bees returned. As soon as the sun had gone down, Maeldun took charge.

'Diuran, Finbar, get your lances and shields and come with me. Machaire, find something that will make a lot of smoke. The rest of you, make the boat ready to leave. If we are not back by sunrise, go without us. We must hope that these bees are like the ones back home, taking their sleep from sunset until sunrise, and that they can be mesmerised by smoke. Let's go.'

The three men set off towards the glade, keeping as quiet as possible and hoping that they would see a hive.

'In the name of Lugh,' ejaculated Diuran, 'look at that mountain! It's not a mountain! It's the hive!'

That stopped them in their tracks. Maybe Finbar was right. Maybe they should just go back to the boat and forget about Oigín. But it didn't seem right. They should at least try to rescue him. The men separated, and squatting at the base of the living mountain, each found a hole through which he could see into the inside of the hive.

'There!' whispered Diuran, excitedly, 'I can see him, in a cocoon near that big thing. Almighty Mother! That must be the queen bee. She's so huge I can't see where she begins or ends.'

'Never mind where she ends,' said Machaire. 'Help me raise some smoke. It's his only chance.'

Machaire had built a fire near one of the holes in the hive wall. As he covered the flames with the dew-damp grass, he prayed as he had never prayed before that the stories of bees being calmed by smoke were true. 'If they're not,' he mused, 'we'll all be in there with young Oigín.'

All three fanned the smoke towards the hole. The smoke was thick and so scented that the men began to feel sleepy. Only fear kept them awake.

'I'll go in and look for Oigín,' Diuran offered. 'After all, it was my idea.'

'Fine,' answered a relieved Maeldun, 'but cover your mouth

and nose. If that smoke gets in your lungs you will be asleep on your feet, like a horse.'

Diuran soaked a cloth in urine and tied it round his mouth and nose. He remembered being told somewhere, sometime that the acid helped to counteract smoke. 'If it's a lie,' he thought as he fought his instinctive nausea, 'I'll remember who told me and break his teeth!' He squeezed in through the hole and made his way to the place where the queen bee towered and billowed into infinity. The smoke was strong and his eyes began to smart, but the wet cloth protected his breathing.

'Oigín,' he whispered, as loudly as he dared. 'Oigín, can you hear me?'

'Diuran, Diuran, is it you? I'm over here.'

'Well, get up and come over here, you fool,' called an exasperated Diuran.

'I can't. I'm caught in this cocoon. Have you got a knife with you?'

Diuran had. Quickly he cut through the sticky, white fibres until there was a hole big enough for Oigín to crawl out.

'Come on, boy,' he urged, 'so far so good, but we don't want to press our luck. Follow me.'

'Will we not take some honey with us, Diuran? Look at the size of the combs; it could be useful.'

'Just one, then, if we can manage it.'

Between them they wrestled out a huge wedge dripping with honey. Then they rejoined Maeldun and Machaire and all four ran for the boat as fast as their legs would carry them.

'Get us out of this place,' roared Maeldun as he clambered aboard. No sooner had the words left his mouth than the crew had the boat underway and they were heading away from the island of the bees.

Once they were safely out to sea, Maeldun clasped Oigín by the shoulder. 'Thank the Mother of All that you are safe, that we are all safe and free. I have had enough of adventure for now. Let's go home.'

Everyone agreed wholeheartedly, but at the back of their minds was the same question, 'Where is home?'

Not one among them knew the direction or the distance, but no one gave voice to their doubts. They might not know how to get home but they all felt that the least they could do was try. And they did. They did. Try, that is.

5: A Year and a Day

Gáire stopped speaking and sat back, wearing a look of quiet satisfaction at a story well told.

'Well?' encouraged Aengus.

'Well what?' asked his host.

'Are you not going to tell me what happened to Maeldun and his men?'

'Well, that depends.'

'Depends on what?'

'Depends on whether or not you plan to pay for your food and lodging.'

'Of course I'll pay, Gáire,' insisted Aengus. 'Yours is a story well worth listening to, but it lacks an ending. Tell me – and cut it short if you wish – did Maeldun ever find his father's assassin again?'

'Young men!' sighed Gáire. 'They want to know the end before they've heard the beginning of a story. Things were different in my day. I would willingly have sat at the feet of the makers of tales and not moved till they moved, not slept till they slept, not eaten until I was invited to eat.'

'Then won't you join me in this wonderful feast?' Aengus asked Gáire with a smile. 'You must forgive my bad manners and my haste, but I cannot stay long. I must find Caillte and I must find her soon. Finish your story, Gáire. Tell me about Maeldun.'

Gáire helped himself to some food, wiped his mouth and said:

'Well and good now, Aengus. I'll do as you bid, but I must tell it in my own way and in my own time.'

'Agreed. In your own way and in your own time, Gáire. Just as long as I hear about Maeldun.'

'You know, you remind me of Maeldun, Aengus. With the help of the powers that be, you won't be wave-tossed as he was, but a journey is never easy, especially if you don't really know where you're going. But enough of that. Where was I? Oh, yes.'

Maeldun's journey continued. Day followed night and night followed day, on and on and on till no one was sure whether they had left home a week before or a month. There was no division to the sea and there was no division to the time. They caught fish and they ate it raw, washed down by rain. If it hadn't been for the comb of honey, they might have died of the boredom of their diet.

Then, when everyone was dulled and lulled into expecting nothing, Oigín cried out: 'Land, I see land, again. I do, I really do.'

The men were on their feet, rejoicing, all traces of hopelessness banished. But Maeldun called for calm.

'I rejoice as much as you do. But let us be more cautious this time. Let us take time to sail around this new land,' advised Maeldun. 'Diuran was right before and we should have listened to him. Let's follow the coast and see that there are no unwelcome surprises awaiting us before we decide to land.'

The men were tired and heart sore of being at sea, and the land looked so inviting that they were tempted to rebel. But sense prevailed and everyone agreed that they had been over-hasty before. As they sailed round, it soon became clear that they had found another island, but this one looked altogether more natural. The grass was green and there were apple trees and everything grew the right way up. And in the distance they could see what looked like horses. They completed one full circuit of the island and then went part way round again, just to be sure.

'I'm for risking it,' said Maeldun's brother, Tirelach. 'I'll go first.'

'I'll go with you,' came another voice.

'And I.'

'And I.'

'Tirelach goes,' announced Maeldun, 'and two other men. Only the three of you. Take a good look over the island and if all is well, we'll join you.'

Tirelach picked his brother Tirechan and another strong man called Aodan, and when the boat was close enough to shore, the three jumped off together and waded onto dry land.

At first they were frightened, for the land seemed to move up and down under their feet, but soon they realised that it was they, not the land that moved. They'd been on the whales' road for such a long time that they undulated to the rhythm of the waters.

The men walked round the island, taking care to steer clear of the horses, which looked perfectly ordinary except for the long nails protruding from their feet, where you would have expected to see nothing but a hoof. The scent of the apple trees lured them to an orchard laden with big, juicy fruit. They weren't the red or green apples that the men were familiar with back home. These hung from the trees like golden suns and their smell was overpoweringly sweet.

'Listen, men,' said Tirelach, 'these apples look good and they smell wonderful but it's possible that they are poisoned, so here's what we'll do. We'll draw blades of grass and the man with the shortest blade tastes the fruit while the other two look on.'

They all agreed and it fell to Aodan's lot to try the apples. Over he went to a tree and shook the branch with his spear. Three juicy apples fell at his feet. Aodan picked up one, wiped it on his tunic, bit into it and tasted ... paradise. In seconds he had devoured the first apple and was starting on the next. He was about to eat the third when he realised that he was totally satisfied and that there was no need to be greedy. He lay down quietly in the sun, put his hands over his contented stomach and closed his eyes.

When Tirelach saw him lying prone on the ground, he became alarmed. 'Are you poisoned, Aodan?' he asked. 'Is the pain bad?'

'Pain? What pain? I never tasted a better apple in the whole of my life.'

'Well, in the name of all that's holy, why are you lying down like a poisoned pup?'

'I'm lying down like a contented man and not like any poisoned pup,' retorted Aodan. 'I've rowed that boat until my hands have moulded to the shape of the oars and my back has curved like a shield. And I've eaten so much raw fish that my skin has grown scales. Now, for the first time since we left home, I've eaten something that tastes better than all the home food I've been dreaming about. All I need now is the ministrations of a beautiful woman and I'd die happy!'

'Would you stop talking about dying unless the apples have poisoned you,' ordered a testy Tirelach. 'Don't you know that there are men back in the boat who are exhausted and hungry? Have you no consideration for anyone other than yourself?'

Aodan pulled himself together and got up.

'I didn't mean to be selfish,' he explained. 'I was just tired. But those apples are the best I've ever eaten.'

On that recommendation, Tirelach and Tirechan could restrain themselves no longer. They decided that, come what may, they'd also eat the apples of gold. They immediately understood Aodan's pleasure. The apples tasted like whiskey but without the burn. They tasted like honey but with the added pleasure of a satisfying crunch. They tasted like edible sunshine and happy days.

'Now who's being selfish?' asked Aodan, as the brothers went into ecstasies over the fruit. 'Need I remind you that there are tired men and hungry men on the boat?'

Tirelach smiled, 'I didn't mean to be hard on you, Aodan, but I got frightened when I thought you were poisoned. Let's carry fifty or sixty apples back to the boat for the others and then we'll rest before we do any more exploring. Who knows what other delights this island may have in store for us?'

Maeldun and the others were glad to see the three return and delighted with the bounty that they brought with them. Having been assured that the three had eaten the apples with no ill effects, they all ate with relish, even the careful Diuran. This, they agreed, was an island where they could rest for a while and recover their strength before trying to get home.

In spite of feeling safe, the men decided to check the boat to ensure that it was seaworthy, and to sleep near the beach – just in case. They also built a semicircle of fires round their camp, forming a defensive wall between them and the island, but leaving them a clear escape route to the sea. The sun had barely gone down when each man curled up on the warm earth and slept. They may have slept for a night or maybe four, but it is probable that they had only been asleep for a few hours when they heard strange noises. Still in a half sleep, each man wondered if he was dreaming. There were two distinct sounds: one had the rhythm of regulated thunder while the second was like voices raised in mirth.

'Is anybody else awake?' hazarded Maeldun.

'Aye, me,' came twenty other voices.

'Sh!' warned Maeldun, 'not so loud. What is it?'

Wide awake now, they listened intently, hardly breathing.

'It's like horse-racing,' suggested Oigín.

'The lad's right,' agreed Maeldun. 'It sounds to me like there are people over the brow of the hill, enjoying themselves and racing horses in the moonlight. Did you see any people when you went for the apples?'

'No, only horses,' answered Tirechan, 'though, to be honest, we were so happy to find that the apples were tasty, that we didn't pay too much attention to anything else. Would you like us to go back and see what's afoot?'

'I want to go too,' decided Maeldun. 'If there's a party going, I don't want to miss it.'

'Nor I.'

'Nor I.'

Each man picked up a piece of burning wood, not to use as a torch, for it was broad moonlight, but in case the horses and the racegoers were less than friendly. Quietly, but with happy anticipation, they climbed the hill. Down below, in the cup of the valley, they saw hordes of men and horses. Well, hordes of beings that were *like* men and hordes of animals that were *like* horses. But they weren't people and they weren't horses. Maeldun signalled, and the men lay flat on the ground, watching and listening.

The 'men' were all short of stature, little bigger than well-developed nine-year-olds. They had pointed ears, cocked like a hunting dog's, pointy beards, and eyes that burned like fire in their faces. There was one other feature that made them different to the men stretched out on the hillside. Each had a tail that was beautifully groomed and ended in a neat, equilateral triangle. They seemed to be betting on the horses, using large amounts of what looked like gold nuggets for their wagers. Each 'man' roared his bet, flicked his nuggets over to the tallyman with the triangular bit of his tail and then waited to see which horse would win.

The 'horses' looked altogether more equine. As Tirelach and the others had noticed earlier, they had long nails on each foot where your average horse had a hoof, but this did not seem to affect their prowess as runners.

The horses set off at such speed that Maeldun and his men could barely restrain themselves from cheering. Lightning would not have been faster than the roan that was leading the race. There were no jockeys, but the horses seemed to know what they were about, going twice around the circular track and half a track up the hill on the other side of the valley. The roan led from start to finish and came in a clear winner.

Some of the 'men' cheered while others cursed their luck, but it was the behaviour of the winning horses that held Maeldun and his men spellbound. The roan and the grey that had come in second lay down on their backs in the winners' enclosure with their feet in the air. The roan turned in its skin, like a ferret trying to escape from a leather bag. Its flesh and bones moved round and round in a clockwise direction, gathering speed as they turned, but its skin stayed perfectly still. In the grey's case it was the skin that was in motion, spinning like a windmill in an anti-clockwise direction, while its flesh and bones remained static.

Maeldun and his companions were dumbstruck. It was as if they had somehow broken into someone else's nightmare.

'Back to the boat, men,' whispered Maeldun and no one needed any further urging. Before the next race had started, they were all aboard the boat and ready to move off, when someone noticed that Aodan was missing. Then, suddenly, there he was on the shore, half walking, half running to join them, and in his hand he carried an enormous branch laden with golden apples.

'Good man, Aodan,' the crew cheered, and for the next forty days and forty nights they had reason to thank Aodan many times over, for the branch repeatedly bore fruit and kept them fed until new land appeared on the horizon.

6: Water, Water, Everywhere

Aengus was as relaxed as a heartbroken god could be. He had eaten and drunk well and was ready to continue his pursuit of Caillte.

'Do me a favour, Gáire,' he urged. 'Just tell me the end of the story. Tell me about when Maeldun's journey finished. Did he get to avenge his father? Did he ever meet a beautiful woman, like I did?'

'What sort of storyteller do you take me for?' asked Gáire. 'I can no more tell you the end of my story than a child can run before it has crawled. If you don't want to hear what happened ...'

'Oh but I do, Gáire. I do. It's just that I don't want to know every little detail. I'd be glad to have the gist of it.'

'If it's only the gist you want,' huffed Gáire, 'you should go to a gist teller. As for me, I'm a story teller and I tell the story my way or not at all.'

Aengus hesitated. He really should be going; he could feel the tug of Caillte's voice on his heartstrings. But his curiosity was fired up now and he desperately wanted to hear how the quest of Maeldun had turned out. And, he reasoned, it was growing dark and it would probably be more sensible to set out in the morning.

'Go on, then Gáire, if you please,' he cajoled. 'Tell me some more – in your own way, that is – about Maeldun.'

'It just so happens,' conceded Gáire 'that Maeldun did meet some beautiful women. It happened like this.'

Back in the boat, Maeldun and his friends were soon longing for sight of land again, although their experiences had taught them to be wary of what the land might bring forth. They sailed on and on in mist and rain and wind until a day dawned when the surface of the water was like green glass. It was so flat and so transparent that they could see right down through it. And there in the depths were the walls and turrets of a fortified town, surrounded by lush green fields where cattle grazed and all manner of fruit trees grew.

'Do you think,' suggested Maeldun's third brother, Forannan, 'that we should swim down? That land is as peaceful and inviting as any I've ever seen. I'm willing to take the chance and go first.'

'Wait a minute,' advised the ever-cautious Diuran. 'Do you see any people? It's true that it looks inviting, but if there are no people there, then it's not the place for us.'

The men debated the matter, some saying they should risk it, with others urging caution, and so they sat, staring at the green world beneath them. The debate was moving in favour of Forannan, when suddenly beneath them they saw a huge bird swoop down from a tree and, with one movement of its curved beak, pick up an ox. Faster than the human eye could record, the ox disappeared. Then the bird turned its attention upwards towards the boat.

'Row men, row,' yelled Maeldun. Before the second 'row' was formed in his mouth, every man was pulling on the oars as if his salvation depended on it. On they rowed and on into an eternity of rowing, day after row, night after row, row after row. They rowed as if in a dream – without enthusiasm, without purpose, without fatigue even.

'I see land again,' whispered Oigín, almost hoping that no one would hear him or that perhaps his eyes were playing tricks on him. 'Maeldun, I see land.'

'What difference will it make?' asked Maeldun, dejectedly. 'These lands are not like home. They are cursed; there is no rest for us on them, no joy. Let's row on and forget about it.'

'Why not at least look it over,' suggested Diuran. 'We are all tired and hungry for food that is cooked and for a drink that puts fire in the belly. Let us try, Maeldun. Almost anything would be better than this unending travel over the waves.'

Diuran was speaking aloud the thoughts of most of the men, so Maeldun guided their craft towards the shore, at first with ill-concealed reluctance, then with gathering interest and finally with vigour.

'Do you men see what I see?' asked Maeldun. 'Are my eyes being tormented by mirages or are there women on the shore beckoning us.'

'If you're seeing a mirage, Maeldun, then so are we,' confirmed a dozen voices.

The nearer they got to the island, the clearer grew the vision. On the shore, waiting to greet them, were the most beautiful women any of them had ever seen. Some were tall and fair. Some were short and dark. But they were all young and healthy and smiling and beautiful.

'Guide the boat straight to the women,' urged the men.

'Wait,' advised Diuran. 'We don't know whether or not it is safe to land. First ... '

'No, Diuran,' replied Maeldun. 'It may be wise to be cautious,

49

but I'll risk death to leave this boat and spend time with these women. Are there any dissenting voices?'

None was heard, not even Diuran's. He too could see the young women smiling and waving, and he too knew he had no choice but to head for the shore. The boat glided swiftly and surely towards the shallow cove where landing would be easiest. The sun was shining and the water sparkling as the boat danced landwards.

'Welcome, strangers, welcome,' sang the smiling women, and tiredness dropped from the men, as one after the other they stepped ashore.

7: It's a Warm Land, the West Land

Maeldun and his men continued to feel the movement of the waves even when they were off the boat.

'Is your land moving?' asked Maeldun.

'No,' the maiden who answered him smiled, revealing teeth more perfect than the finest row of pearls. 'You have been on the whale's road too long,' she said gently, 'so long that you have become one with the rhythm of the waves. What you and your retainers need is a period of rest and tranquillity. Then your body and mind will be attuned to earth again and you will find that this island is not only beautiful but utterly immobile. Come, let me take you to the quarters set aside for our honoured guests.' She spoke in a strange, singsong voice that reminded Maeldun of the falling notes of a harp.

The palace towards which the men were conducted gleamed white in the sunshine. Seeing Maeldun's admiration, the young woman explained:

'All our buildings are constructed of a stone we quarry locally. It is similar to the shells that the sea animals wear. In sunlight it appears pure white, but at sunset it shimmers with the colours of a distant rainbow. My name is Áluinn,' she added, 'and I am queen of this island. And now I see a conflict in your face: fatigue is fighting with curiosity. Let the fatigue win for now. Tomorrow, we shall satisfy your curiosity.'

The men allowed themselves to be led first to the baths, then to a meal of fruit and deliciously flavoured bread, and lastly to their rooms. The beds were large and the silk sheets smelt of sunshine and flowers.

If this is death, thought Maeldun as the bed rose and fell under him, then it is better than life. And Áluinn is so beautiful.

He woke to find the light streaming into the room through an open door that looked out over the sea. 'It must be close to midday,' he concluded, and realised with pleasure that the room had stopped moving. He could once again stand on firm legs on a still floor in a steady world. He made his way to the baths, only to find that most of the others were already there, being bathed and barbered and pampered. Even Oigín, who did not yet have a beard, was having his hair attended to by a girl of his own age.

Once they were clean and refreshed, they were offered a vast array of food – exotic fruits, nuts of every variety and the sweet, perfumed bread that they had eaten yesterday. When they had filled their bellies, Áluinn appeared, looking happy and even more beautiful than the night before.

'Maeldun,' she smiled at him, 'last night I promised to satisfy your curiosity. If you would like to accompany me, I shall endeavour to make all clear.'

Together they climbed the hill to Áluinn's palace, and Maeldun learned about the island where they had landed. It was called Tirnaman – the land of women – for it was inhabited only by women. From time to time, they sailed to other islands for the purpose of procreation. The girl children were kept and the young males returned to the lands of their fathers. Once, long before, men and women had lived together on the island, but there were so many problems associated with co-habitation, and so many broken dreams that the women of the time had driven the men out. Since that time there had been peace and tranquillity.

'Are you never lonely?' asked Maeldun.

'I did not think so,' replied Áluinn, 'but now I perceive that there has always been a void in my life, a void that I now wish to fill. And I am not the only one. Many of my friends desire you to stay with us, living in our homes, sleeping in our beds. We should like to invite you to end your journey and to abide here.'

For answer, the entranced Maeldun put his arm round her shoulders and bent to kiss her face. 'I accept your invitation, Áluinn, and I'm sure my brothers and friends will also want to accept it. We are tired of the endless seas and the cold and the loneliness. I willingly agree to stay and never again will I think of returning to my old home. From now on, home is where you are.'

And when he said it, he meant it, Gáire told Aengus, but young men will say anything to please a young woman, and Áluinn was well worth pleasing.

Time flew by without counting, days and weeks and months. Tirnaman was indeed a paradise, full of happy men and smiling women with no thought of the past or the future. Then one day Maeldun thought he would go and look at the boat, just for old time's sake. When he got there, he was surprised to find that it had been hauled out of the water and cleaned and waterproofed.

'It's ready to sail,' Forannan broke into his thoughts. 'Some of us have been coming here to make it ready for our journey home.'

'Home?' queried Maeldun. 'But this is our home, now. Aren't you happy here?'

'Happy, yes,' Forannan assured him. 'I've never been so happy in my life. There is so much peace on the island that it is almost palpable. I'm happy, but I'm not content. I think of our mother and the court and I even think with affection of our diet of raw fish! I want to go back. And have you forgotten why we set out in the first place? Let me remind you that you have yet to avenge your father's murder.'

'Do the others also want to leave?' Maeldun asked.

'No one really wants to leave,' he was told. 'We are all happy and healthy and well looked after here, but we began our journey with a purpose, a purpose we have not fulfilled. We are agreed that we must leave Tirnaman and follow our destiny.'

'Forannan's right,' came another voice and Maeldun realised that one by one the men had all assembled, drawn like a magnet to the boat. 'Forannan's right. Tirnaman is beautiful and the women are kind, but we are not among our own people. It is time for us to go.' It was Diuran who spoke and although Maeldun saw sadness in every eye, no one spoke out against him.

'I must first say goodbye to Áluinn,' Maeldun whispered, grieved that he would have to leave.

'No, Maeldun,' insisted Diuran. 'We daren't say goodbye or none of us would ever leave. I too love my woman. I too love my life here, but it is not home and these women are not our people.'

Maeldun knew that his duty was to his father and to his men, so in spite of the pain in his heart, he walked to the boat.

'Let's go,' he ordered gruffly, and soon the men and the boat were again riding the waves, following a destiny that would take them they knew not where.

The sea was calm and the wind light, so the salt on Maeldun's cheeks had nothing to do with the weather. Diuran began to speak.

'Not so much as a word from you, Diuran,' ordered Maeldun. 'What you said was right, but I'm sorry you said it. Doing what is right means hurting our women, ourselves, our unborn children. It seems right to us, but what about them? What about them?'

No one answered. No one could. Choices are never easy and they had made their choice. Duty before joy – surely they had made the right decision? No one looked back. They were afraid that if they did, they would turn the boat around. Their bodies already ached for the life they had just left. They thought of the voices of the women, and the memory became almost real.

Each man heard his name in a litany of song, ringing out over the waves. Aodan heard it and Athrú; so did Cathal, Colman and Conan; the song echoed in the hearts of Diarmuid, Diuran, Donal and Dorman; it raised lumps in the throats of Feilim, Finbar and Forannan; it echoed in the ears of Maeldun, Machaire, Manus and Murchú; it struck chords in the brains of Oigín, Olas and Osnan; and to Tirechan and Tirelach it seemed so real that they looked back and found it was real. The women were standing on the shore, calling for them, and one by one, the men on the boat turned to look back.

8: A Maiden with a Ball of Twine

'Don't go back,' urged Diuran. 'Forge ahead.'

'No. Row back a little,' ordered Maeldun. 'We at least owe them the courtesy of hearing what they have to say.'

The men rowed back with greater joy than they had rowed away, and when they were within earshot they rested their oars and listened.

'Maeldun,' called Áluinn, 'what did we do that you treat us like this? What did we fail to give you? We took you in when you were tired and cold. We fed you. We clothed you. We loved you. Maeldun, I loved you. I shared everything with you. Come back, Maeldun, come back.'

'We can't,' Maeldun replied sadly. 'We must avenge my father's murder. We must return to our own country.'

'And what about your own child? Does he not deserve a father?' Áluinn raised her arm, 'Here, Maeldun, catch.'

Maeldun was taken off guard and, without thinking, he reached up to catch what Áluinn had thrown. It was a ball of twine, one end of which she still held in her hand. The ball stuck firmly to Maeldun's palm and he was unable to detach it. Áluinn began to pull on the twine and slowly, then more quickly, the boat and the men were reeled back to shore. The women ran into the water to hug their loved ones. Only Áluinn waited on the shore.

'Maeldun,' she whispered when he joined her, 'why did you leave me?'

All the words about duty and loyalty faded from his lips and he knelt on the sand before her.

'Trust me, Áluinn, I'll never leave you again,' he said and he meant what he said, because love is warm and duty is cold and there are few who wouldn't choose the warmth.

Gáire sat back and rested. So did Aengus. He thought about the story he had just heard. If he had been in Maeldun's shoes, would he have left the lovely Áluinn? Has a man a greater duty to his father or to his child, or indeed to the woman who loves him, he wondered. Can you continue to love a woman if she has stopped you from doing your duty? Could she continue to love you if you put your own happiness first?

'I can't answer any of your unspoken questions,' smiled Gáire. 'I can only be glad that the problem was Maeldun's and not mine. What choice would you have made, young Aengus? Your lover or your father? Your happiness or your duty?'

'Perhaps a man has to be in such a situation to know how he would react,' answered a diplomatic Aengus. 'But forget about me. Did Maeldun stay? Tell me what happened next.'

Gáire drank slowly and stared into the middle distance until his mind's eye focused again on Maeldun.

For a year and a day, Maeldun was at peace. His child was born and his wife meant more to him than the sun that warmed him and the air that sustained him. But, just as shadows lengthen with the fall of the day, so dark thoughts spread in the mind of Ailill Ochair

Aga's son. There was no one alive now to avenge the death of a brave man. No one who would be able to give the murdered man's spirit its deserved rest.

In spite of his good intentions and his promises to Áluinn, Maeldun found his feet moving towards the shore and he found his hands repairing the outer skin of the boat and lovingly carving new oars. And he was not alone for long; first Cathal and then Colman came to help. And the next day, Finbar and Tirelach joined them. Soon the men were meeting regularly on the beach and laughing as they remembered the giant bees and the crazy horses. They forgot the danger and the storms and the taste of raw fish. And each man agreed when Diuran said:

'We have no choice. We must go.'

So they set off again. But once more their hearts were heavy and once more the women called and the men looked back and listened.

'Catch, my love, catch,' called Áluinn as she threw the ball of twine to Maeldun. He caught it, and Áluinn and the women were again able to pull the boat ashore. The men hugged and kissed the women as if they had been away for a long time and the women promised to make their life so sweet that they would never want to leave again. After all, a man has a duty to his children as well as to his father and friends.

The happiness they all knew during the next weeks was like the happiness the birds know in Foghmhar, the month of the harvest. The air is still warm. There is more food than they can eat. The nestlings can fend for themselves. But there is an inherited memory that tells them that this time is passing and will soon have passed.

And the day came when the men launched their boat into the sea for the third time. This time the women were joined in their calling by the little children.

'Don't catch the twine when she throws it,' Diuran advised Maeldun. 'I'll catch it.' He caught the ball in his left hand and it stuck there. Slowly, gently, Áluinn began to pull and slowly, eagerly, the boat headed for the shore.

'Give me your sword, Tirechan,' instructed Diuran. He hacked at the twine, but the cord immediately blunted the blade so that the sword made no more impact on it than if he had tried to cut water. 'Another sword, quick,' he shouted and before anyone could blink, Diuran had cut off his hand and let it and the ball of twine fall into the sea.

'We're free, Maeldun,' he called out, raising the bleeding stump of his arm triumphantly in the air. 'We're free to go home.'

Yes, they were free, free to roam the seas again in the hope of finding the way home. Freedom shouldn't taste bitter, but it did to them. They continued to glance back until the women and the shoreline became a memory and the task of ploughing a straight furrow through the sea replaced it.

9: Behind the Whaling Wall

For days the men rowed on, conscious that each second took them further from their island of contentment. On and on they journeyed, still strong from their good food and their extended rest. No man spoke of the women and some would have thought it a dream if Diuran's hand had still been on the end of his arm. But it wasn't.

'It's healing well, Diuran,' Maeldun assured him.

'It is,' Diuran agreed. 'It hardly gives me any pain now. The brine has cauterized the wound and soon a new skin will grow. If only I could go to the silversmiths of the north, I could get myself a new hand.'

The men smiled as they remembered the northern silversmiths. As children, they had heard about them from Fáidh, an old, blind visionary. Fáidh could see the future as clearly as he saw the past, and he often told the boys about the great heroes of times to come. No one knew why Fáidh had this gift but everyone believed that what he saw was true. Fáidh had first discovered it when he had lost his sight. On that day he had stopped for an instant to listen to a bird. Its song was more beautiful than any he had ever heard.

When the last note faded, Fáidh found that he was totally blind and he soon realised that years had passed in that moment of ecstasy.

Diuran had once asked him how he could know about great heroes who would not be born in their lifetime. Fáidh thought for a moment and then explained:

'Time is not like a river that starts in one place and ends in another, Diuran. It is more like a crystal circle that has no beginning and no ending. Everyone who lives makes notes on the crystal, but some people set up reverberations that last forever.'

Diuran did not understand what the old man meant and he did not care. He and the other children loved his stories. One of their favourites was of a northern warrior called Niall. He had lost his hand in battle, but the silversmiths were so adept that they fashioned him a new hand and taught him to use it. At first, he could only make staccato movements. Open ... close ... open ... close. But gradually he learned to scratch his head and rein in his horse and stroke the soft roundness of girls. Indeed, many of the girls found his stroking irresistible, and responded willingly to his silvered touch. If Diuran could get a hand like that, it would make up for his heroic sacrifice.

Thoughts of silver hands can occupy a man's mind when he needs to forget living hands and responsive bodies. Maeldun and his men travelled on by day and night, lost in the eternal and unending sea. They did not know where they were going, only where they had left.

Oigín's keen eyes were again the first to spot land.

'I can see land ahead,' he muttered, not knowing whether to be glad or sorry.

In silence, they all watched the approaching landfall. It did not look very inviting. Scattered on the shoreline, as far as the eye could see, were the skulls and bones of whales. Many were in groups, as if they had been killed at the same time, males with large skulls and long backbones, the smaller skeletons of the females, and calves of varying sizes.

'They're glorious creatures, whales,' murmured Conan. 'I remember Fáidh telling me stories about them. They can grow so big that their length surpasses the length of a river and their mouth could encompass a flock of sheep. And yet, in spite of their size, they can jump for joy in the water and sing to tell the other whales where they are.

' There was one story about a holy man called Brendan. He set out one day with nothing but a fish for himself and another for his cat, Pangur Dubh. For weeks Brendan and Pangur were tossed on seas that had mountains and valleys and ridges and hills, but all made out of water. When they were tired beyond all tiredness, Pangur started miaowing. "There's no pointing miaowing, my little Pangur," Brendan told the cat. "We may reconcile ourselves to a watery grave." But Pangur went on miaowing and standing up on the rim of the vessel, like a small rampant prow. Up Brendan got, and there in front of him, not more than an hour's walk away – if you could walk on the water, that is – was the most beautiful land that eyes could behold. "Is it heaven, do you think, Pangur?" asked Brendan, but Pangur only miaowed.

'Well, they made for the island and they walked on it and Pangur caught fish in the pools. Brendan cooked the food and for three days and three nights they knew the joy of total fulfilment. Then, suddenly, a terrible earthquake shook the narrow end of the island. Pangur ran to the boat and Brendan followed the wise instincts of his feline companion. He had just managed to get the boat a short distance from the island when the entire sea erupted.

'Brendan watched, more in disbelief than in fear, as the front of the island rose high into the sky and two sloe-black eyes peered out at them. A huge mouth opened to reveal rows and rows of sharp white teeth. The head moved, the tail flicked and before Brendan could say *Seaninmacbunnainbuidhe*, the island had leapt into the air, uttering a song that was like nothing Brendan or Pangur had ever heard and would remember as long as they lived. Their 'island' was nothing more and nothing less than a gigantic whale.'

While Conan talked, Maeldun was directing the boat ever closer to the shore. From the evidence of the whale kills, they had expected to see lots of large fishing vessels, but there were none to be found. All they could see were small gatherings of people sitting on the ground. The groups ranged in size from six to eleven, but no larger. And every group was crying piteously, which was strange in itself, but what made it more remarkable was that the faces being drowned in tears were purple-skinned.

'Is it a dye that they've used, Maeldun?' asked Oigín.

'It looks like no dye I've ever seen,' he answered. 'The colour reminds me of the innermost band of the rainbow. Look at their hands and feet; they're purple too.'

'Could it be that they are cold, then?' continued Oigín. 'Perhaps they are crying because they are so cold.'

'It doesn't make sense,' Maeldun responded. 'If they were cold, they could congregate around the fires, or put on extra garments. No, I don't think that's what has them in such a state.'

'Well,' persisted Oigín, determined to get to the bottom of this mystery, 'maybe they are crying because they killed all those whales?'

But Maeldun had no answer to these speculations.

They called out to the wailing people, but they ignored the boat and carried on crying.

Maeldun was perplexed. 'They don't look dangerous,' he said, 'but you can never tell. Let's draw lots to see who goes ashore.'

The task fell to Tirelach, and he swam ashore. Slowly he walked towards the first group of people. With each step, his colour changed, until he, too, turned purple. Sadly he sat down beside his new friends and started to cry.

His companions on the boat could not believe their eyes. But it was undoubtedly Tirelach, their Tirelach – the same in every feature and detail – except that he was now purple.

'Tirelach, Tirelach, come back,' they called, but although Tirelach looked towards them, he made no move to join them. He only cried a little more loudly.

'We'll have to go and fetch him.' said Tirechan. 'I'm not going to leave my brother sitting there, crying.'

'And neither am I,' agreed Forannan.

'Go then and get him,' urged Maeldun, 'but be careful.'

The brothers swam to the shore and walked gingerly towards Tirelach. With each step their colour altered and their expressions grew sadder. They bent down as if to pick Tirelach up, but as they did so, big tears rolled down their purple faces and they sank to the ground.

'Are my eyes tricking me?' asked Maeldun, 'or have my three brothers turned purple?'

'If your eyes are tricking you,' answered Diuran, 'then mine have joined in their deceit, for I see what you see. What are we going to do?'

'They're my brothers,' said Maeldun. 'So I should be the one to go ashore next.'

'We'll go too,' chorused a dozen voices.

'We can't risk more than two more men,' Diuran's voice was quiet, but firm. 'If we lose five in all, we can still manage the boat. More than that and we all die.'

'Diuran's right,' announced Maeldun. 'We need one volunteer to accompany me.'

'Let me go,' suggested Oigín. 'I'm the fastest runner and I have the best eyes.'

'He's right. Take Oigín,' advised Diuran, 'but we'll have to use some cunning if we are to avoid losing you both. Do you remember Fáidh's story about when Colm of the Birds was banished to Alba and forbidden ever again to put his foot on his native land? Do you remember what he did? He took some soil from Alba and put it in his shoes so that his feet never touched his homeland even though he walked on it. We must do something similar.'

'In the name of all the powers, Diuran,' exploded Maeldun, 'where are we going to get soil, and us surrounded by water?'

'We can't get soil, but we can use oars.'

'Oars?'

'Yes, oars,' said Diuran. 'I know you won't be able to run fast with oars on your feet but, at the same time, your feet won't come in contact with their land. That way, you have a better chance of not turning purple.'

The men discussed Diuran's scheme and, in spite of its drawbacks, decided that it was worth trying. Oigín saw the humorous side of walking on oars, but Maeldun complained that it was an unnecessary encumbrance. His complaints were only half-hearted, though, because he could see the value of Diuran's ruse.

Slowly, painfully, Maeldun and Oigín oared their way to the shore and up the beach. At first they had to cling to each other to maintain their balance, but they soon grew more stable on their strange footwear. When they were confident of staying upright, they made for the group. Maeldun took Forannan by the arm, while Oigín raised Tirechan to his feet. The brothers went with them readily enough, but seemed unable to utter any sound but a high-pitched wail.

'Come on,' urged Maeldun, 'back to the boat. Then we'll come back for you, Tirelach.'

Tirelach did not seem to hear his words. He just sat and wailed as Maeldun and Oigín awkwardly led the brothers back towards the boat. They were within a few strides of their target when a spear struck Maeldun's arm.

Oigín looked back and saw a group of purple men pursuing them. 'They've turned on us, Maeldun,' he warned. 'And those spears look deadly.'

On they struggled, and as the feet of Tirechan and Forannan touched the water, the purple drained away and they returned to their old selves.

'What happened?' queried a bemused Forannan.

'Now's not the time for questions and answers, brother. On to the boat, quickly.'

Diuran had steered the boat as close to the men as possible and Tirechan and Forannan were swiftly hauled on board, followed by Maeldun and Oigín, who were almost thrown in, as there was no time to disentangle them from their oars. Only when they were out of spearshot could they unstrap the awkward appendages and attend to Maeldun's injured arm.

'It's only a flesh wound, Maeldun,' Conan assured him. 'It won't cause you any trouble. But I'm not too happy about the condition of the boat. So many of the spears have pierced the outer skin that it looks like a porcupine. If it begins to leak we are in serious trouble. We'll have to make for land and mend it as best we can.'

Maeldun stood up and looked back. It was just possible to see Tirelach, still sitting on the spot where they had left him, purple and no doubt wailing. 'I'm sorry, brother,' Maeldun silently assured him. 'Sorry to have taken you on this terrible voyage in the first place, and sorry to be leaving you now, but we can't risk the boat or any more of the men.'

The boat moved further and further away from the strange island until the sound of the wailing could no longer be heard by human ears, but it echoed in their hearts like a lament for Tirelach.

10: Won't You Walk into My Parlour?

Gáire and Aengus were now so involved in the narrative that neither thought any more of curtailing it. For a while they both sat back and contemplated the fate of Tirelach and the people on the island.

'Do you think the islanders were being punished for killing the whales?' asked Aengus.

'Are you asking me, man, or telling me?' queried Gáire, a little testily. 'Do we ever know the answers to the most interesting questions? Our role is but to watch and to see. Understanding is beyond us. Just as it was beyond Maeldun and his friends. Still, luck was with them after that. The sea remained calm, Maeldun's wound healed and soon they found an island where they could patch up their boat and revive their spirits.'

'No purple wailers on the next island?' encouraged Aengus.

'None, but it had, as you might have guessed, its own interesting features.'

Oigín, as usual, was the first to spot the island and it looked a lovely place, quiet and peaceful. As they approached the shore, they saw an old man beckoning to them.

'Welcome, friends. Welcome. Come ashore.'

Not even the ever-cautious Diuran distrusted this old man despite the fact that the description 'strange' did not even begin to do him justice. He was old in the way that hills are old and trees are old, still strong but weathered. He was naked too, in the sense that he wore no clothes, but the hair of his head covered him from his neck to his heels and the hair of his beard reached from his chin down to his toes.

'Welcome, welcome,' he kept calling, and even when they were all ashore and sitting in his hut, he kept running around touching them and telling them how welcome they were. He fed them cooked fish and succulent fruit and apologised for having no meat or wine.

'I don't have such delicacies,' he explained, 'but what I do have is yours. Rest, my friends, rest, and tomorrow we will mend your boat and you will tell me why you are here. Rest, be at peace, and whatever you do, don't go to the other side of the island.'

The warning was unnecessary. Maeldun and his men were in no mood to go anywhere. Tired and drained of energy, they lay down and slept. It was so good to stretch out to one's full length. It was so good not to feel the undulating motion of the waves. It was so good, but still it was not their island of contentment.

Next day, they worked on the boat, mended their clothes and told the old man of their adventures so far. When evening came and they were congregated round his fire, he told them his tale.

'My name is Uaigneas and I was once young and strong like you. I had a wife and children, three sons and a daughter, and I had land and prosperity to spare. I had all that any man could want, but

I needed more. I heard the call of the wind, "Uaigneas, Uaigneas," it would sigh, "come and see where the winds find rest." I heard the call of the waves, "Uaigneas, Uaigneas, come and explore the many shores that we wash." And I heard the call of the terns, "Uaigneas, Uaigneas, come and feel what freedom is." I listened to the calls and they drowned out the pleas of my wife and the needs of my children.

'One day, I heard another voice in my head, not the voice of terns or of waves or winds. It was the voice of the Mother of All. "Go then, Uaigneas, go. As you are, you are of no use to your family or your friends. Go and my spirit will be with you. You will see where the winds find rest, and explore the lands that the waves wash, and know the freedom of the terns. But you will learn the value of wife and warmth and home and hearth."

'The voice in my head led me to the shore, where a large sod of earth was floating. I got on without a backward glance, and the winds drove me and the waves carried me and the terns led me on. I lost count of how long I travelled, but it may have been years or tens of years. What is a day or a week or a year if days all are alike and there is no change of season? The sod on which I journeyed grew larger until it became this island you are standing on now. Birds dropped seeds so I had trees to tend and fruit to eat. The sea spawned fish of all kinds so I had fish to sustain me.'

'And were you not lonely, Uaigneas?' asked Maeldun.

'Lonely? I may have been lonely. Yes, I think I was lonely. I was certainly glad to see you, but it is a long time since I was conscious of being lonely. You see, the Mother of All kept her promises. Her spirit has been with me always. I have been guarded and protected and preserved. I have even had my children for company.'

'Your children?' asked Maeldun, 'but we thought you were alone.'

'Alone, no. The spirits of my children are in the birds that nest in my trees. They talk to me and sing to me and, in my own way I'm happy. But I keep away from the other side of the island. It is dangerous there and I have all that I need here, all that I need. I do not want the webs of silver and gold that are spun there.'

Silver and gold! That night the dreams of Maeldun's men were filled with thoughts of the bounty that lay within their reach. They knew they could not eat it or sleep on it or use it to make their journey easier, but the thought of it drew them and when morning came Forannan said:

'I think I'll wander to the other side of the island.'

'Don't get into trouble, brother,' Maeldun advised. 'Our boat is ready and we should leave here tomorrow when we have gathered some fruit.'

'I won't get into any trouble,' laughed Forannan. 'Uaigneas is a nice old man but he has been on his own too long. He sees danger where none exists. After all, he's still alive, isn't he?'

'Still, I'd be happier if you didn't go alone, Forannan,' Maeldun insisted.

'I'll go with him,' offered Diuran. 'One hand is not much use for gathering fruit, but it can carry a sword and Forannan will have good company.'

Off they walked towards the other side of the island, passing under the trees where the spirits of Uaigneas's children sang, walking on lush grass and bountiful soil. Beyond the trees they saw a gently sloping hill with tall trees on the top.

'It's beautiful, Diuran, isn't it? And look at those trees; it may be a trick of the light but it appears to me as if there are lacy curtains of silver and gold strung between the trees.'

'If it's a mirage that you're seeing, Forannan, then I'm seeing it too. This must be the silver and gold that Uaigneas spoke of. If we could take some home, we'd be rich for life. But take care – Uaigneas also spoke of danger, and while it looks peaceful maybe he was right.'

'Right? Diuran, you've been at sea too long! Think of what else that old man told us: a sod that grows into an island! Birds that drop seeds that grow into trees! Children in the shape of birds, talking to him! Surely, you didn't believe all that nonsense.'

'I did at the time. Stories that are true at night often appear foolish in the light, and I grant you that his story does seem odd.'

They talked and joked as they walked towards the draperies, for that's what they were, hanging in strands of the purest silver and gold.

'Wait here, Diuran, while I check things out. I'll call you as soon as I'm sure everything is fine.'

Forannan walked towards the gold and touched it. It was the finest gold he had ever touched, but slightly sticky. The silver had traces of what looked like dew on it and had a consistency similar to thick honey.

'Everything's fine, Diuran,' he called, and raised his sword to cut through the gossamer gold. The first stroke slit it and blew it away from him. The second carried the lace towards him, wrapping it around him. 'Diuran,' he shouted, 'I'm caught.'

But Diuran had already seen what lay behind the lace curtain: an enormous spider, which even now was drawing the golden threads, and Forannan, towards it. He ran to save Forannan, but his pace was no match for the spider. Forannan shrieked as the thick, black arms encircled him and he was hauled deep into the spider's lair. And then there was silence.

With his one good arm, Diuran hacked at the web, cutting off pieces of gold, but never with any real chance of reaching Forannan.

'Forannan, Forannan,' he called desperately, but there was no answer, only the swishing sound of Forannan being bound into a spool of gold. 'I'll get the others, Forannan,' he shouted, 'I'll be back.'

'I tried to warn you,' whispered Uaigneas, when Diuran had told them what had happened. 'I told you there was danger. But, what was meant to be will happen. Take your gold thread with you, Diuran, and lay it on the altar of the Mother of All, for you will get back home, but not all of you. Not all of you.'

So, for a second time, the men had to leave a friend on an alien shore; first Tirelach and now Forannan. A second time they turned their backs on one of their own. Their hearts were heavy as they rowed their boat away from the shore.

Maeldun was filled with sorrow and guilt. He should never have allowed his three brothers – the extra men expressly forbidden by Seanfhear – to come on the voyage. It's all my fault, he thought.

And Tirechan was thinking: They'll never get home while I'm alive. I'm the next one. I'm the one holding them back.

11: Refreshing Waters

The weather was fair and the seas calm, so for the next two days they made good headway. Maeldun found himself watching Tirechan closely. He had lost two brothers and had no intention of losing a third.

'We must ensure his safety, Diuran,' he confided to his friend. 'I know my brothers insisted on coming with me, but the fault is mine, not theirs. Tirechan must survive.'

'Don't worry, Maeldun,' Diuran assured him. 'Thanks to the loss of my hand, I am now capable of little more than watching. You have my word. From now on, whenever we are on dry land, Tirechan will never leave my sight.'

Maeldun knew that Diuran was the best guard on the boat, and some of his apprehension left him. But he still felt the loss of Tirelach and Forannan grievously.

'Are we heading for home, Maeldun?' Oigín asked.

'We have been heading for home since the day we were blown off course, Oigín, and I promise you I would take you there tomorrow if I could. But there are two problems: we don't know where we are and we don't know where home is. All we can do is follow the Guide Star and hope.'

'Wouldn't it be great to be home with our families?' continued Oigín. 'I dream of eating my mother's fresh bread, hot from the oven.'

'Or fresh vegetables from our fields,' added Feilim.

'Or milk,' suggested Olas. 'Do you know, I wouldn't drink milk when I was a boy. I didn't like it. Now, at night, I dream about its sweet smell and soft texture and I'm just on the verge of tasting it when I get somebody's foot in my mouth or the rain wakes me up.'

'What's that straight ahead?' called Diuran suddenly. 'Oigín, for once you've missed it. It's land, isn't it?'

Oigín shaded his eyes with his hand. 'It's land, all right, Diuran,' he agreed. 'A fine land, too, by the look of it, although it's not home.'

The land ahead was laid out like a well-bent crescent moon, and Maeldun guided the boat towards the central point. At first glance they could see neither trees nor people on the island, but there was a small group of houses a short distance in from the shore, houses similar to those they had left at home.

'I'll go ashore, Maeldun,' volunteered Tirechan. 'It looks safe, but you never know.'

'No, you've done enough volunteering for a while, brother,' answered Maeldun. 'We'll draw lots and three men will go ashore, one after the other.'

'Let me go,' urged Oigín. 'I'm quick and I'm lucky. Let me go.'

'And me,' pleaded Feilim.

'And me,' insisted Olas. 'I've never been given the chance to be the first explorer and my legs are so cramped that I'll be the shape of a chair if I don't stretch them.'

There seemed little danger, so Maeldun agreed that the three young men should go ashore. Steadily, they moved up the beach, first Oigín, then Feilim, then Olas. Oigín walked straight ahead while Feilim checked to the left and Olas to the right. The men in the boat watched their backs to make sure that no one crept around them. Oigín headed for a house that looked just like his mother's. It had the same round window above the door and the same well-swept step. But surely it couldn't be? Surely he wasn't at home? The house looked the same but the surroundings were different. And what was that he smelled? Surely it wasn't fresh bread?

Oigín walked in through the doorway and before him on the table was a tray of still-cooling bread. All his favourites were there: small, round, sweet baps; rich, dark, fruit-laden loaves. It took all his strength of purpose to leave the bread and go outside. He called for Feilim and an answer came from the house on his left.

'I'm in here, Oigín, and you'll never guess. This house is the dead spit of the house I was born in. It's even got my own bed in it and, Oigín, best of all, the table's laden with food of all descriptions, including fresh vegetables. Can we eat it, Oigín, do you think?'

Before Oigín could reply, there was a shout from a third house nearby.

'Olas,' they called. 'Are you all right, Olas?'

'All right. No indeed, I'm not all right. I'm out of my head with pleasure! This is my grandmother's house, the house that I used to visit every *Samhain*. It's got food hanging from the rafters, meat and poultry of all kinds, and right in the middle of the floor is a meskin of the loveliest smelling milk my nose has ever come across. Oh God, tell me it's not a dream! Tell me I'm not going to wake up with somebody's foot in my mouth!'

'If you're dreaming, then we're all dreaming,' Oigín assured him. 'Let's go and tell Maeldun what we've found. One thing for sure, I don't care if it poisons me, but with the help of Lugh, I'll eat that fresh bread tonight.'

Maeldun and the others heard the stories with a mixture of joy and disbelief.

'Right,' Maeldun ordered, 'we will go ashore, but with caution. So far there seems no cause for alarm, but we can't be sure. Keep alert, men, and, Diuran, keep all your wits about you.' He looked at Diuran and nodded meaningfully in Tirechan's direction.

To their astonishment and joy, each of the men, except Athrú, found a house exactly like one he had once lived in. Some recognised the walls or the doors or the beds or the chairs. Some recognised objects that they could not have described two minutes before, but they all recognised the peace that went with the house. And while Athrú did not find his own house, he found plenty to please him elsewhere. He ate fresh bread with Oigín and newly cooked vegetables with Feilim. He drank milk with Olas and the water of life with Finbar. He found music and laughter in Donal's house and was warmly greeted in Maeldun's house by a woman who was the image of Áluinn. Athrú shared the joys of many men as he moved from one house to the next.

Only one house was unexplored. It didn't look anything like Athrú's own home and yet somehow he felt it calling to him. The house was round and high with slits for windows and only one door. As he approached, his breathing grew heavy from a mix of fear and anticipated pleasure. There was something wonderful inside, something he'd dreamed of. Slowly, Athrú walked through the door, his sword in his hand, his eyes looking from left to right, his feet carefully feeling the floor before taking each step. It was dark in this house, so much darker than in the others, but there was a glimmer of light straight ahead and quietly, resolutely he made for it. One step, two, three and four, just a few more, and there it was. On a large wooden table in front of him a big black cat was curled up, and to judge by its steady breathing, fast asleep. Behind it was an open chest festooned with jewels of the rarest kind.

Athrú was speechless with amazement. For long minutes he just stood, eyeing his treasure. There were pearls that the dark unfathomed depths of ocean had unwillingly given up, diamonds that glowed like luminescent raindrops, emeralds so big that no finger could bear their weight. 'Mine,' he thought, 'all mine. I saw them first. The others have all got their prizes. This one was meant for me.'

'Maeldun! Oigín! Come and see what I've got. Come and see my house.'

Reluctantly the others left the pleasures of their houses. One after the other they arrived and stood mesmerised in front of the jewel-laden table. Even Maeldun found it hard to put his thoughts into words.

'It's the greatest treasure I've ever seen, Athrú,' he said at last. 'A windfall that will make all of us rich.'

'Not all of us, Maeldun. It's my treasure. I found it. You've all got your own houses and your own treasures. This one is mine.'

As he spoke, he stretched out his hand and picked up a glowing, red ruby. The cat opened her eyes, arched her back, hissed and leapt towards Athrú. Athrú put out his hand to ward her off, but she jumped straight through him. At the spot where she had disappeared, a charred hole appeared in Athrú's body. It was as if a heated poker had been pushed through paper. First there was a black-rimmed hole, then smoke, then conflagration until, on the floor at the men's feet were the ashes of their friend.

For what seemed an eternity, there was complete silence. The spell was broken by the cat, who jumped back on the table, curled up and went to sleep.

'I've seen it,' whispered Maeldun. 'My eyes have seen it and I still can't believe it.'

'Believe it, man,' insisted Diuran. 'That cat will not let us touch a single one of those jewels and no matter how rich they might make us, I, for one, prefer to be poor and alive. Some of you go and collect food from the houses to take back to the boat; we will gather up poor Athrú's ashes and give them a decent burial at sea.'

'Aye,' they all agreed, but when they went outside they discovered that the houses had vanished. So they made their way sorrowfully back to the boat, yet again decreased in number.

12: The End of the Road and the Beginning

'Money's not everything, is it, Gáire?' Aengus mused. 'Far from it, my friend,' replied the storyteller. 'Far from it, but you're beginning to look tired. It's time for me to finish my tale and send you to bed.'

It was a weary and dispirited group of men who returned to the boat. They were no nearer home and no nearer knowing which way to sail.

'We will continue to follow the Guide Star,' Maeldun told them. 'It's the only thing we can do.'

Day followed day with unremarkable sameness. The men had been on the sea so long and rowed for so long that time had lost any meaning for them. Then one day their boat was encircled by gulls. Birds mean that land is close, and it was. Facing them, rising high into the sky, was an island that was all mountain. It was the sort of mountain that children draw, wide at the base and rising smoothly and rapidly to a peak. Except that there was no peak on this mountain. It was as if someone had sliced it off with a giant sword.

Despite being heartsore of the sea, the men were not too keen to land, their previous experiences having made them fearful.

'Shall we bother stopping?' asked Oigín.

'We must,' Maeldun told him. 'We need fresh food and a change of exercise.'

'Who's to go ashore?' asked Diuran.

'Anyone who wants to,' answered a dispirited Maeldun. 'Maybe Tirelach and Forannan and Athrú were the lucky ones. Maybe we'll never find our way home.'

The men shared Maeldun's depression, but their spirits rose as they approached the land. Built into the mountain was a long hall and standing at the entrance was a raven-haired little woman with the reddest cheeks and cheeriest smile that anyone had ever seen.

'Come on in, boys,' she called. 'I knew you were coming and I've your meal ready. Come on, lads, there's a small cove here to your left and you're as welcome as the rain is to the parched earth.'

The men all realised how much this woman reminded them of their mothers and at the same time they knew they had missed their mothers every day of the voyage without realising it.

'I'm Bandraiocht,' she told them as they reached the shore. 'I've been here on my own since, well, since I don't know when. What is time if you have no one to share it with? I cannot begin to tell you how happy I am to see you. Come in. I have a fire going, warm water for bathing and good hot food and drink. Are you ready for it, lads?'

They were indeed, and they did justice to the meal she had prepared. How long was it, they wondered, since they had eaten real food off a plate or drunk the water of life from a goblet? However long it was, it tasted better than any food or drink they could remember.

'Sleep around the fire, boys,' Bandraiocht invited. 'I have feather-filled quilts for all of you and tomorrow, if you are willing, I'll show you my island.'

Tomorrow came and each man felt new strength and new hope in his body. Bandraiocht led them up the mountain with the speed and grace of a deer. Several times she had to stop and wait for them.

'Your legs have grown weak,' she told them, 'from all that sitting. You must exercise while you're here. A run up and down my mountain every day and you'll be as fit as I am.

When they got to the top of the mountain, they saw that it was hollow. Deep down inside it was a lake of icy-looking water.

'You can swim in it, if you want to,' Bandraiocht invited. 'I'll show you the way down.' But no one took her up on her offer.

After showing them around, Bandraiocht left them to their own devices. Tirechan lay on the rim of the crater, with Diuran protectively nearby. Together they watched the birds and the small animals and felt the sun warm on their skins.

'Look at that bird, Diuran. What is it?'

'I don't know, Tirechan. I've never seen anything like it.'

It was a large bird with a wingspan to match a man's outstretched arms. Its feathers were grey, like the grey of an old person's hair rather than the young grey of a northern goose. It was like an eagle in its majesty, but its beak was straight, not curved like the beak of a bird of prey. The men watched as it flew slowly, wearily overhead, circling lower and lower until suddenly, without warning, it plunged into the lake.

'Is it fishing, do you think?' asked Diuran, but there was no need for an answer because they could both see what was happening. The bird dived deep into the lake, leaving circles on the surface.

They watched as it plunged, deep, deep, out of sight. Then it re-emerged, flying slowly at first, then faster and faster until it soared so high into the sky that they could barely see it.

'Did you see what I saw?' asked Diuran. 'Did you see that? It went in an old bird and it came out young and strong. Did you see it?'

'I saw it, Diuran, but I still can't believe it. Let's call the others.'

'You call the others if you like, Tirechan, but I'm going to dive into the lake, and I think you should too.'

'But it could be dangerous, Diuran. You don't know what it will do to you.'

'I don't,' replied Diuran, 'but I'm prepared to risk it.' And without another moment's hesitation, he dived headfirst into the lake.

Tirechan watched him hit the water and then ran for the others. Diuran swam and swam. It was like swimming in a bath. It was like flying through the air. It was like being stroked and stretched and pleasured beyond words. His legs moved with a strength and vigour that he might have had years before but had long forgotten. And his arms moved through the water like finely tailored oars. 'My hands seem to stroke the water as they cut through it,' he thought and then shouted, 'My hands, my hands!' For he had two whole hands again.

Diuran moved effortlessly to the edge of the lake, and just as effortlessly up to the rim of the mountain. He walked and leapt with the unlaboured motion of wind or rain or bird or dolphin. His muscles and veins and bones and skin exulted in their liberation. He had already reached the mountain rim when his friends were still making their way up. Only Bandraiocht was there to meet him.

83

'You followed the bird in,' she smiled.

'I did,' agreed Diuran. 'You've been in too, haven't you?'

'I have, Diuran, I have. I was this age when I followed the bird in many lifetimes ago and since then, I have not lost a tooth. Nor has a hair of my head turned grey. You've found youth and strength, as I have. We're the lucky ones.'

By this time Maeldun and the men had struggled up the mountain.

'Diuran,' said Maeldun, 'You look so well! And your hand! You've got your hand back.'

'Don't stand marvelling, man,' Diuran urged. 'Get into the lake. Look what it did for me.'

'It's too late,' sighed Bandraiocht. 'The effects disappear almost as soon as the bird leaves the water.'

Tirechan and several of the men jumped into the lake anyway, but Bandraiocht was right. They felt refreshed but they did not look or feel like Diuran.

'When will the bird come back?' asked Tirechan. 'We're not in a hurry. We can wait.'

'It won't be back in your lifetime, son,' Bandraiocht told him. 'I know when it will come only days before it happens, but it does not come often. I expected it this morning. That's why I brought you all up here.'

'But you should have told us, Bandraiocht,' complained Maeldun, 'then we would all have followed the bird in.'

'Nobody told Diuran,' she replied and led the way down to the hall. 'I cannot give any of you perfect health, but I can give you the next best thing, good food.'

While Maeldun checked and rechecked the boat, Diuran ran about the island touching sand and stone and tree. 'I've never

before appreciated my hands or my feet. I took them for granted,'
he thought, 'but not any more. Every day of my life, I'll look at the
gift of my hand and remember what it was like without it.'

After their meal, Tirechan followed Bandraiocht to her resting
place.

'You're not just an ordinary woman, Bandraiocht, are you?'

'Who is ordinary, son?' she replied. 'Look at Diuran's hand. To
you or to me, it might seem a very ordinary hand and yet, to him,
it is the most incomparable hand that has ever existed. When we
have lost something, we learn to value it. When we are alone, we
learn to value thought, and thought makes us wise.'

'You know our story, don't you?' he asked.

'I do.'

'Will we ever get home?'

'It is sometimes better not to ask such questions,' Bandraiocht
smiled.

'I need to know, Bandraiocht.'

'All will get home, Tirechan, but one,' she told him and saw
from his eyes that he understood.

Days of pleasure and peace passed quickly on the island, but at
last it was time to go.

'We'll have to leave now, Bandraiocht,' Maeldun told her, 'or
Diuran will start swimming home!'

'Yes,' she agreed. 'I'll miss you, but it is time to head home. May
the powers that rule our lives and our worlds go with you! May the
winds be gentle and always at your back! May you all know peace!'

Off they went, sad to leave Bandraiocht, but no longer depressed.

'Home, lads,' Maeldun assured them.

'Home,' they all replied.

The wind drove them gently but powerfully during the day and throughout the night. There was no need to row, so each man slept when darkness fell.

'Wake up, Maeldun,' yelled Diuran. 'It's Tirechan.'

'What's wrong with him?' asked Maeldun.

'He's not in the boat,' answered Diuran. 'He's not here. I watched him when we were on the island, but I didn't think I had to watch him on the boat.'

'What's happened?'

'Where is he?'

'I saw him late last night, sitting near the stern of the boat,' volunteered Oigín.

'Well, he's not there now, is he?' shouted an angry Diuran. 'We must go back for him. He's lost overboard. We can't just leave him.'

'Go back to *where*, Diuran?' Maeldun asked. 'We've let the wind blow us for a day and a night. We don't know which direction we've come from, so we can't go back.'

'Well, we can't just leave him.'

'We've had to leave the others,' Maeldun answered. 'The choice is not ours. I should have obeyed Seanfhear and I didn't. My action has cost us four men and, for all I know, we may never see home again.'

'We'll see it all right,' shouted Oigín, 'for we're nearly there as it is. Look, Maeldun, I know those hills. They are not far from home. I know the way back from here. We'll soon see our homeland.'

Gáire paused and drew a deep breath. He looked at Aengus, who was waiting expectantly.

'And they did, Aengus. They did see their homeland. Soon, they were safe again and back home after years of wandering.'

'Did Maeldun punish his father's murderer?'

'No, Aengus, he did not. The man had drunk himself into a stupor years before and had died in his own vomit.'

It was late, very late and it was time for Aengus to rest before setting out again.

'How many islands did Maeldun visit, Gáire?' asked Aengus, just before he lay down to sleep.

'Thirty-seven, Aengus, and each one different.'

'But you've only told me about what happened on ten of them.'

'Next visit, Aengus. I'll save the rest for the next visit.'

BOOK TWO

Through Hollow
Lands

13: Wandering and Wondering

Midsummer morning came sharp and bright and early. The day would be long and the search for Caillte must begin. In his sleep, Aengus had seen her face and heard her voice urging him to follow her.

'I'll follow you, Caillte, to the ends of the earth, if necessary,' he told her.

'Will you eat something, Aengus?' Gáire's voice broke into his reverie.

'No, Gáire, no. I've wasted enough time.'

'There's always time for a bite and sup, Aengus, just enough to keep you going until you find another hostelry and another host.'

'But Caillte's waiting, Gáire.'

'And do you think her love is so fickle that she will not wait a little while longer, Aengus? Eat a little of my wife's food, and drink a little milk. Then pack all that remains in a bag. Food for the road, Aengus, for none of us knows if it will be a short road or a long road. Where will you go?'

'To the west, Gáire, towards the setting sun.'

Soon it was time to leave. 'It's time to say farewell, Gáire,' said Aengus. 'And it's a sad farewell because I'm leaving good friends. I'm leaving not just you and your wife, but also Maeldun and Diuran and ... '

'You never leave the people you love, Aengus,' smiled Gáire. 'You carry them around in your head. For you, my wife will always be preparing the best food in the world, and I will be getting ready to tell you another tale. May the Powers of Light guide you, Aengus, and till we meet again, may they keep you always in the palm of their hand.'

Aengus walked westward, the sun strong on his back. He did not know why he took this direction or where he would find Caillte, but his stride was that of a man who knows where he is going and why.

After several hours, he came to the banks of a winding river, its waters tranquil and inviting. It was broad enough so that an ordinary man would hesitate to jump across, but to someone of Aengus's abilities it presented no problem. He took a few steps backward and gathered himself for the leap. Then, before his eyes, the river seemed to stretch until its furthest bank was almost on the horizon. Aengus stopped, puzzled. As he did, the river contracted to its original size. Aengus pondered his next move; if the river expanded while he was in mid-leap, he would be lost. He decided to follow the course of the river in search of a means of crossing. And where the river disappeared around the base of a hill, he found stepping stones. He crossed quickly, his feet barely touching each stone. Once safely on the other side, he lengthened his stride, putting a good distance between himself and the treacherous river.

The mid-day sun burned directly over his head and he decided to look for a shady spot to rest. In the mountain range to his left he spotted a small opening, barely big enough to crawl into. But once inside, he discovered that the space quickly opened up into a wide rock chamber. The further in he went, the higher and wider and brighter the chamber grew.

'That's the sky I can see,' Aengus murmured in surprise.

'Well. and if you live long enough,' came an exasperated voice, 'you'll hear every degree of stupidity! And what else would you expect up there but the sky? Were you expecting the sea?'

Aengus looked round, but in spite of the light that illuminated every nook and cranny, he could see no-one.

'I'm down here, you great big, ignorant being. My mother used to say that if people grew too tall, their brains became addled. Are *your* brains addled, Aengus?'

'No, they certainly are not,' exclaimed Aengus in annoyance. 'But where are you and how do you know my name?'

'I'm here, one stride in front of your left foot.'

Aengus looked down at his foot, but could see nothing but the bare ground all around.

'I still can't see you,' he insisted.

'No brains and no second sight,' came the exasperated voice. 'I'll have to make things easier for you.'

And suddenly, right where he had indicated, and as if he had materialised out of thin air, appeared a small, cross-looking man. Well, although his white beard proclaimed him to be a man, by his size he could be taken for a two-year-old child.

'Are you a midget?' asked Aengus.

'A midget!' the little man exclaimed indignantly. 'I most certainly am not. I'm a perfect size. You, on the other hand, are like an overgrown mushroom, too big and too coarse to be of use for anything.'

Aengus was about to tell the little man that he was a god and not to be trifled with, but the little man anticipated his words.

'Oh, you don't have to tell me, Aengus. I know all about you. I know your seed, breed and generation,' sniffed the little man. 'Your credentials are, I suppose, acceptable. Your family is a reasonably well established one, though in no way comparable to my own. We have been overlords here since time immemorial. Your family only goes back to time memorial. By the way, my name is Lord Luchorpan, but I won't stand on ceremony. You may call me Luch.'

Aengus looked at Luch. Despite his size, he was perfectly formed, and there was no doubting his aristocratic bearing.

'You have me at a disadvantage, Luch,' said Aengus. 'You seem to know everything about me, but I know nothing about you.'

Luch sighed, but indulgently, as if he were dealing with a very young, and somewhat stupid child.

'It's hard for me to understand your mental and psychic limitations, Aengus. My people are the Fomorians and we have lived here since living was possible. We developed with the land and became as much a part of its cycle as wind and waves or sun and streams. It's a small land so we stayed small in our symbiotic relationship with it. Then your people came. Whereas we had concentrated on developing our minds, all your development had gone into growing big bodies. At first, we tried to live with you, some even inter-married with you, but it was like crossing a sunbeam with a snail. It just did not work, so we drew ourselves apart. Now, our peoples inhabit the same land but not the same dimension, so you do not see us. Occasionally, however, we enter your world or allow you to enter ours. Do you understand what I'm saying, Aengus?'

'I understand the words you are saying, Luch, but I'm not certain what those words imply.'

'Don't let it bother you,' answered Luch, kindly. 'Can the stone understand a tree or the spider a wolfhound? They don't have to, and they can live in harmony. We do not blame your people for coming to our land; we can give the land to you and yet still have it for ourselves. You don't understand that, do you, Aengus?'

'Not really,' admitted Aengus.

'Let me try to explain. Do you know what it is to feel that you have a destiny, Aengus? To feel that you must follow a light wherever it leads, irrespective of the cost?'

'Oh yes, I understand that. My destiny is that I must follow Caillte even though I don't know who or where she is.'

'Do you have a name for this feeling, Aengus?"

'No.'

'We do. The name we use is *freet*. Now, when I give you that word, do I lose it?'

'No, you still have it and I have something that I didn't have before.'

'Exactly, Aengus. And it is the same with this land. We were able to give it to you without losing it ourselves. Your freet links you with me. I'm here to help you, but before I do that I must teach you who you are. When you know who you are, then you'll begin to know where you are going.'

'At the moment I don't have time for your teaching, Luch,' answered Aengus. 'At any other time I would have welcomed it, but I must follow my freet. I must find Caillte.'

Luch looked up at his big companion, his face a mixture of

sadness and exasperation.

'No time for my teaching? No time to learn? When we stop learning, Aengus, we start dying, because learning is growth. Nobody knows everything, not even me, although I must confess I know a great deal more than you.'

'Do you know where Caillte is?'

'Yes.'

'Then take me to her, Luch. Help me fulfil my destiny.'

'Aengus, there are two ways to do everything: the right way and the wrong way. I can show you how to find Caillte, but we must do it my way – the right way. If you agree to that, there is one condition: while you are on your journey of discovery, you must not use your divine powers. You must act like a man and feel like a man. That way, you will learn about weakness, and such knowledge will teach you true strength. Otherwise, you must find Caillte on your own.'

'But I don't know where to find her,' Aengus confessed. 'This morning, I felt I knew exactly where I was going. Now, I'm not sure.'

'You knew where you were going this morning, Aengus, because I called you and I led your feet. But now it's time for you to choose. Will you look for Caillte in *my* way or will you journey alone? My way will seem strange to you, but it will lead you to Caillte. Your way will be more natural to you and it may lead to Caillte. What's it to be, young man?'

'My way *may*. Your way *will*. That's what you said, Luch?'

'That's what I said.'

'Then it has to be your way.'

'Perhaps there's hope for you big people after all,' smiled Luch.

'Come on, Aengus, follow me.'

14: The Race of Macha

Aengus followed the little man, not knowing where they were going or how long the journey would be. He was sure of only two things: that he would find Caillte and that Luch could cover ground faster than he himself could.

'Am I going too fast for you, Aengus?' Luch broke into his thoughts.

'Well, just a little,' admitted Aengus. 'How can you travel so fast on such little legs?'

'We're not here to discuss my legs,' answered an exasperated Luch. 'Can you not see that my legs are perfect for me? If they were any bigger, they'd be out of proportion. In any case, I don't need long legs because I don't walk all that often. Normally, if I want to go somewhere, I just think myself there. It's quite simple.'

'*Think* yourself here? Can all your people "think themselves" where they are going?'

'Oh, certainly, and when our two races interbred, some of that ability passed on to you.'

'It did? How do you mean? I can't think myself to another place, and neither can anyone else I know. In fact, you are the only creature I have ever met who could do that.'

'Sit down for a moment, Aengus, and I will explain. Do you remember your mother?'

'Of course.'

'Do you remember what she looked like?'

'Of course I do.'

'And the way she used to teach you.'

'Oh, yes. I remember how she would tell me who I was and what I would be and why I should never betray a trust. When she taught me, she never said: "Don't do this or don't do that." She would tell me a story and leave me to draw my own conclusions.'

'She was a good teacher, by the sound of it.'

'She certainly was. I remember the time she told me the story of Macha. It was springtime and so warm that it might easily have been summer. A friend and I were wrestling and he threw me. I hit my head on a stone and was very angry so I shouted that I was a god and that I would turn him into a toad.

'My mother called me over. She said nothing about my threat, which she had obviously heard, but began to tell me about Macha, a kinswoman of hers.'

Macha was tall and beautiful and strong-willed. Every god in the country had sought her hand, but Macha scorned them all. She would choose a husband of her own. Nobody was going to tell her whom to pick. Besides, she might not get married at all. She was very happy as she was – riding her horses, writing her poetry, singing her songs and watching how the humans lived.

There was one particular group of people who lived in a valley between two high hills near where Macha herself lived. They were good people, hard-working and brave, and Macha often sat on the hillside watching them working in the fields and tending their animals. She found herself thinking about what it would be like to live with them and work with them.

One day while she was watching, she heard a voice from behind her:

'And who might you be, my lady of the shining hair?'

Macha turned and saw before her a man who was tall and fair and more attractive than any of the gods who had wanted her in marriage.

'I'm Macha,' she told him.

'And I'm Comhgall,' he smiled. 'I'm on my way home. I live in the valley but I have been away for some time looking at horses.'

They sat together on the hillside, talking and laughing. They discovered much in common: their love of horses, their love of music and poetry.

'Sing to me, Macha,' Comhgall urged as he lay back in the grass. 'Sing me one of your own songs.'

Macha raised her voice in song:

> *Arrows from a bow wound deep,*
> *Piercing the body's screen.*
> *But deeper still are the wounds of love*
> *Gaping though never seen.*
> *Like a sailor tossed on the white-waved sea*
> *Love-lamenting nights I spend*
> *Awaiting my lover who will not return*
> *In a love-wounded world without end.*

Comhgall listened as she wove words into a melody. 'Your song tells me that love can bring pain,' he said, 'but I find that hard to believe.'

He took her hand and pressed it to his lips. 'Macha,' he told her, 'I've seen many women who would have been mine for the asking, but you're the first one that I have wanted. You are the only woman I will ever love. Will you stay with me, Macha, here in our valley? Will you marry me and love me?'

Macha stretched out her hand and touched his hair and his face.

'Yes, Comhgall, I will marry you and love you and live with you, but you must never let anyone know that I am not human. If they discover that I am a god, there will be no place for me among your people and I will have to leave you.'

'I promise I will never tell anyone, Macha. I never want to lose you. Now, come home with me and meet my family. We have much good news to tell them.'

Soon Macha was as much a part of life in the valley as her husband. She looked human. She behaved like a human, but she knew things that no ordinary mortal could know and her wisdom helped Comhgall grow rich and comfortable. He still travelled and bought horses, but he always rushed home to Macha, especially now that she was carrying his twins. Macha knew that her unborn children would be boys, and when she told Comhgall, his joy was so great that he went out to celebrate.

When he was drinking with his friends, a traveller arrived. He introduced himself as a horse trader, but in reality he was one of the suitors that Macha had turned down.

'I am looking for a man named Comhgall,' he announced. 'I believe he buys horses, and I have the fastest horse on earth.'

Comhgall went up to the stranger. 'It is true that I buy horses,' he said, 'and at any other time I might have been interested in your horse, but tonight I am not thinking of horses. I'm about to become a father. What's a horse compared to a son?'

'So they lied when they told me that Comhgall was a man interested in horse racing?' sneered the stranger. 'They lied when they said that you were a man who would take up a challenge. I am telling you now that I have the fastest horse on earth. Are you afraid to bet against my horse? No one told me that Comhgall was a coward!'

'I'm no coward,' roared Comhgall. 'I do not refuse a challenge. Bring your horse here and let us see it.'

The stranger's horse was old and tired, sagging in the middle from carrying too much weight. Comhgall and his friends laughed.

'Go home, young man,' Comhgall dismissed him. 'That beast could not outpace any of my horses! Why, even my pregnant wife could run faster.'

'Done,' said the stranger. 'I'll wager all my gold that my horse can run faster than your pregnant wife.'

Comhgall trembled. What had he done? He loved Macha more than his life, but what about his honour? What about his word? When he got home, he told Macha what had happened and asked for her help.

Macha's face clouded over with sadness. 'If I run faster than his horse, Comhgall,' she told him, 'everyone will know that I am not human. Once they know that, I'll have to leave you.' She looked at her beloved husband and she knew that he could never live with the shame of dishonour. 'I'll run for you, my husband.'

And she did. She ran faster than the wind and Comhgall won the gold. That night Macha gave birth to twin boys.

'While you have our sons, you will always have part of me,' she told a distraught Comhgall as she bade him goodbye. He watched her go and felt love and youth ebbing from his veins.

When Aengus had finished the story, Luch sat silently for a few minutes. Then he asked: 'Where were you when you were telling me that story, Aengus?'

'Where was I? Well, I suppose I was back home. For a while, it was as if it was all happening for the first time and I was once again at home with my mother.'

'That's what I meant when I said that some of our power to travel from one place to another had passed to you. The difference is that you can do it only in your minds. You can't take your bodies with you. Are you well rested now, Aengus?'

'I am, Luch.'

'Let's go, then.'

15: Ballydran

For a while, they walked in silence.

'Did you make me recall that story in order to teach me that some lovers are doomed to be apart, Luch, or to remind me that I must use only human powers on this journey?' asked Aengus.

'I wasn't trying to teach you anything, Aengus. I merely put you in the position where you could learn something. If that's the conclusion you have drawn, then you have learnt a valuable lesson.'

'Where are we going now, Luch?' he enquired.

'Straight ahead, lad, straight ahead.'

'Yes, but straight ahead *where*?'

'Young men are so impatient,' sighed Luch. 'We'd get there quicker if we didn't have to talk all the time. But I'm probably being hard on you. Your breed needs to talk about everything. You substitute words for actions. You'd rather write songs than sow seeds. It's not your fault. As a wise woman once remarked, "To know all is to understand all and to understand all is to forgive all." Knowing all about you, Aengus, means I can understand your tendencies.'

'What do you know about me, Luch?'

'Don't you know your history, Aengus?'

'Well, I know that my people came here from a country far to the south and to the east. Some say that we were brought by a whirling wind. Others claim that my ancestor, Danaan, led us across the lands and seas. She was a queen and the bravest warrior of her time. We trace our family name, the People of Danaan, to her. And when we came, we brought with us fire and light and poetry. There's much more to it than that, but those are the main points.'

'And what do you know about the people who were here before you?'

'Not much, Luch, but I believe they were short and dark and not very intelligent ... '

Aengus broke off, partly because Luch had stopped and partly because he realised that his words might seem a little offensive.

'Offensive?' snorted Luch, 'a little offensive? Oh, it's my own fault for reading your mind! Sometimes it's better to shut off the power. One rarely reads anything kind about oneself.'

'Were your people in charge of this land before we came, Luch?' asked Aengus, trying to be conciliatory.

'We were, Aengus and, in a very real sense, we still are. Your people were known as the people of light because you were fair and came from the south and you carried weapons that flashed in the sunlight. We, on the other hand, were known as the people of lightning. We were short and dark and we controlled the elements, sometimes appearing in mists, but more often riding the lightning shafts.

'At first, we welcomed you. You seemed so pretty and so childlike. We loved you. We taught you. We even intermarried with you. But soon we found that you could be cruel and unthinking. And in the end we fought you. At the Battle of Magh Tuireadh, on the plain of the pillars, your people and mine met. Force and strength fought wit and wisdom, and wit and wisdom lost. We, who had prided ourselves on healing and helping, killed and were killed. Many of us died on the battlefield and the rest of us felt like dying of shame. We withdrew to our place of refuge, a place that your ancestors called Lugnangall, the hollow of the strangers. We left the surface land to you, to the invaders, and since then we've lived separate lives, meeting only by chance or by request.'

'Did we meet by chance, Luch?'

'No, Aengus, not by chance.'

'But I didn't request anything.'

'Didn't you, Aengus? Haven't you been asking all the powers in existence to help you find Caillte? But no more talk now, we have a lot of ground to cover before we sleep. If only your people had learned to think themselves from one place to another!'

On they walked, Luch leading the way, sure-footed as a squirrel, Aengus following, unwilling to admit that he found it hard to keep up with a man who barely came up to his knee.

'If we are to proceed at the speed of your foot, Aengus, we'll take three days to reach our destination and we must stop and rest soon. Where would you like to spend the night? To our left, we have Annaghmore where there is a fair in progress. The people there are the ones who ousted Danaan's race, just as surely as hers ousted mine. Their fair is a celebration of life and love. They put a live goat on a pole and the young, unmarried girls dance round it. If you haven't seen it before, Aengus, you will enjoy it. After the dancing, many of the following year's marriages are arranged, if you get my meaning.'

'Aother time perhaps, Luch, unless we may meet Caillte there.'

'No, she will not be there, Aengus. Then you have another choice: over to our right, we have Glenagealt, the glen of the lunatic. That's where King Goll found refuge when he lost his wits on the battlefield. Shall we go to Glenagealt and talk to King Goll?'

'If you will not be offended, Luch,' answered Aengus. 'Let's not take any diversions. I'm eager to get on, so let's go straight ahead and find somewhere on our route where we can rest for the night. Do you know of such a place?'

'There is a little settlement called Ballydran.'

'Do they have a fair?'

'No.'

'Or a mad king?'

'Nothing like that, Aengus. It's just a quiet little village with quiet, ordinary people. Put an inch into your stride, man, and we'll be there before you know it.'

Luch and Aengus put their energies into walking and soon they were on the outskirts of Ballydran. In size it was half-way between a large village and a small town and the first impression was one of peace and order. There was one wide street down the middle of the town, with houses arranged on either side. It was a strange street, sloped to one side like a long, low hill. If you stood on the low side you could just see the upper half of the houses on the other side and yet, if you walked down the middle of the street, you could see both lines of houses. There was no dirt on the street and no dogs wandering about.

Not like Ballycook, Aengus thought, remembering a tale he had once heard about a town with the lovely name of Ballycook, the settlement of the cuckoo.

On a cold winter's day, an old beggarman called Bacach had arrived at Ballycook, looking for a bite to eat and a hayshed to sleep in. Everywhere he looked, the doors were shut tight against him. Only the dogs wandered the streets, and dogs don't like beggars. They started to growl and move towards him.

Bacach tried to pick up a stone to rattle at their heels, but the stones were frozen to the ground. Slowly, painfully, Bacach made his way out of the town. When he had reached the outskirts, he turned and cried out: 'My curse upon you, long, hungry Ballycook, where your stones are chained and your dogs are loose. May you feel the pain of hunger and cold and loneliness every hour of every day until you learn to treat strangers more kindly!'

Fortunately, Ballydran was no Ballycook.

'You're right about that,' Luch broke into his thoughts. 'Poor old Bacach got a very uncivil welcome in Ballycook, but in Ballydran you will find all the doors are open. Now let us go to the temple. It is dedicated to the Mother of All and it has been set aside for travellers. We'll spend the night there. I think you'll find it of interest.'

Luch led the way to a building that was similar in design to the other houses, but constructed on a grander scale. As they approached, they could hear voices raised in praise of the Star of the Sea, the Guide of the Wanderer, the Lamp of the Night and the hundreds of other names reserved for the Mother of All. Luch entered the temple quietly, Aengus close on his heels. It was quiet and cool. The central section was shaped like a boat, but in place of a sail, it had a silver net. A group of young men were chanting the litany, their hands raised.

When the singing ended, Luch said: 'Diuran built this temple, Aengus, and placed the silver net in the centre. It was his act of thanksgiving for returning home after a perilous journey on the oceans of the world.'

'Diuran!' Aengus exclaimed in amazement. 'You don't mean

the Diuran who sailed with Maeldun?'

'Did someone ask for me?'

The question came from one of the singers. He walked toward the travellers, smiling.

'Greetings, friends,' he said as he approached them. 'You are most welcome, here. What we have to offer is simple – water to wash in, food and drink to sustain you, a bed to sleep in and good company if you have the desire for it.'

'Are you *the* Diuran?' asked Aengus.

'I don't know any other,' the young man replied. 'I see you looking at my hand. Yes, it's in perfect condition as, indeed, I am too; not a day older nor a hair greyer over these many years. But there'll be time to answer some of your questions when you've washed and rested.'

Diuran showed them to a room.

'Warm water will be brought for you, and when you're ready, I will join you for some food.'

'Don't rush him, Aengus,' advised Luch when Diuran had left. 'There'll be time enough for your questions.'

'Why didn't you tell me it was Diuran's town?'

'I told you it was Ballydran.'

'But this country is full of towns called Bally this or Bally that!'

Luch looked at Aengus pityingly. 'I can't help it if you cannot make a simple connection. Anyway, never mind that now. When we eat with Diuran, ask only the question that you most want answered. Otherwise we will get no sleep tonight and you will not be fit for an early start in the morning.'

When the food arrived and Diuran sat down with them, Aengus was in a fever of frustration as Luch kept Diuran talking about the land and the weather and the problems of travelling. Finally, there was a break in the conversation.

'Diuran,' Aengus gasped, his words tumbling out, one chasing the other as he tried to forestall another interruption from Luch. 'What happened to Maeldun? Does he live near here? Did he find it easy to settle down? Did he ever ...'

'One question at a time, Aengus,' laughed Diuran. 'To be honest, I can answer all of them and none of them. After Maeldun arrived home safely, he was greeted as a hero everywhere he went. He had power and prestige and could have married into any of the wealthy families in the land. For a time, he seemed happy, but one day he sought me out and asked for a small corner of my silver net, to bring him luck on his journey. 'I'm going to find her, Diuran,' he told me. 'I'm going back to Áluinn and my island of contentment.' Later that day, he set out alone and no-one has seen him since.'

And with that, Diuran rose from his seat and left, wishing them a peaceful night.

But Aengus was too restless to sleep. There were still so many unanswered questions.

'Did Maeldun ever find Áluinn?' he asked.

'What do you think, Aengus?'

'What sort of an answer is that?' retorted Aengus.

'Some questions can only be answered by a question,' Luch told him.

'I don't believe that.'

'All right, Aengus, I'll answer yours if you answer one of mine. Why do young people only understand their parents when they are the same age as their parents were when they couldn't understand their parents?'

'What?' asked a puzzled Aengus.

'Exactly,' replied Luch. Then he added, 'Maeldun found peace, Aengus. We can be sure of that. He knew where his contentment lay and he went after it. Only the very brave or the very lucky can do as much.'

16: No Flies on Me

Aengus found himself alone in Coll Wood. There was no Gáire, no Maeldun, no Luch. Only the silence in the noise of the night. He knew where he was going and he knew with total certainty that he'd find his love, the maiden with apple-blossom in her hair. What was her name? He couldn't have forgotten. Her name meant more to him than his life. But look, there ahead: a house of glass and she's there.

He rushed to the house that glimmered and shimmered in the moonlight. His love was smiling and calling him in.

'Aengus, I've been waiting for you. What took you so long? Don't you know me? Don't you remember? I'm Etain and we have an hour together.'

'Of course,' thought Aengus. 'It's Etain, my Etain. How could I have forgotten?'

Aengus held her in his arms and remembered the first time he had seen her. She was so tall and beautiful, walking beside her husband, Midhir. But what could Aengus offer that Midhir could not surpass? 'I'll give you joy beyond words,' his eyes told her. 'And I'll take it,' hers replied. Somehow, they had found one another later that night and had melted into one another as dawn melts into day.

'I'll never leave you, Aengus,' she told him. 'We will live together always.'

'Will you? Live together, always? Will you?' came the rasping voice of a betrayed husband. 'Never leave him? I'll see to that. Fuamnach, I order you to transform her. Transform her into a creature no man will ever love.'

Fuamnach breathed heavily and uttered words in a language known only to the most powerful of magicians. Aengus felt Etain changing in his arms. Gone was the softness, the strength, the beauty, and on his arm was a purple fly.

'Etain,' he moaned, 'Etain?'

The fly looked up at him with large, sad, purple eyes.

'You wanted her. You've got her, Aengus,' laughed Midhir. 'She's all yours now.' And he stormed off in a fury.

'Fuamnach,' pleaded Aengus, 'Fuamnach. Have pity, I beg you. Will she ever get back her human form?'

'For one hour a month when the moon is full, she will have her own body,' the magician replied. 'You must build her a house of glass, Aengus, and you may visit her there. I can do no more. Except for that one hour, she will be a fly, but no ordinary fly. She will be the most beautiful fly in the land, just as she was once the most beautiful woman.'

Sadly, silently, Aengus constructed the house of glass. For twenty-eight days, Etain was a fly but, for one hour, once a month, she was again the most beautiful woman in the land. During the month, Aengus fed her and sang to her, and during their hour, she sang to him and loved him and wove harp strings from his hair.

When Midhir found out that Fuamnach had not punished Etain

fully, he sent a wind to the house of glass. While Aengus watched in horror, the house shook and shivered and fell. Etain was caught up by the wind and blown high, high into the air.

'Etain,' he called, 'I'm coming. I'll follow you.'

The gale blew Etain up and down and backwards and forwards and Aengus struggled to follow her. Up and over the trees she went and down towards the river. There was a young couple lying beside the river, talking of love. The wind seemed to subside and Aengus had almost reached Etain when she was snatched from his fingers and blown into the girl's mouth.

The young couple left and Aengus sat alone and bereft on the edge of the river.

Months passed and Aengus continued to sit and mourn for Etain. Then, one day, the same young girl came to the river, carrying a beautiful child.

'I've brought you back to the river where you were conceived,' she told the child. 'I'll call you Etain, and one day, men from all over the land will come to look at you and marvel at your beauty.'

It was Etain, all right. Aengus could see her golden hair and beautiful purple eyes, and he knew that he would never again hold her in his arms or taste the warmth of her body.

'Etain,' he cried. 'Etain.'

A hand shook Aengus's shoulder. 'Wake up, Aengus,' Luch called. 'It's time for us to continue our journey, although I doubt that you are much rested. You were tossing and turning all night.'

17: Threads of Gold

Aengus was very disturbed by his dream. It had seemed so real, but it couldn't have been, could it? Was there a time when he had known and loved Etain? Had he won her and lost her? Should he try to find her again after he had found Caillte? He was so confused.

'Young men!' sighed Luch. 'Yesterday, you had only one thought: to find Caillte. Now you're dithering between Etain and Caillte. Young men have high ideals, Aengus, but they are lacking in two essential ingredients: constancy and consistency.'

'And when, old man, do we gain these two essential virtues?' Aengus asked disrespectfully. He was growing a little tired of being lectured to by this small man.

'Only when continence is no longer a restful interlude.'

'What?' interjected a surprised Aengus. 'Luch, were you ever in love?'

'I was wrong,' smiled Luch. 'Young men suffer from *three* deficiencies. The third is their assumption that they invented love-making.'

'*Were* you in love, Luch?' Aengus persisted.

'That's for me to know and you to wonder about, Aengus. But I have no intention of telling you about my affairs, moral, spiritual or pecuniary, until I know you a good deal better. Put your curiosity into your walking! We have a good distance to cover before we rest.'

Aengus's thoughts of love were gradually ousted by the necessity of keeping up with a man less than half his size who could cover the ground twice as fast as he could. Aengus tried to match Luch's walk. It seemed to him that Luch took a normal step, but then somehow slid his foot forward, covering a second step's length for every one of Aengus's.

'It's what the men of the mountains call "mountainy gait",' Luch explained. 'They developed it for climbing hills after their sheep. It takes years of practice and it helps if you start learning it when you are five or six.'

'How did you learn it?'

'I spent some time helping an old couple who lived alone on the mountains. Their only son had gone, and they couldn't really cope. One evening, they sat at the fireside, cold because they had no wood to burn, hungry because they had no food to eat, and they thought about what it would be like to have a little one to live with them and share their burden. They were thinking of a human child, of course, but I was little and I could be more help than any child. Next morning, when they got up, I had the house cleaned, fresh water drawn, the cow milked, firewood in and fresh bread baking on the griddle.

The old couple were astonished :'Is it the fairies, do you think, woman of the house?' asked the old man.

'I'd say it must be, for who else would do this for us? But I'm not asking too many questions. I'm just going to wash myself and then sit down and eat. If you examine luck too closely, you can lose it, man of the house, and I for one have no intention of losing it.'

'And they didn't. I stayed with them and learned to walk like them. Strange, isn't it, Aengus, that you Danaans pushed us, the people of lightning, aside and you, in your turn, were replaced by such ordinary humans? Do you ever wonder how it is that intelligence and power are no guarantee of ascendancy?'

Aengus was concentrating all his energies into keeping up and had none to spare for philosophising.

'Sorry, lad,' Luch told him. 'When I get involved in a subject, I often speed up.'

'You must have been very involved in the last one,' Aengus gasped, 'because you've almost been flying. Shouldn't we rest for a while?'

'Very soon, Aengus,' Luch assured him. 'There's a lake just ahead where we can rest.'

And there was. Very soon, Aengus could see the water shimmering in the sunlight. When it came into full view, the lake was what Aengus could only describe as two-tier. The first lake was high up, almost filling a valley that was itself cradled within a larger valley. The second lake was smaller, lower down and fed from the first lake by an overflow that turned into a waterfall.

'That valley, ' Luch pointed to the inner valley surrounding the top lake. 'It's called Glen Suaimhneas, valley of peace.'

'Let's rest there then,' Aengus suggested. 'I am in need of some peace.'

Together they climbed up and sat under a tree, a little way back from the lake. As they rested, silent, the valley's peace flowed into them. They saw the sheen of the water break as fish rose to the surface and watched as birds flew quietly, lazily overhead.

Two large birds flew together, circling in a synchronised dance. Lower and lower they flew until Aengus and Luch could see that they were bound to one another by plaited threads of gold that tied the left leg of one bird to the right leg of the other. The birds had two bodies and four wings, but their motion was that of only one sentient being.

They came to rest at the edge of the water, a short distance in front of Aengus and Luch. The birds dipped their beaks in the water, and when they had drunk, they started to sing. At first there was melody only, but it was a melody that needed no words to speak its message of pain and loss. Then came the words, which may not have been words, but they imprinted a meaning in the mind that was as clear as if they had been spoken.

While they watched, the birds were transformed into women of such beauty that Aengus's eyes filled with tears just looking at them.

'Sing to me, sister,' urged Laban. 'Sing to help us understand and bear our fate.'

'Our fate is a hard one,' Fand answered. 'For you and I are joined by fate as surely as by these golden threads. But I still remember the happy times.'

'I remember when Conchubhar was struck on the head by a stone from a sling. His golden hair was soon the colour of an angry sky but I, with a thread of purest gold, mended his head so that no one, save me, could see the wound.

'And I remember the moment that Conchubhar told us about Cúchulainn and his deeds of courage and love. I already had a husband, Mannannan, but what was that when I saw the young warrior? I watched him arrive in the early morning, striding in his pride through dew that seemed to flame where his feet fell. "Come with me, Cúchulainn," I sang to him. "Come and I shall heal your wounds. Where I shall take you, there will be no pain in mind or body, no loss of strength and vigour, only joy and peace and fulfilment."

'He came with me. Of course he came, and you helped us to escape. For one moon we lived and loved and I never wanted it to end. "Fand, my love," he whispered one day, "I must go back to my world to see Emer, my mortal wife. I must ensure that she has all that she needs."

'Could I deny him the right to look after a loved one? Could I deny Emer a little happiness when I had so much? Sadly, I told him to go, but made him promise to meet me when the moon was full again, under the Yew-at-the-World's-Edge. One moon passed slowly, but it passed, as I prepared for Cúchulainn's return. In my eagerness to meet my love, I stood under the tree long, long before the moon was up. Strongly it rose and slowly it slipped lower and lower in the sky but still Cúchulainn did not come. Was that a noise? Was it Cúchulainn? No, it was the mad laugh of Mannannan.

'"Your wait is in vain, faithless woman", he cried. "Cúchulainn has treated you as you treated me. Your pain may be great now, but you will soon discover what real suffering is. I will turn you and your sister into birds. Together you will fly the skies and sing of love and of betrayal."

'And this has been our fate ever since. My greatest joy is that you are with me, Laban. My greatest sadness that you must share my fate.'

Still singing, still flying as one, Fand and Laban flew up into the still air, up and away.

Aengus watched them until they were out of sight.

'Will they ever be free from their spell, Luch?' he asked.

'Will men and women ever stop hurting the ones they love most?' Luch replied.

'Another question that can only be answered by a question, Luch?'

'Are you asking me or telling me? Come, Aengus, we have another half-day's journey ahead of us.'

18: Never Give All the Heart

'What are you humming, Aengus?'

'It's a song I wrote once about a singer who loved too long and too well and who learned too late that what he had always wanted was not to his liking when he finally got it.'

'That sounds a fairly typical piece of writing for a young man – contrived.'

'And I suppose you could do better?'

'Well, I'm not a poet, Aengus, so perhaps I lack your sensitivity, but I've only heard two poems that I'll never forget and they are both very short and very simple, on the surface, that is. One is by a man called Quinn, who never went to school but who learned all that he knew by being a good listener and a good observer. He called his poem 'The Watcher' and he wrote it in the idiom of the people:

> *I seen them come*
> *And I seen them go*
> *Like summer rain and winter snow.*
> *I seen them go*
> *And I seen them come*
> *And I watched them, dumb.*

119

'What do you make of that, Aengus?'

'Interesting,' answered Aengus, 'although it's not something I would want to have written. And what's the second one?'

Luch thought for a moment and said, 'It's about a merman.'

> *A merman loved a maiden once.*
> *With jewels bright he decked her hair.*
> *He took her home to share his life*
> *And learned too late she needed air.*

'So what did you think of that, Aengus?'

'I can't say that I share your taste in poetry, Luch,' Aengus answered truthfully.

'Ah well, never mind, Aengus,' smiled Luch. 'Tomorrow, we'll be visiting a school for poets and musicians. You might find something there more to your taste. But now, we must get on with our journey. By the way, I should congratulate you. You have learned to cover the ground much better today. You are not so tired either, are you?'

'No, I'm rarely tired when I have something to think about. I was turning over the story of Fand and Laban in my mind and trying to remember how they were associated with Conchubhar, the king of Uladh. There's a tale about Conchubhar that is tickling the surface of my memory. But I just can't remember it.'

'Think with less agitation, Aengus, and I'll see if I can extract it for you. Ah, yes, I might have known. It's a story of love. Shall I tell it to you, lad, to help make our journey speed by?'

'Please, Luch.'

'It's a story that I have heard many times and in many places, Aengus. All tellers add their own twiddles but, as stories go, this one needs neither fancy words nor music to hide the seams.'

When Conchubhar was king, he was feared throughout the land, because he had the best warriors and fought the best wars that ever a storyteller could want to relate, but the tales of valour and chivalry will have to wait for another time for this is a story of power and love and the power of love.

Conchubhar was the son of Nessa, a woman of might and guile. She managed to trick her husband, Fergus, into giving up his kingdom to his stepson.

Luch paused. 'And do you know how she did it?' he asked Aengus.

'No, but no doubt I'll hear!'

'Well that's where you're wrong, you overgrown Danaan, for I have no intention of telling you that saga. Though, mind you, you could learn from it! No, I'm telling only one small slice of a loaf of a story.'

When Conchubhar was young, he was tall like you and, like most young men, he had a weakness for a beautiful face, especially when it kept company with a beautiful body. As he got older, his passion for women decreased for a time, until he set eyes on Deirdre. Every poet who has ever lived has tried to describe Deirdre. That she was beautiful is beyond dispute, and kind and loving too. Think, Aengus, of all the qualities you admire most in a woman. Think of them and then multiply them by the biggest number you can think of. Then Aengus, you will have just the smallest inkling of what Deirdre was like.

As you might expect, there were suitors queuing up for the pleasure of being rejected by Deirdre for, although Deirdre could have had kings or lords or gods, her heart was set on Naoise, an ordinary mortal who had only four claims to fame. Firstly, he was the son of Usna, and I don't have to tell you who he was.

121

Secondly, he was the brother of Ainnle and Ardan and, as you know, with the possible exception of Usna himself, their stories are widely known and rehearsed throughout the length and breadth of the land. Thirdly, he could talk to the deer. He would call them and ask them where they had been and what they had seen and he would warn them when they were in danger.

'But what was his fourth claim to fame?' interrupted Aengus.

'I'm beginning to think that I overestimated your intelligence the first time we met, Aengus! Do I have to draw everything out for you? What else would it be than that Deirdre loved him and had vowed to marry him?'

One day, shortly before the wedding, Conchubhar rode up on a visit to Usna and his eyes fell on Deirdre. Just gazing upon her caused the dimness to clear from his eyes. Listening to her made him hear sounds that his ears had long forgotten. And loving her, he knew, would make his years fall from him like snow from a ditch when the sun rises.

'I must have Deirdre,' he told Usna.

'She's not mine to give, Conchubhar,' Naoise's father reminded him. 'She is here, of her own free will, learning what her life will be like when she marries my son.'

'I want her, Usna, and I must have her. Give Naoise any other woman in my land. Give him any ten that he chooses, but Deirdre is for me alone. If necessary, I will lay waste to all your lands and enslave all your children, but I intend to have Deirdre as my queen.'

Usna was worried. He knew that Naoise would never take one woman or ten or ten thousand in place of Deirdre, but he also knew that Conchubhar had grown cruel with age and would stop at nothing to achieve his desires.

'Should we not ask my diviner for advice?' Usna suggested.

'Ask him, if you wish,' Conchubhar agreed, 'but Deirdre will marry me, whatever he or anyone else says.'

Usna's servant, Culaith, had overheard the exchange and ran to tell Naoise, who was preparing to go riding with Deirdre, Ainnle and Ardan.

'Conchubhar will not be dissuaded,' Culaith assured them.

'What can we do?' Naoise asked.

'We have no choice,' Deirdre replied. 'I will never warm that old man's bed. You and I, Naoise, will go across the sea to Alba. I have kinfolk there. We may not live in much comfort there, but we will live together and in peace.'

'Agreed,' answered Naoise.

'I'm coming too,' said Ainnle.

'And I,' added Ardan. 'When that old man hears that we have foiled his plans, he will seek vengeance from any one close to you, Naoise.'

'In that case, I'm also going with you,' insisted Culaith. 'Besides, there's safety in numbers.'

'Get a horse, then, Culaith,' urged Deirdre, 'for we must leave at once.'

They left with all haste and got safely to Alba. The rage of Conchubhar when he discovered what had happened would take a book to describe. For miles around Usna's home, the crops blazed and the people fled or died. A land of plenty was transformed into a dead and dying landscape. Not even the wild animals escaped the savage vengeance of a king who felt that, in losing Deirdre, he had lost his youth and his joy and the promise of a blissful future.

When news reached Alba, Deirdre and Naoise lamented the fate of their land and people. Ainnle and Ardan wanted to return and avenge the savagery meted out to Usna and his people, but Culaith advised against it.

'Can a wren kill a hawk or a rabbit a hound?' he asked. 'Then neither can gentle men defeat a wounded bull.'

So they stayed in Alba. Ainnle, Ardan and Culaith knew peace and contentment, while Deirdre and Naoise grew together like two cuttings grafted on to the one stem. Time passed, pain subsided and thoughts of home returned. Sometimes Culaith would stand on the edge of the sea and look at his homeland, less than one day's rowing away. Alba was beautiful and the people kind, but home was over there. Home was seeing places that you knew better than the lines of your own face. It was hearing voices that sounded exactly like your own. It was knowing the time from the strength of the sun and intuiting the weather from the movement of clouds and trees and animals. It was wearing clothes in a particular way – like those men rowing their boat towards him.

'They're from home,' Culaith realised with a start, and ran to warn the others.

Deirdre and Naoise stood at the shore with Ainnle, Ardan and Culaith behind them.

'It's Conchubhar's step-father, Fergus,' said Deirdre, 'and six others. We must be careful.'

'It's me. Fergus,' a voice from the boat called. 'We come in peace. Look, we have no weapons.'

The men raised their cloaks and it was clear that they carried neither sword nor spear nor knife.

'Come ashore,' Naoise invited and soon they were listening to stories of home.

'I come from Conchubhar,' Fergus told them, 'and I come in peace. You know me well. You know that I have no reason to love Conchubhar. His mother, Nessa, tricked me into giving my kingdom to Conchubhar for one year. Year has passed year and decade has passed decade, but still he keeps my kingdom. I know now that I will never rule my land again because Conchubhar is a better king than I was or could ever be. He is recognised as the strongest man in our world, and the richest. Under him, the land has been able to grow fertile, for no one dares attack us, and the people have grown comfortable. Conchubhar is sorry for what he did to your people. He has settled wealth on Usna and returned all his property. Now he wants the sons of Usna to come home. He needs your strong arms and he wants your forgiveness.'

'And what about me?' asked Deirdre.

'You may also come home if you wish, Deirdre,' Fergus told her. 'What Conchubhar felt for you was no more than a passing whim. You made him feel young. But now he realises that friendship is more important than physical fulfilment and that self-respect endures longer than lust. You are all invited home. You too, Culaith. You have his word that you will be safe and unmolested.'

'I don't trust Conchubhar,' Deirdre told Fergus.

'Do you trust me?' he asked.

'I do,' she admitted. 'You are not one to lie for Conchubhar.'

'Then, you have my word, Deirdre, that all of you will be safe. I will die rather than break that word.'

'We should go home,' Ainnle and Ardan agreed. 'It will be good to see our father again and our friends.'

'I, too, want to go home,' added Culaith. 'Here, we only exist, but at home we can begin to live again.'

125

'I still don't trust, Conchubhar,' cautioned Deirdre. 'I know Fergus believes what he says, but I feel we are safer here.'

'I'm with Ainnle and Ardan and Culaith,' Naoise told her. 'I know how you feel, Deirdre, and I will not force you to change your mind; if you stay, I stay. But think about it, just think about it. Home! Our children would grow up at home, not strangers in a land that is not truly ours. My father is old. He has suffered a lot because of us. We must do all that we can to fill his declining years with the joy that can only come from being surrounded by children and grandchildren.'

They talked well into the night, but the decision had already been made in four out of the five hearts.

'If we are to take advantage of the morning's tide, we must leave soon,' Fergus told them.

'I'm ready,' came the eager voice of Ainnle.

'And I,' agreed Ardan.

'Don't go without me,' smiled Culaith.

'I too want to go home,' admitted Naoise.

'And what about you, Deirdre?' asked Fergus.

'I go where Naoise goes,' she told them.

Naoise swung her high in the air. 'You'll see, my love,' he assured her. 'You'll see. Just this once, your womanly intuition is wrong. We'll look back on today and laugh at these doubts. You'll see.'

After the five had thanked Deirdre's kinfolk for their kindness and hospitality, they set out with Fergus. The journey home was one of unbroken joy. The sea was calm. The wind was at their back. The eagerness of the exiles seemed to speed the boat westward, homeward.

When they landed, the shore was lined with men and women welcoming them, and with children, giving them flowers and kisses. Fergus led the way up the shore to the ranks of warriors surrounding the chariot in which Conchubhar was standing.

'Conchubhar, my lord,' he spoke with joy, 'I've brought home our friends. I gave them my word that their safety was assured and I'm happy to say that they trusted me.'

'I've had to swallow too many of your words, Fergus, since the day my mother married you,' Concubhar replied harshly.

'Kill the old fool,' he instructed his guards.

He turned to Culaith. 'It does not suit a servant to have attitudes beyond his station. Killing is too good an end for you. Guards! Lock him in the kennels with the hounds until I have thought of a suitable punishment.

'And now, my fine sons of Usna, – Naoise, Ainnle, Ardan – did you really think I would allow you to get the better of me? Remove their heads,' he ordered his guards, 'and dispatch their father in the same fashion.'

The brothers were dragged off to their deaths. And Deirdre stood there, too proud to let Conchubhar see her cry, too numb even to whisper a word of love when Naoise was torn from her side. She did not even complain when Conchubhar summoned a priest and ordered that their marriage be sanctioned immediately.

Afterwards the king grasped Deirdre by the arm and shoved her before him into his chariot. 'Now you will stand with me as my queen in front of all the people,' he told her triumphantly, as he drove through the crowds.

'Drive faster,' she encouraged him.

'So, you are as eager for the marriage bed as I am?' he gloated, tightening the reins and urging the horses faster. 'I swore I would marry you and that promise, at least, I have kept.'

'And I promised I would never warm your bed,' she shouted, as she leapt on to the rim of the chariot and flung herself to her death.

For a while, Luch said nothing and listened while Aengus thought.

'We don't often find that sort of love in men or women, Luch, do we?' Aengus said, eventually.

'Do we not, Aengus?' his guide asked. 'Well, whether we do or not, there's no more time for stories or questions either, for we have reached our destination. Before us you see the rarest settlement in the world, for it's here that all the poets and songmakers come to learn their trade.'

There was no need for Luch to urge Aengus to a last burst of speed. He was already outstripping his guide in his eagerness to meet the men and women learning the skills to which he, too, aspired.

19: The Poets' Secrets

This settlement was different from any other town or village Aengus had ever seen. The houses were built in rows of concentric circles, and all faced a round building, which was at the heart of the hamlet. Every door stood open. There were no windows in the houses and no chimneys. There were no children on the street and no dogs. There were no market traders or hawkers. There was some noise, all right, but it was the sound of scales and chords, not the resonance of human speech.

As Aengus and Luch approached the central building, a man and two women emerged from the doorway.

'Welcome, strangers,' sang the first woman, who introduced herself as Máthair.

'A thousand welcomes, travellers,' chanted the man, known as Athair, although his real name was Obaoighill.

'A hundred thousand welcomes to our visitors,' intoned the second woman, who was older than the others and addressed as Máthair Mór. 'You have come just as we are about to retire for the night. I shall call one of our scholars to take you to your quarters. We welcome you as strangers. During your stay, we shall respect you as gods. And, when you leave, let us hope it will be with tears at the parting of friends.'

Máthair Mór clapped her hands and a young person emerged from the shadows. The newcomer was wearing a loose-fitting over-garment, woven from coarse wool, which concealed the body so completely that Aengus was unable to say if it covered a man or a woman. A roughly woven cincture encircled the waist and the garment was topped by a large, oversized hood that covered the head and face.

The scholar bowed first to Máthair Mór, then to Athair and to Máthair and finally to Luch and to Aengus. He (or was it she?) said nothing but led the way to a small well-built house, which from a distance was indistinguishable from the many others in the settlement. It was, however, the outermost house and when they got there, Aengus realised that it had one singular feature. It had a window in the wall that faced away from the settlement and towards the road that Luch and Aengus would take on leaving.

When they had been shown their accommodation, the scholar again bowed, first to Luch and then to Aengus and left.

'Could you make out if our new friend was male or female, Luch?' enquired Aengus.

'Does it matter?' asked Luch.

'Well, yes. I like to know whether I'm talking to a man or a woman.'

'I didn't hear you doing much talking then,' smiled Luch.

'Oh, you know what I mean, Luch, don't you?'

'Yes, I do. We are fortunate that I can read your mind, because your verbal expression leaves a lot to be desired,' admonished Luch.

Then relenting a little, he added, 'The scholar was a female, a fifth-year student of versification. Her name is Maedhbhín. We may see her again tomorrow.'

'Why did she not talk to us, Luch?'

'Don't you think we should leave these questions for tomorrow, Aengus? We've had a long day and, since my slumbers were disturbed by your dreams last night, I am looking forward to sleeping long and deeply tonight. Good night, Aengus.'

'Good night then, Luch,' came the reply, followed almost immediately by the comment. 'But I still wonder why our guide didn't talk to us.'

'Wonder away then, Aengus,' replied a callous Luch as he prepared for sleep.

'I have a feeling,' said Aengus, 'that if I don't find out, I mightn't be able to sleep. Well, I'll just have to toss and turn, like last night.'

'All right, all right, you inquisitive Danaan! I know what you're up to. I'll tell you, but I must say that I find your ignorance beyond belief. I thought everyone knew about the teaching traditions of poetic establishments. I thought ...'

'Oh, please don't give me a lecture, Luch,' pleaded Aengus. 'I'm tired too. I just want a few facts and then we can both get to sleep.'

'Briefly, then, Aengus, not everyone can be a poet. You must at least know that. It helps if you come from a line of renowned poets, but even that is no guarantee that you will be accepted here. You have to show that you have intelligence, industry, sensitivity, musical skill, a good memory, a quick wit and, most of all, the dedication necessary to devote at least seven, but preferably twelve years of your life to learning your craft. Are you satisfied now, Aengus? Do you think I could possibly be allowed to let my eyelids rest over my eyes and my tongue lie quietly in my mouth?'

'Just one last question, Luch, and I promise I'll let you sleep.'

'Just the one, Aengus.'

'Well it has two parts, two very little parts.'

'Hurry up, then.'

'Why was Maedhbhín wearing that terrible robe and why did she not talk to us, and, oh yes, why are there no windows in the houses – or chimneys?'

'That's four parts! You're either non-numerate, Aengus, or you're trying to cheat me. Either way, it does not matter because I can give you one answer that will, with intelligent application, apply to all parts of your question. All those wishing to become poets must show serious dedication to their craft. They must learn to subjugate their physical desires – even their desire for normal conversation – so that all their strength can be channelled into poetry. Even sunlight, the symbol of all-powerful Lugh, must be avoided, so that the light of the inner mind may enhance the poet's artistry. As Máthair Mór once wrote:

> Both task and joy are one.
> I wrought to write and wrote aright.
> Dim rooms shone light on the inner eye
> In darkness, it's begun.

Think about it, Aengus.'

'Luch ... '

'Goodnight, Aengus.'

'Goodnight, Luch.'

20: Art and Craft

Morning came, as mornings always do, whether they are dreaded or longed for. Maedhbhín brought them a simple meal of bread and fruit and spring water.

'I'm still hungry,' Aengus confided when they had finished eating. 'I take it these aspiring poets think it's wrong to enjoy good food?'

'You're wrong, Aengus,' Luch assured him. 'They understand and respect all the good things of life – food, drink, music, language, games, love – but they are willing to forego some of the joys that we take for granted so that they can pour all their energies into producing the greatest song and verse that they are capable of. They are here because they have a dream and because they are talented. During their years here, they will study their craft. They will learn about sounds as a smith learns about metals. Just as he learns how much heat to apply to melt silver or lead or gold, they learn how much pressure it takes to make sounds melt into words and words into music. Their first task, however, is to control the instrument of their own bodies. It must serve them rather that causing them to serve it.'

'Can we stay here for a few days, Luch?' enquired Aengus. 'As you know, I'm a poet, a good poet, but not yet the great poet I plan to be. I could learn something here. I'm sure of that.'

'A few days, Aengus? Do you think that will be enough?' Luch asked quietly.

'Oh yes, I'm a god, so I can learn a lot faster than these humans.'

'There's at least one thing you haven't learnt in all your life, Aengus, and that's humility!' exclaimed Luch. 'Do you honestly think you could master twelve years' work, or even seven, in a few days, especially since you are only permitted to use human powers? These people empty themselves of pride and lust and envy so that they can be filled with words and music, which they can then give us. You're so full of your own worth that there's no room for anyone else's beauty.'

For a time, they were silent, Aengus thinking about what Luch had said, Luch listening in to what Aengus thought.

'Would it be possible for us to stay a while, anyway?' asked Aengus, 'just to learn about learning?'

'What about Caillte?'

'When I told Gáire that Caillte was waiting for me, he said that waiting a little longer would not hurt. I think he was right.'

'What you are really telling me, Aengus, is that, at the moment, it is more important to satisfy your curiosity than your lust. Isn't that it?'

'Well no, not really. What I meant was ... well ... Yes, Luch, I suppose I am saying that, for the moment, curiosity comes first. But it's not idle curiosity. I want to be a maker of songs and poems. It is my destiny, Luch, my freet. One day, I'll be able to sing so that even the birds will come to listen and my words will be so honey-sweet that the bees will congregate around my mouth. I may not be able to learn as much as I think I can in a few days or hours, but, even if I acquire one solitary piece of knowledge, I will have gained something.'

'Yes, Aengus, you will have gained something. You will have added to a store that cannot be stolen from you and that will not weigh on you when you travel. We can stay for one day and then we must continue our journey.'

Aengus and Luch were sitting listening to the scholars practising when Maedhbhín appeared. She stood at the door for a moment and then removed her habit. Underneath it, she wore a simple one-piece dress.

If she hadn't been wearing the habit when I first saw her, thought Aengus appreciatively, I'd have had no difficulty knowing that I was dealing with a woman!

'Máthair Mór has asked me to show you what we do,' she smiled, 'and to explain some of our techniques. Our habit is a symbol to others and to ourselves that we are trying to live by what we call the 'Three Custodies': custody of the eyes so that we see only what we should, custody of the mouth so that we say only what we would and custody of the body so that we need only what we have. For the duration of your stay, I am to set aside these custodies, so I have removed my habit.'

'Three custodies!' repeated Aengus. 'I've been listening to some of your chants. You do a lot of things in threes, don't you?'

'We do,' answered Maedhbhín, looking up at him and smiling, and Aengus couldn't help noticing that her eyes were as deep and as dark as an untroubled lake.

'We often learn traditional wisdom in what we call triads. The more we carry in our heads, the less we have to write down to carry in our hands.'

'What's your favourite triad, Maedhbhín?' Aengus asked.

'I don't know that I have a favourite,' she replied, 'but I like this one. There are three slender things that support the world: the milk from the breast, the grain on the grasses, and the thread in the hands of a woman.'

'I'll tell you what my least favourite triad is, Aengus,' Luch told him, curtly. 'The three signs of poor breeding: staring, overlong visits, and the constant asking of questions.'

Maedhbhín laughed and, in spite of himself, Aengus joined in.

'Perhaps you could show us around, please, Maedhbhín,' Luch suggested. 'We would be delighted to listen to anything you have to tell us, wouldn't we, Aengus?'

'We would, indeed,' Aengus assured her.

Maedhbhín led the way through the settlement, pointing things out as she went.

'We have a system,' she explained. 'The most important buildings are in the centre of our settlement. In those, we have the houses of our teachers and our most senior scholars, those that have been in the institution for at least ten years. Radiating in circles around this centre are the houses of scholars, with the newest students and our visitors being in the houses furthest from the centre. The houses on the periphery are the most comfortable, by the standards of the outside world. Yours, for example, has a window and simple, comfortable furniture.'

Luch remembered the bed he had slept on the previous night and smiled ruefully at the different meanings people could apply to the word 'comfortable'. He had little further time for reflection, however, because Aengus had just begun to question Maedhbhín.

'How does this institution support itself?' he asked. 'There must be at least fifty houses.'

'Fifty-seven,' she corrected.' We do not need much money. We rarely wear anything other than our habits. Our food is simple. We grow what we eat and we eat what we grow. In a good year, like this one, the food is plentiful. Most scholars come with a gift, often a big one, from their local chieftain. It is assumed that, in time, the poet will return to the home of the chieftain and repay such kindness by composing genealogies for the family and by commemorating their heroic deeds. Chieftains and visitors have learnt to be very generous. No one wants to be immortalised as mean.'

'No indeed,' agreed Aengus, reminding himself to be more liberal than he had intended with his parting present.

'Perhaps that will teach you not to ask so many questions!' Luch whispered, as they followed Maedhbhín between houses and closer to the centre.

Maedhbhín stopped in front of a building where students were chanting triads.

'We have two types of scholar,' she told them, 'those who stay here for as long as twelve years and who intend to be *filí*, and the others who study for only seven years. They will be bards. It is my intention to be a fully-fledged *file*. We all learn to chant triads, to chain sounds so that they chime and clash and hunt out meaning, and to sing the praises of the good, the brave and the generous. Listen to the thoughts-in-words of that third-year scholar:

> *If poetry were suppressed, people would be poor,*
> *Without guide, without guard, without gaud.*
> *Dying, they would die a direful death,*
> *With deeds undone, unheard, unsung.'*

'Interesting,' thought Luch.

'That's so good,' Aengus enthused.

'For a third-year, it's acceptable,' Maedhbhín admitted. 'It has power but little subtlety. In a few years' time, he will allow the art to conceal the craft and let the craft caress the art.'

Throughout the day, Aengus and Luch listened to Maedhbhín as she introduced them to teachers and scholars, men and women, all of them striving to outdo their best. Bells rang to remind them of the passing of the day. After the first bell, the scholars stopped working, went to their houses and ate in silence. The second bell called them to their duties in the fields, in the kitchens or in the area where furniture was made or mud bricks baked.

'They are remarkably obedient to the bell,' Aengus commented. 'Is it really necessary to leave a phrase unfinished?'

'We feel that it is. We choose this life and we believe in the paradox that discipline sets us free. Máthair often tells a story to the new acolytes to stress the importance of immediate obedience to the bell.

Years ago, a talented scholar was illustrating his verse. He was drawing a circle when the bell sounded. He finished his circle, put away his work and then answered the bell. Máthair invited him to leave the settlement. 'But why?' he asked, 'What have I done?'

'It's what you have not done,' Máthair informed him. 'You heard the bell and yet you finished what you were doing'

'But Máthair,' he reasoned, 'I was drawing a circle. Everyone knows that a circle must be drawn with one movement of the wrist or it is not perfect.'

'You aspired to a perfect circle,' she told him. 'We aspire to perfection.'

The scholar left later that day.

Aengus was quiet for a while. He knew he would find it very

difficult to leave a circle that was only half drawn, but he did not feel that Luch or Maedhbhín would agree.

'I assume,' he asked, choosing what he hoped was an uncontroversial topic. 'I assume that there are three bells each day?'

'You are right,' agreed Maedhbhín. 'We do not need a bell to call us to work and we choose for ourselves when to retire for the night. The three bells regulate our working day.'

'Careful, Aengus,' Luch advised him, but Aengus could see no reason for following such advice.

'What do you do after the third bell?' he asked.

'Normally,' Maedhbhín smiled her most beautiful smile. 'Normally, we retire to our houses, eat if we need to and practise our crafts. Tonight, however, we will not be doing this.'

'Why? What will you be doing?' pursued Aengus.

'Máthair Mór, Athair and Mathair feel that, in honour of our guests, we should have a feast.'

'A feast,' enthused Aengus. 'That's a wonderful idea!'

'There's more,' Maedhbhín assured him. 'Because you are a god and a poet and a man of means, you are to be allowed to supply the feast. We feel certain it will be a feast to remember.'

21: Entertaining Aengus

Aengus and Luch went to make the financial arrangements for the feast before returning to their house.

'Don't tell me I asked for it, Luch!' Aengus pleaded. 'I didn't know we were going to be cajoled into providing a feast!'

'You're really improving under my expert tutelage,' laughed Luch. 'You're even reading my mind now. But you were excessively generous, Aengus. Half that amount would have provided ten feasts, but I suppose you felt like being open-handed.'

'I felt like nothing of the sort, Luch!' Aengus admitted. 'I was forced into providing this feast. But I daren't risk being mean. With all these poets around, I'd never be able to hold my head up in society if I didn't provide them with what they so poetically describe as "lashings and leavings"! They'll be eating and drinking our health for the next moon or more!'

'Ah well, now, your money couldn't go to a more worthwhile cause than the upkeep of impoverished poets. And besides, we'll enjoy ourselves. I have a feeling, Aengus, that tonight is one neither of us will forget.'

In time, Maedhbhín called, to lead the honoured guests to the feast. From the central house could be heard sounds of music and merriment.

'We're not late?' Aengus asked.

'By the sound of it,' she confided, 'we're just in time. We felt it was our duty to get things ready before collecting you. After all, it is some time since we have had such rich food to eat and such fine beverages to drink. We needed a little practice to get the feast going.'

'I'm glad they only needed a little practice!' thought Aengus, as he walked into a room where everything seemed to be swaying. Gone was the darkness, banished by tens of torches whose flames flickered and fluttered, casting multicoloured lights on the young men and women. Some were dancing, some were drinking, all were laughing.

'They're not wearing their habits,' Aengus noticed.

'There's a time and a place for discipline, Aengus,' Maedhbhín explained. 'Tonight is a time for pleasure.'

She led the way to a place where Máthair, Athair and Máthair Mór were sitting, deep in conversation. They stood up to welcome Luch and Aengus.

'Aren't you going to enjoy the feast?' Aengus asked them.

'We are already enjoying it,' Athair assured him. 'Good food, good company, good drink and good conversation. At our age, who could ask for more?'

'Are you still talking about poetry?'

'Still?' exclaimed Máthair. 'For us, poetry is food and drink and life. It is a subject matter which never tires.'

'Aengus wonders how we can find any intellectual subject so fascinating,' smiled Máthair Mór. 'But Aengus, our subject matter will outlive us. It will last when you and I are but a shadow of a memory. Athair has been telling us about his invention. He has worked out a technique that allows us to use the strokes of the Ogam alphabet as a system of musical notation. This means that we can teach our scholars ways of memorising words and music. It has always been our motto that:

A tune can outlive the song of a bird
The wealth of the world is outlived by a word.

Now we can cause word and tune to live together and forever.'

'How?' asked Aengus.

All three laughed. 'Not now,' they advised him with one voice. 'You are still young. Leave the intellectualising to us.'

'Eat and drink,' advised Máthair.

'Sing and dance,' added Athair.

'Live and love,' encouraged Máthair Mór, as Maedhbhín led both guests away.

'Let's listen to Speansa,' Maedhbhín suggested. 'He is composing a verse in your honour.'

Speansa was very young and very handsome. He had a goblet in his right hand and his left arm was around the waist of a girl who would inspire many love songs in her lifetime. Speansa was not, however, eulogising his love. He was commemorating the generosity of Aengus.

Bright was the night and through the plangent air
Sweet sounding harps and flutes did gently play,
To noble spirits, that gen'rously did pay
For this great feast, which we have come to share.
For we tonight will cast aside our care
Our discontent with our full lengthy stay
In cloisters dark, with expectations dear
Of fun-filled days, though young days fly away
Like untamed birds which fly through fear
And leave us lone though we would hold them dear.

Tonight, at least, all sad thoughts are undone
They fought with joy, but joy in triumph won
And we have decked its victory march with flowers
And lightened dark with our own torched sun
Which later shall lead men to ladies' bowers
And crown our hopes of finding love-filled hours.
Rejoice tonight, for joy will not last long.
And all toast Aengus, patron of our song.

'He's perfecting a new form of verse stanza,' Maedhbhín told them. 'It has eighteen lines and an intricate pattern of rhyme and rhythm. It's better suited to a wedding celebration, but by the time he has finished all ten stanzas, it will be flowing as freely as the wine is. Perhaps you would like to leave the other nine for another time and listen to one of the others?'

Aengus was keen to hear the remaining stanzas, but Luch's frown encouraged him to take up Maedhbhín's suggestion and they moved to another group, where Liamor was singing the merits of wine under the guise of lamenting a bird's death.

Look at you now, my bonny bird,
Your sweet life gone for good,
You've lost your life; we've lost the song
That livened yon distant wood.

You're lying there with wings outstretched,
Your bones on a stony bed
And it wasn't for the lack of food
That caused you to be dead.

You ate your fill, I know that's true.
But you've died while still a youth.
Nor was it man that laid you low.
No, you died of the druth.

> *You sang to me throughout your life.*
> *You sang of men and mice.*
> *And now you're dead, you've left me with*
> *One last piece of advice.*
>
> *Oh, skip your food if you're in haste*
> *The loss won't make you shrink,*
> *And skip your woman, if you must,*
> *But never skip your drink!*

Each group had a song or a verse, or both, and the torches were burning low when Aengus realised that Luch was no longer with them.

'Where's Luch?' he asked. 'Has he gone to bed?'

'He has gone,' Maedhbhín told him, and then added, 'but not to his own bed, if I'm any judge. And you, Aengus, would you like to walk with me? It's lovely walking at this time.'

Perhaps it was the music or the poetry or perhaps it was simply that Maedhbhín was beautiful. They walked together under the stars and, for a time, Aengus was in the stars and of the stars, flying higher than Fand, swimming stronger than Diuran and reading minds more easily than Luch.

22: The Twelve-legged Crow

When morning came, Aengus found himself alone and went quietly back to the house. He listened at the door but could hear nothing. He tiptoed in, hoping that Luch was still asleep. He had just sat down on his bed, convinced that he had escaped detection, when a loud voice asked:

'And what time is this to be coming in at?'

Aengus turned to see Luch perched on the windowsill.

'What are you doing up there, Luch?' he asked.

'I'm pretending I'm a bird, Aengus! What do you think I'm doing? I was waiting for you to turn up. I assume from your late arrival that you enjoyed yourself last night?'

'I did, Luch,' Aengus admitted, 'but nothing would have happened if you hadn't left us.'

'I'm your guide, not your guardian, Aengus,' Luch told him, 'and besides, I was invited by Máthair, Athair and Máthair Mór to visit a neighbouring town and help give judgement in a serious case.'

'What case, Luch? Did I miss something?'

'Your curiosity is a source of wonder to me, Aengus. It's an endearing but dangerous quality. Yes, you did miss something, but, from the look in your eyes, I'd say you also gained a lot last night.'

'I did, Luch. I did. But aren't you going to tell me what happened? That way, I'll have gained two things.'

'A young poet once wrote, "Knowledge enormous makes a god of me!" Was that you, Aengus?'

'It wasn't, I'm sad to say, Luch, but I certainly know what he meant.'

'I suppose I might as well tell you about last night,' said Luch. 'After all, we have to wait here until our hosts send us on our way.'

'While you were listening to versifiers, I went into the corner where Máthair, Athair and Máthair Mór were philosophising. There comes a time in all our lives, Aengus, when a lovely idea is as attractive as a lovely body. I thought they would be continuing their discussion of the use of Ogam for musical notation, but by the time I got back to them, they were talking about a problem in a neighbouring townland, Aiteaconn.'

The people in Aiteaconn had for years been among the most blessed in the country. The earth there was so fertile that they could harvest corn three times in a season. Their cows and their sheep regularly gave birth to twins. And their hens laid two eggs a day. Their chieftain, Conn, was honourable and peace loving. His wife, Buainne, was kind and generous, and their son, Art, was as honourable as his father and as kind as his mother. The future well-being of the people of Aiteaconn seemed assured.

Then, one day, Buainne fell ill. Conn sent couriers to all parts of the land asking for help. Men and women skilled in herbal remedies came, but Buainne grew thinner and weaker. It was clear to everyone that she would die. One morning, she asked to be taken outside to feel the sun on her skin and the wind in her hair, perhaps for the last time. Conn and Art knelt beside her.

'I want you both to promise me something,' she told them.

'Anything, mother,' answered Art.

'Anything that is in my power,' replied Conn.

'Art,' Buainne whispered, taking her son's hand. 'I want you to promise me to obey your father and never do anything to hurt or offend him.'

'I promise, Mother.'

'And Conn, I have had a good life. The only thing that saddens me now is the thought that you will be lonely. Promise me that when I am gone, you will take another wife. Promise me.'

Conn tried to tell her that no one could ever take her place, but Buainne was so frail that he did not want to oppose her.

'If that's what you want, Buainne,' he agreed, 'then I promise I'll take another wife.'

Within minutes, Buainne was dead. There was weeping and wailing throughout Aiteaconn and beyond for nine days and nine nights. Then it was time to let the dead rest, so the mourning ceased and life in Aiteaconn went back to normal, almost.

Art was young. Of course he missed his mother but there was still much for him to do and plenty for him to learn. Conn, on the other hand, was desolate. He was like a man walking in a storm. There was noise and motion all round but he didn't know whether he was walking to the east or the west or whether, indeed, he was walking in circles. His advisers watched him for a year and then went to him.

'Conn,' they urged, 'it's time for you to keep your promise to Buainne. It's time for you to marry again.'

At first, Conn rejected the idea, but slowly he realised that, for all his love of Buainne, he couldn't join her in the grave. If he married again, at least he wouldn't be so lonely. As luck would have it, that very day, a beautiful stranger arrived in Aiteaconn. Her name was Becuma, and Conn could not help but be moved by her comeliness. Whereas Buainne had the loveliness of warm sunshine and gentle rain, Becuma had the brilliance of spun gold and well-cut diamonds.

'I'll marry Becuma,' Conn told his advisers.

'Wait until we have found out who she is and where she comes from,' they counselled.

'I'll marry Becuma whatever you find out,' he told them. 'I've been alone for too long and I am only doing what Buainne wanted and what you yourselves recommended.'

Conn married Becuma and for a while life seemed to continue as before, although the corn was less plentiful and the hens were not as productive.

'It's because of your son,' Becuma told Conn. 'He hates me. He looks at me with ill-concealed contempt. I've tried to be a mother to him, but he scorns my gestures of love. He is calling down bad luck on all of us, Conn. You must banish him.'

'Banish my son? Banish Art? But everybody loves him. He wouldn't bring bad luck to anyone,' insisted Conn and, for a time, he remained adamant that his son should not be banished. But, day after day, conditions deteriorated in Aiteaconn. Blight appeared on the corn. Animals died. And, for the first time in living memory, cries of hunger began to be heard in the townland.

'You must do something, Conn,' urged his advisers.

'You must banish Art,' pressed Becuma.

One day, as more and more reports of misfortune were brought to Conn, he sent for Art. In front of the people, his advisers and Becuma, Conn banished Art.

He took a rod in his hand, broke it and gave it to Art:

'Art, son of Conn, it has become clear to all of us that you are a source of evil in this townland. From this moment, you are banished from it. Never set foot on our soil again. Never turn your face in our direction. Never expect help or sanctuary from us. You are no longer my son. You are no longer my heir. You are no longer welcome here. This broken stick is yours to remind you that we have broken all our links with you. Only when you can make the two parts of the stick unite and grow together again, only then may you return to Aiteaconn.'

Art tried to tell them that he had done no harm, that he had never wished evil on anyone, not even on Becuma, but no one listened. Conn turned his back on his son. Becuma, the advisers and the townspeople did the same. When they turned around again, Art was gone.

Luch paused. 'I suppose you can guess what happened next, Aengus. But let me tell you.'

If times were bad when Art was in Aiteaconn, they were infinitely worse after he had left. The rain stopped falling. The sun grew oppressive. The young seedlings shrivelled and failed. The animals grew listless and, without sustenance, they died. At last, the community could no longer suffer in silence.

They went to Conn and told him: 'Our land has been poisoned, Conn. There is neither milk to drink nor corn to eat. We shall all die if we don't purge the evil that is blighting us.'

'I banished my son,' Conn insisted. 'What more can I do?'

'Go to the Druids,' they advised. 'If we don't get help soon, we will all die.'

Conn sought out the wisest druid of them all, a woman called Seanós.

'What can I do?' he asked her. 'How can I bring back the peace and prosperity that Aiteaconn was famed for?'

'You will never be able to do that, Conn,' Seanós informed him, 'but you can help the land of Aiteaconn to yield again.'

'How can I do it?'

'You must first find a boy like Art, a boy without blemish who is willing to come with you to Aiteaconn. He must then pass a test that I will set. And you, Conn, you will have to banish Becuma. These things must be done, and done in that order, if Aiteaconn is to be saved.'

Immediately and without looking back, Conn set off to find a boy without blemish. He travelled the length and breadth of the land, but failed to find a boy of the quality of Art. Leaving the land, almost in despair, he took a boat and set sail, hoping that the deities would guide him.

After a time, he came to a lovely island where the grass was lush, where birds and insects sang and where animals were fat with grazing. It reminded him of Aiteaconn when Buainne was still alive. Conn approached the palace and spoke to the queen.

'There is such a boy, here,' she agreed, 'but he is my son, Gealt, and I will not let him go.'

'Let me go, Mother,' Gealt pleaded. 'Let me help Conn and his people. I will do what is necessary. I know I can help them.'

The queen could have forbidden Gealt to accompany Conn, but she thought of how comfortable she and her people were and how sad it must be in Aiteaconn. At length, she agreed:

'Gealt can go with you, Conn, but on one condition only. You must swear that you will guarantee my son's safety.'

Conn immediately agreed to the condition and he and Gealt set out for Aiteaconn.

'And last night, Aengus, was the night that Gealt and Conn arrived back in Aiteaconn,' Luch announced. 'While you were philandering, Máthair, Athair, Máthair Mór and I went to Aiteaconn to see the outcome.'

At this point, Luch stopped and looked out the window.

'I'm surprised that our hosts haven't come to bid us adieu, Aengus. Do you think we should go to them?'

'I do not,' replied an indignant Aengus. 'You must tell me what happened in Aiteaconn.'

'There'll be plenty of time for that, Aengus,' smiled the little man. 'Duty before pleasure, you know.'

'You always do this,' exclaimed an irate Aengus. 'You always stop at a crucial point in the story, leaving me gasping to know what happens. Did you see what happened last night?'

'I did.'

'And do you think you could possibly share the experience with me.'

'I could.'

'Please, Luch, please tell me. Our hosts have their own method of doing things. They will come to us when it is their time and we must have the courtesy to fit in with their wishes.'

'Such courtesy, Aengus! Such new-found sensitivity! But you're right. We must not try to impose our will on our hosts. We will await their pleasure and, in the meantime, let me tell you what you missed.'

Last night, we were all congregated in Aiteaconn: Becuma in regal splendour, the people in pain and poverty, Conn and Gealt tired and footsore, and Seanós ready to carry out her part of the bargain.

'Aiteaconn is sick,' announced Seanós. 'It must be cured. There is only one cure that I know of. Gealt must be killed; his blood must be mingled with the barren earth and it must touch the roots of withered trees.'

'No,' answered Conn. 'This cannot happen. I guaranteed Gealt's safety to his mother. You will have to think of something else, Seanós.'

'There is nothing else,' she insisted.

'It's all right, Conn,' said Gealt. 'I'm willing to give my life to save you and all these people.'

'If you are willing, Gealt,' answered Conn, 'then I thank you, and my wife and my people thank you.'

Just then, a cow walked into the middle of the proceedings, swaying under the weight of two bags that were hanging on either side of her flanks.

'Open the bags, Conn,' Seanós instructed and Conn did so. From the bag on the cow's left flank he took out a little bird with one leg. He dropped it to the ground, but the bird used its wings to hop about and seemed unconcerned by all the people.

From the bag on the cow's right flank, Conn took out another bird. It was like a crow but it had twelve legs and could move as fast on the ground as a hawk swooping through the air.

'These birds will fight, Conn,' Seanós told him. 'Which do you think will win?'

'The bird with twelve legs,' answered Conn. 'He is bigger, stronger, swifter. The outcome is obvious.'

'Put them to fight,' Seanós instructed.

Conn collected the birds and put them in a pit. Everyone knew that the twelve-legged bird would win, but it didn't even try to fight. It stretched its wings, took the air and seized its freedom.

'Who is the winner?' asked Seanós.

'The one-legged bird,' answered Conn, 'because the other bird fled.'

'The one-legged bird and the innocent boy have proved their worth where you failed, Conn,' Seanós announced. 'You must now banish Becuma from Aiteaconn, and you yourself must seek the road of exile. Instead of the blood of Gealt, the milk from this cow will be spread on the land and the earth will become fertile again.'

So Máthair, Athair, Máthair Mór and I watched as Becuma was driven off to the north and Conn set out, alone, to the west.

'And speaking of our friends,' said Luch, 'here they are now.'

Máthair, Athair, Máthair Mór and Maedhbhín approached the house.

'We have come to wish you safe travel,' sang Máthair.

'Safe travel and joyful arrival,' added Athair.

'Joyful arrival and the hope of a return visit, friends,' enjoined Máthair Mór.

Aengus looked at the hooded form of Maedhbhín, anxious for one last smile from those deep, deep eyes, but Maedhbhín bowed first to Luch, then to Aengus and quietly went back to her studies.

'I'm sorry to be leaving, Luch,' Aengus said as they set off. 'I was happy here, but I'll come back and visit them all one day soon.'

'You should never revisit a place where you've been happy, Aengus,' Luch told him quietly. 'You can never recapture that same happiness.

'When we're young and we're happy, we often associate the happiness with a place. But happiness does not only come from a place, Aengus. It comes from what our poet friends would call a "confluence triad". It is the result of the coming together of a time, a place and a group of people. We can return to a place. We can return to a group of people. But we can never return to a time.

'Enjoy what you have at the moment, Aengus. Even as you enjoy it, it is fading as surely as the light on a perfect day.

'But that's enough philosophising for one day. We've a long way to go before we rest our heads tonight.'

23: Changeling Ways

The sun was already high when Aengus first indicated that he would be glad of a rest.

'I didn't get much sleep last night,' he murmured by way of explanation.

'Oh didn't you?' retorted Luch, 'and whose fault was that, may I ask?'

'It was nobody's fault, Luch,' answered Aengus, 'but that doesn't alter the fact that I could be doing with a rest.'

'A rest for the body, Aengus, and one for the spirit. Let's find a stream where we can put our feet in the water and we'll eat some of this food that Maedhbhín left for us.'

'I didn't see her leaving us any food, Luch.'

'That's because you were looking for what she didn't do, rather than for what she did.'

Luch led the way down into a little valley and found a place for them to rest. The stream was little more than a ribbon of cool water, but there was a tree to give them shade and soft grass to lie on. For a while, the only sounds were those of nature, singing with the birds and frolicking with the stream. Then Aengus turned to his friend.

155

'Luch,' he began.

'Don't you ever get tired of asking questions?' Luch responded.

'But I haven't asked one yet, have I?'

'Well, that's one for a start,' Luch laughed, 'but there's a whole host of questions queuing up in your head.'

'Can I ask one, just a little one?'

'Haven't you learnt anything yet, Aengus?' Luch joked. 'There's no such thing as a little question! All questions, or all questions worthy of the name, lead to a consideration of ultimate truths, so how can they ever be little?'

'Well, can I ask one question?'

'Just the one, Aengus.'

'Let me phrase it right, then, because, if I don't, you'll answer "yes" or "no" and I'll lose my opportunity.'

'So you're learning after all, Aengus?'

'I hope so, Luch. I've been wondering about the old couple you befriended. Do you remember you told me about them when you explained how you learned to walk like a mountain man? There must be many old couples who need help and friendship, but you don't go to all of them. My question concerns them. Why did you go to stay with that particular old couple?'

'That's a long story, Aengus.'

'I hoped it might be.'

The old couple I told you about were called Ádh and Miádh and, as I mentioned, they did have a son, once. He was born when Ádh thought herself to be beyond child-bearing and there wasn't a happier couple in the entire land.

'He's a gift from the fairies,' Ádh told her husband, 'and we must treat him well or they'll take him back.'

Nobody could have treated a child better. They would have

given him the coats off their backs and the bite out of their mouth, but gradually it became clear that Dramhlas was not as quick as other children. He didn't talk as much or run and jump as much, and although Ádh would not hear one word against her son, it seemed to Miádh that Dramhlas would be a burden on them all their lives.

Often, as he tilled his land or fished the streams, Miádh would sigh: 'Oh, if only there was some way of making a wise man out of my son!'

One day, Miádh and Dramhlas visited a nearby port, where people were buying and selling goods that had travelled over the oceans of the world. All the traders seemed so clever that Miádh did not know how to bargain with them, so he wandered down to the shore, holding Dramhlas by the hand.

'Oh, if only there was some way of making a wise man out of my son!' he sighed.

'But there is,' came the answer.

'Who? What?'

'It's me, here, in the boat. I'm Gruagaire and if you let me have Dramhlas for a year, I'll bring him back to you a wise man.'

'Is it possible, Gruagaire?' asked Miádh. 'Is it really possible that you can take my son, Dramhlas, and turn him into a wise man in the course of a year?'

'It is and I can,' answered Gruagaire.

'Let me go home first and ask my wife,' Miádh pleaded. 'She dotes on Dramhlas and it would break her heart to lose him.'

'She won't lose him,' Grugaire assured Miádh. 'I'll have him back here next year and I'll guarantee that his wisdom will amaze you. What do you say, Miádh? Make up your mind. The tide is about to turn, so I'm leaving with or without Dramhlas.'

Miádh didn't know what to do. He turned to his son and asked: 'Do you want to go, Dramhlas? Do you want to go with Grugaire?'

'Eh?'

'Do you want to go with Grugaire, son?'

'Eh?'

Miádh hesitated no longer. 'Take him, Grugaire,' he pleaded, 'and bring him back a wise man. I'll be waiting here for you both at this exact time next year.'

Grugaire took Dramhlas on to his boat and soon the tide took the boat and its cargo out of sight. Miádh went home and told his wife what had happened.

'It was for the best, Ádh,' he assured her.

'You've given my son to a stranger,' she accused, 'and you tell me it's for the best? How can it possibly be for the best? How do we know that Grugaire will feed Dramhlas? You know he's very particular about what he eats.'

'Stop worrying, woman,' Miádh insisted. 'I'll go and collect Dramhlas next year, I promise you.'

'Well, see that you do,' urged Ádh, 'and don't give my son away for love or money again.'

The year passed slowly for Ádh and Miádh. Dramhlas was not the brightest of children but he was someone to talk to, somone to work for, and Ádh in particular, missed him. But the time did eventually arrive for Dramhlas to return.

'Let me go with you,' pleaded Ádh. 'I want to be there to tell Dramhlas how much we love him and how we've missed him.'

'No,' insisted Miádh. 'I don't want Grugaire to think that I'm not master in my own home. Besides, Dramhlas will be hungry and you can have all his favourite food ready.'

Ádh agreed that it would be a pity if Dramhlas had to return to a home where there was no welcoming food waiting for him, so Miádh set out alone. He stood on the spot where he had first seen Grugaire, and at the exact moment, a boat came into view. In it was Grugaire, but who was that agile young man with him? Miádh could hardly believe his eyes. The young man was rowing with skill and power.

'Father,' he called, 'it's me, Dramhlas.'

'Welcome home, son,' shouted Miádh. 'Welcome home. Welcome home.'

As soon as the boat was berthed, Miádh hugged his son and shook Grugaire's hand warmly.

'I don't know how to thank you, Grugaire,' Miádh kept saying. 'I don't know how to thank you. You've turned my boy into a wise man.'

'Just think, Miádh,' Grugaire told him, 'if I could do so much in one year, what would I able to do in two? I could turn him into a genius.'

'It's true,' thought Miádh. 'It's true. Look what you've done in one little year! All right, Grugaire, take the boy and turn him into a genius.'

Grugaire and Dramhlas got back into the boat. When they had sailed a short distance from the land, Grugaire shouted:

'I made you no promise to return the boy this time, Miádh, so he's mine.'

Sadly, slowly Miádh made his way home. From a distance, he saw Ádh standing at the door waiting for her son.

'Where's Dramhlas?' she asked her husband when he approached the house, and Miádh had to confess what had happened.

Ádh gave out a great cry of despair. 'You've given away my son for the second time,' she accused her husband. 'I didn't want a genius for a son. I didn't even want a wise man. I was content with my own son. Foolish he may have been and slow, but he was company and he would have been a help to us in our old age.'

The old couple sat down at the table, which was covered with Dramhlas's favourite dishes. 'You must eat,' Miádh told her.

'How can I eat when I don't know whether or not I'll ever see my son again?' asked Ádh, as she began to wrap the food up in a bundle.

'What are you doing, wife?' Miádh enquired.

'I'm packing the food for our journey,' she answered, 'for I'm setting out this very day and I won't return until I have Dramhlas with me.'

Miádh tried to explain that they didn't know where Dramhlas was and that their journey would be futile, but Ádh had made up her mind. That very day, they set off looking for Dramhlas.

Need I tell you, Aengus, that they travelled over hills and through woods and across water? Indeed they did, and one day they came to a large house where Grugaire lived with his six sons.

'It's Grugaire,' Miádh told his wife. 'I'd recognise him anywhere.'

Ádh went up to Grugaire and threw herself on her knees in front of him. 'Please give me back my son, Grugaire,' she pleaded. 'I don't care if he's a genius or a wise man or a simpleton. I just want Dramhlas back.'

'I'm a fair man, Ádh,' Grugaire told her. 'I didn't steal your son. Miádh gave him to me and I have taught him all that I know. It would not be right just to give him back to you, but I'll give you a chance. Tomorrow morning, I'll turn Dramhlas and my six sons into doves and I'll let you pick. If you pick the right bird, Dramhlas can return home with you, but if you pick the wrong one, Dramhlas is mine forever.'

Ádh didn't like this arrangement very much, but she agreed to it because a little hope was better than no hope at all. 'I'm going to get some sleep, Miádh,' she told her husband.

'How can you sleep at a time like this?' he asked.

'I must rest, so that I'll have all my wits about me tomorrow morning.'

Ádh lay down and was soon fast asleep and dreaming. In her dream, she saw Dramhlas and he told her: 'Listen to me, Mother, and trust me. Do you remember that I had a birthmark under my right arm?'

'I do, son, it was a dark ring.'

'Tomorrow, look for that ring under the dove's wing, Mother. Do as I say and all will be well.'

Ádh told no one about her dream, but she felt happy, and to Miádh's surprise, she ate a hearty breakfast before going to Grugaire's house.

'I don't know how you can eat food,' Miádh grumbled, but Ádh advised him to eat up too because, with luck, they would soon be on their way home with Dramhlas.

Ádh and Miádh made their way to Grugaire's house and Grugaire led them to a hut where he had seven doves. They were all males, all the same size and they all cooed sweetly as Ádh approached. She picked them up, one by one, and examined them under the right wing. The first four doves were perfectly white, but the fifth one had a small dark ring under its right wing.

'This is my son,' she called out. 'This is Dramhlas.'

Suddenly, the dove changed into Dramhlas. Mother and son hugged each other and then they both hugged Miádh. They were so happy that they failed to notice how angry Grugaire was as they left him.

'I'll pay you back for this,' he muttered, but Ádh and Miádh were too full of joy to hear what he said or to care. They had their son back.

'How are we going home, Mother?' Dramhlas asked.

'We're walking, son,' she answered. 'Your father and I have a little money left, but it will only be enough to buy food for the long journey home.'

'You and Father deserve to travel in style, Mother. Listen to me and do exactly what I say. There's a fair in the next town we pass through and there's always a race at a fair. I'll turn myself into a horse and I'll run so fast that I'll win the race before the other horses have even started. All the dealers will want to buy me, Mother, and you must sell me to the one who offers most. But remember, Mother, don't let the buyer keep the bridle. You must sell the horse, but keep the bridle. Do you understand, Mother?'

'I do, son,' she answered, 'but is it not dangerous?'

'Not if you do exactly what I've told you, Mother.'

'I'll do everything you say, Dramhlas.'

So Dramhlas changed himself into a horse and Ádh and Miádh led him to the fair. There were many men there with horses that looked as if they could outstrip the wind, but Ádh approached the group and entered Dramhlas for the race.

'That horse of yours hasn't a hope of winning,' one owner told Ádh, but she said nothing in reply, knowing only what her son had told her and certain that he knew what he was doing. The race started, and from the moment the horses took off, Dramhlas was in the lead. He raced as no horse had ever raced before, getting stronger with every stride he took. By the time the race was over, many of the owners were clamouring to buy him.

'I'll give you a bag of gold for your horse,' one offered.

'Two bags of gold.'

'Three bags and my two horses. I've never seen a race like it!'

Ádh waited patiently until all the bids were made and then agreed to sell Dramhlas for seven bags of gold and three horses. The buyer's eyes gleamed as he handed over the money and his own horses. Ádh quietly removed the bridle.

'What!' exclaimed the buyer, 'Are you taking the bridle?'

'I am,' answered Ádh, 'because I sold you the horse only, but if you don't want the horse I can sell it to one of the others.'

'I'll take him without the bridle, then,' grumbled the buyer, 'but you drive a hard bargain, ma'am.'

Ádh and Miádh rode away from the fair, leading their third horse. When they were some distance from the town, Ádh shook the bridle vigorously and there, standing beside her, was Dramhlas.

'We're rich, son, rich!' she told him. 'Your father will never have to work again and the three of us will live in comfort for the rest of our lives.'

So they rode back home and, for a while, they lived in peace and comfort. Then one day, Dramhlas approached Ádh.

'Mother,' he said, 'you and Father are getting old and the time is coming for me to take a wife.'

'I was thinking the same thing, son,' she agreed. 'It's time we had a few grandchildren to liven up this old home.'

'But I can't bring a wife in here, Mother,' Dramhlas continued. 'The house is old, the land is poor and we are not living in the style that I enjoyed when I stayed with Grugaire.'

'There are still three bags of gold left, son,' Ádh informed him. 'Take them and buy what you need to make this home more comfortable for you and your wife-to-be. Your father and I lived in poverty so long that I have all that I need and more.'

'But Mother,' Dramhlas went on, 'I know how we can earn

more money than you've ever dreamed of. We can buy a castle and rich land and you can live like a queen.'

'I'm living like a queen now, Dramhlas,' she assured him. 'I've got you and your father, and a roof over my head and food. I've got my health and strength. What queen in the wide world has more?'

'But we can have all these things and be rich as well, Mother,' he insisted. 'Look, there's a horse race to be run in a few day's time not far from here. We'll do as we did before. I'll change into a horse and win the race. You'll bet money that I will win and then you'll sell me as you did before. That way we'll have all the money we need to last us the rest of our lives.'

'We have enough now, son,' she assured him. 'Let's be content with what we have.'

Dramhlas then went to his father.

'Did you hear what I was saying to Mother?' he asked.

'I did, son. Your mother's a good woman, but she doesn't understand money matters.'

'Will you take me to the race, Father?' Dramhlas asked.

'I will, son. I'll do all that you ask.'

'Remember, you must not sell the bridle, Father.'

'I'll remember, Dramhlas.'

So, early the following morning, Miádh and Dramhlas left home for the races. They travelled to the outskirts of the town where the race was to be held and Dramhlas turned himself into a fine, brown horse. Miádh led him into the fair and headed straight for the race.

'I bet three bags of gold that my horse will win,' he told them, proud that he had money to spend.

'Your horse is a good one, old man,' a young farmer told him, 'but it will never beat my mare.'

'We'll see about that,' boasted Miádh.

The race began and for a short while Dramhlas held back. Then he ran as no one had ever seen a horse run. His hooves moved so quickly, it was hard to tell whether he was running or flying.

'I've never seen a horse like it,' one trader said. 'I'll give you ten bags of gold for him.

'Twenty bags of gold,' offered another.

'Thirty bags of gold and my silver bridle,' offered the young farmer. 'With your horse and my mare, I'll breed the swiftest runners the world has ever known.'

'Done,' agreed Miádh. 'Thirty bags of gold and your silver bridle.'

The young farmer handed over the bridle. It was the most beautiful piece of workmanship Miádh had ever seen.

'Hold on to that, old man, until I go and get my money.'

Miádh fingered the bridle and thought how well it would look on Dramhlas when they decided to play this trick again.

'Dramhlas,' he thought. 'Where's Dramhlas?'

Miádh looked all round him but the young farmer was nowhere to be seen. He ran around the fair and searched in every corner of the town, but there was no sign of the farmer or of Dramhlas.

The old man went home sorrowfully. He had lost Dramhlas and the money, and he and Ádh would have to live as best they could without them.

'And that's why I went to stay with the old couple for a while, Aengus,' Luch explained. 'I wanted to ease their pain a little. I couldn't make up for their son but I was company. And now, Aengus, it's time we set off again. We're almost there.'

24: The Hill in the Hollow

There were many other questions that Aengus would have liked to put to Luch, but it was already late in the afternoon and Luch was walking at a pace that indicated they had a good distance to travel before nightfall. They were in mountainous country now and the walk was upwards, ever upwards. The bright sky of day slowly darkened and first one, then several stars appeared in the sky.

'Watch this, Aengus,' Luch advised.

Aengus wasn't sure what he should watch, since he could see nothing strange at first. Then, as his eyes grew accustomed to the greying world of the night, he saw a beautiful girl looking up at the stars.

'How I would love one of those stars!' she sighed.

'Which one do you want?'

It was the voice of a youth, standing just a short distance from Aengus.

'That one,' she replied. 'The one that twinkles blue and green and yellow and red. That's the one I would love to have.'

'Will you come away with me if I get it for you?' he asked.

'No one can give me a star,' she answered. 'No one can climb up there and bring it back to me.'

'But if I *can* give it to you,' he persisted. 'Will you come away with me then?'

'I will certainly leave all that I have and come with you, if you can give me my star, but I am certain that no one can climb so high.'

'Perhaps I cannot climb up,' agreed the youth, 'but I may be able to persuade the star to come down.'

He put his hand in his pocket and took out four coloured stones, a blue one, a green one, a yellow one and a red one. He held the blue one between his finger and thumb, bent to the ground and hurled the stone with all his might at the star. Up and up the stone flew, making unerringly for its target. The stone collided with the star, which flickered brightly before dimming.

'Oh,' cried the girl, 'you've put out the blue light.'

Without answering, the youth selected the green stone. Bending again to give power to his wrist, he discharged the second stone. It too flew unwaveringly to the star, striking it at its centre. The star quivered again.

'You've put out the green light, now,' sobbed the girl. 'Please don't hurt it any more.'

'But you said you wanted it,' he reminded her, aiming the yellow stone at the star, now displaying only yellow and red beams. The third missile hit its target and the star shivered from the jolt.

'It's only got one colour left,' she wept. 'It's red and sore. Leave it where it is.'

But the final stone was already rushing to smite the star for the fourth and last time. The star trembled like a guttering candle before plummeting to the ground at her feet.

'There's your star,' the young man told her. 'I've kept my part of the bargain. You must keep yours.'

The girl knelt on the ground and gently picked up the dull, dead star. She cradled it in her hands for a moment, then slipped it into her pocket and followed the young man.

Aengus stared after the couple's departing figures, wondering who they were and where they were going. He was about to put these questions to his friend when Luch whispered:

'It's time for me to leave you now, Aengus.'

All thoughts of the young couple vanished.

'But you can't go, Luch. I need you. I don't know where I am. I don't know where I'm going. You told me you knew where Caillte was, but she's not here. Help me, Luch, help me.'

'I have helped you all I can, Aengus, my friend. I've shown you what I have seen and helped you to see for yourself. Caillte is not here, but she is close and you will find her. It was my task to bring you to the middle of the world and leave you.'

'But we're nowhere near the middle of the world, Luch,' Aengus complained.

'Oh yes, we are, Aengus.'

'Where is it?'

'Here, my friend, beneath your two feet.'

Aengus held out his hand to bid a reluctant farewell to Luch.

'Don't be sad, Aengus,' his friend told him. 'It's part of your nature that you want what you can't have or have no longer got. Saying goodbye to a friend who is well and happy should be as easy as a child of six saying goodbye to the time when he was five.'

'But a child of six hasn't the sense to realise that his childhood is slipping away and that he'll never have it back again.'

'Is it the child who is lacking in sense or the man looking back? In one way, I'll always be with you, Aengus. I'm part of this time of your life. You'll only have to close your eyes and think of now and I'll be with you.'

'It's not the same, Luch,' the young man struggled for words.

'No, it's not the same, lad,' came Luch's reply, and it seemed to come from a long way off.

'Luch, Luch,' called Aengus. 'Luch, not just yet, please. I want to tell you ...'

But Luch was gone.

BOOK THREE

The Apples Of
The Moon

25: Time and Tide

I t was close enough to mid-summer for the night to be short.
Short nights or long hardly mattered to Aengus as he sat alone
on a hill, watching the stars and the moon. Everything in the sky
was so beautiful, so bright and shining and alone. There weren't
two moons or two Guide Stars or two of anything. Of course,
there were many stars, thousands of them, but they didn't touch or
interact. They were, like Aengus, suspended in their isolation.

As Aengus sat, too saddened by the loss of Luch even to think
about Caillte, a pony wandered up the hillside. It was a young
pony with a dark brown, shaggy coat, strong, short legs and deep
brown, thoughtful eyes.

'Can I help, Aengus?'

'Who? Is it Luch?'

'No, not Luch. I'm Capaillín.'

'You're a horse?' asked Aengus, incredulously.

'Well, a pony actually.'

'I must be going mad,' thought Aengus. 'I'm seeing dying stars
and listening to talking ponies! I'll just sit quietly and maybe I'll
recover.'

'I'll stand here quietly too,' agreed Capaillín. 'To tell you the truth, I've had a very long day. I knew I had to meet you tonight, but I wasn't sure of the exact time, so I rushed. I was upset when I saw you sitting here. Have you been waiting long? Am I late?'

'Late for what?' queried a bemused Aengus.

'Late for our appointment! Aengus, are you all right? You didn't fall and hit your head or anything?'

'To the best of my knowledge, I didn't hit my head,' replied Aengus, 'but I must have fallen asleep because I seem to be dreaming.'

'Oh, and is it a pleasant dream? Tell me about it and I'll help you interpret it. I'm actually very good at interpreting dreams and better than average when it comes to reading ashes,' encouraged Capaillín.

'I don't know that you'd call it *pleasant*,' Aengus replied, 'but it's certainly odd. I'm having a conversation with a talking horse.'

'Oh, if you're referring to me, you're not dreaming. I'm real and I'm talking. But I'm not a horse, just a pony. You see, I'm only thirteen hands high,' Capaillín confessed. 'Of course, I probably look taller, because you're sitting down and I'm standing up.'

'I'll just sit here with my eyes closed,' Aengus murmured reassuringly to himself, 'and maybe it will go away or maybe I'll wake up.'

'I'll go away if you don't want me here,' huffed Capaillín, 'but I must say you're not very polite. Here I am, tired out from rushing to meet you, and all you can do is sit with your eyes closed and hope I'll go away! You haven't even the courtesy to refer to me by the correct pronoun. I'm a female, you know.'

'I didn't mean to be rude,' explained Aengus, 'but I must admit I wasn't expecting to meet a talking horse.'

'Who were you expecting to meet?' Capaillín enquired politely.

'I don't honestly know.'

'Well, if you don't know who you expected to meet, why are you surprised that it has turned out to be a talking pony? That doesn't seem very logical to me.'

'I've got it!' exclaimed Aengus, 'you're Luch in disguise! You *are* Luch, aren't you?'

'I'm really beginning to worry about you, Aengus. I've told you three times already that I'm Capaillín. Surely you don't have difficulty with that word. And you can see that I'm not a *Luch,* whatever that is, unless your eyes are giving you trouble?'

'No, I can say "Capaillín" all right and I can see you clearly,' smiled Aengus, 'but you must forgive me. It's not every day I meet a talking horse!'

'A pony, not a horse, remember? Oh, I'm a lot like a horse, I agree, and I have some distant relatives who are horses, although I don't particularly like talking about that branch of the family.'

'But, there's no such thing as a talking horse, sorry, pony,' insisted Aengus.

'Who told you that?' enquired Capaillín, with genuine interest.

'Well, nobody actually told me,' admitted Aengus, 'but everybody knows that horses, or indeed ponies, don't talk. I'm really sorry if my information hurts or offends you, Capaillín,' he went on, 'but we can't be having this conversation, because ponies can't talk!'

'Listen carefully, Aengus, and don't give me the first answer that comes into your head. What am I?'

'You're a horse. No, you're a pony.'

'All right, let's try another small step. Can you see my mouth moving?'

'I can.'

'And can you hear the words that my mouth is forming?'

'I can.'

'And are those words meaningful?'

'They are.'

'And are my sentences well-formed?'

'Well-formed?'

'Are my sentences grammatical? Are the words put into structures that you can interpret?'

'Yes, I think so.'

'What do you mean, you think so?'

'Well, I'm not absolutely sure what you mean by grammatical.'

'You're taking me away from my main line of argument, Aengus,' Capaillín complained. 'It really is too bad that someone of your station has had such a poor education. Let me try to put it simply. When we communicate by language, meaning is carried in two main ways: by words and by structures. When I say "man" you get an impression of someone who is human and adult and male. So far so good?'

'Yes.'

'But meaning is also carried by the order in which the words occur. If I say to you, "Aengus ate the fish", that's very different from saying "The fish ate Aengus", isn't it?'

'It is.'

'Simply put then, we know what another person means if we know what the words mean and if the word order is correct. Do you agree with that?'

'I suppose so,' agreed Aengus, 'but I don't see where this is getting us.'

'It's getting us back to the question of whether or not I'm able to talk. Do you understand what I'm trying to communicate?'

'Of course I do.'

'Well then, it's clear that I've been talking to you. And, if I've been talking to you and I'm a pony, then we can conclude that I'm a talking pony.'

'I have a feeling that I haven't fully understood your argument and I think that I may still be dreaming, but all I know is that we are here together at the top of a hill and we're talking. Why are you here, Capaillín?'

'I'm here to help you.'

'Help me to find Caillte?'

'Yes, if that is what you wish.'

'Do you know where she is?'

'I know how you can find her, Aengus, but the journey won't be easy.'

'No journey is too difficult if it will lead me to Caillte,' Aengus insisted. 'Where do we have to go? What do I have to do?'

'We must travel to a faraway land, Aengus, and we must find some silver apples. Each apple will give you a wish, and one of your wishes can be Caillte. It's not going to be easy, Aengus, because you cannot use your godly powers in the search. Are you sure you want to go on?'

'Can you promise me that when I find the apples I will be able to see and touch and talk to Caillte? She won't disappear again?'

'If you find the apples, Aengus, you will be able to fulfil your dreams.'

'Then I'm willing to go. How do we get to this strange land?'

'I'll lead the way, Aengus, but we will rest here until morning.'

26: The High Road

The dew was still wet on the ground when Capaillín gently nuzzled Aengus awake.

'It's time for us to be off,' she told him.

'So you really exist? I felt sure that I'd wake up this morning and find that I'd been dreaming.'

'It might have been easier for you if you had been dreaming, Aengus,' Capaillín assured him, 'but we have a long way to go and no time for idle chat.'

They walked down the other side of the hill that Aengus had climbed the day before with Luch. It was stony and rough and there was little time for conversation as Aengus and Capaillín both watched their footing. The descent took longer than the climb had, but at last they reached the bottom. Stretching ahead of them was a wide, swift-flowing river.

'We must cross,' Capaillín declared.

'We'll never be able to get across that river,' Aengus insisted. 'The current's too fast. We'll be swept away.'

'We have no choice, Aengus. We must get across. Cling to my coat.'

Aengus and Capaillín stepped into the water, which whirled and eddied around them. It was deeper than they could ever have imagined. There was no possibility of walking across. They would have to swim and hope that they could avoid the rocks.

'Swim on my right side, Aengus,' Capaillín told him, 'and hold on to my mane with both hands. You're too light to be able to withstand the current. Hang on tight.'

Aengus did exactly as he was told. There was water in his eyes and mouth, and the noise of roaring water in his ears. Capaillín was strong, but the current was soon sweeping them along.

'We'll never make it, Capaillín. The current's too strong,' he cried despairingly.

'Stop talking and push with your legs. Use all your strength to help me.'

Never had Aengus felt so weak. Every muscle ached. Every bone seemed pulled and stretched as they forced their way across.

'Not much further, Aengus,' gasped Capaillín. 'Try just a little harder.'

Aengus's mind screamed that he couldn't try harder, that there was no strength left in his body, that it would be so much easier to let the river take them, but he felt Capaillín making even greater efforts and he, too, found extra strength. One last, strong push and they could feel ground under their feet.

'We're nearly there, Aengus. But don't relax just yet,' Capaillín advised.

Capaillín had barely finished speaking when Aengus felt an undertow seize his legs, forcing him under the water. He used his hands to steady himself and lost Capaillín.

Up and down Aengus bobbed as he was carried back into the centre of the river, but just as suddenly as he had lost his legs, he felt himself being yanked towards the riverbank. Capaillín had caught his clothes in her mouth. With Capaillín pulling with all her strength and Aengus thrusting his legs against the force of the water, they just managed to scramble to the far bank, where Capaillín hauled her almost-drowned companion up on to the grass.

'We've made it, Capaillín,' he whispered before falling on the ground and immediately into an exhausted sleep.

'Are you all right, Aengus?' He woke to the sound of Capaillín's voice and the gentle pressure of her nose against his cheek. 'Have you rested enough? We must try to find some food for you before night falls.'

Aengus sat up and looked around. A vast plain stretched as far as the eye could see. There were no hills, no trees, no houses or other signs of habitation. Some grass grew in isolated tufts and only a few outcroppings of rock broke the monotony of the landscape. Aengus got to his feet and found that his legs trembled.

'Get on my back, Aengus,' Capaillín invited. 'We'll be able to travel faster that way.'

Aengus did as he was told. He was feeling light-headed from his exertions and from lack of food, so he was quiet while they headed westward. Suddenly, he started to laugh.

'You're feeling happier?' asked Capaillín, turning her head back to look at Aengus.

'It's not that, Capaillín. It's just that I've remembered a silly rhyme that I heard when I was very young.'

'No doubt, you're going to tell me the rhyme,' sighed Capaillín.

'I certainly am. It went like this:

> *The Thunder God went for a ride*
> *Upon his favourite filly.*
> *'I'm Thor,' he cried. The mare replied:*
> *'You forgot the thaddle, thilly!'*

'Witty, isn't it?' laughed Aengus.

'Puerile, I think is the word that describes such wit. But are you uncomfortable without a saddle?'

'Only a little, Capaillín,' he admitted, 'and it's much easier at the moment to ride than to walk.'

On they went again in silence, both of them scanning the horizon in search of food.

'Over there, Aengus, to the left, do you see it?'

'See what?'

'A black pig, hoking around that little rock.'

Aengus looked closely and there it was!

'Do you think we could catch it, Capaillín?'

'We can certainly try, Aengus. Now hold on tight. It's easy to lose your grip when you have neither saddle nor bridle.'

Aengus wound the mane around his fingers and dug his knees into Capaillín's sides. With a leap they were off. For a moment, it looked as if the pig could neither see nor scent them, because it remained unperturbed, but, just as Aengus's thoughts were turning to roast crackling, the pig turned its head, spotted them, and headed off to the north.

Aengus had never chased a pig before, so he didn't know what to expect, but he was amazed by the speed and the agility of the animal. On and on they rode, turning left or right, as the pig turned, until they came to a wide expanse of sea.

'We've got him now, Capaillín,' exulted Aengus.

'Have we?' panted Capaillín.

And Capaillín was right. Just as it seemed as if the pig was trapped, it leapt into the water and began to swim.

'After him, Capaillín,' shouted Aengus, and they too plunged into the water. It was invigorating to feel the cool water after the long ride in the sun and they had no difficulty keeping up with the pig. Unfortunately, although they could keep up with the pig, they could not catch it! Aengus was about to call off the hunt and settle for a meal of fish, when the pig seemed to rise up in the water.

'Capaillín,' Aengus shouted, 'the pig's walking on the waves!'

'Nonsense, we've reached land. I can feel it beneath my feet.'

The pig was running up the beach and heading for a clump of trees.

'Keep going, Capaillín,' yelled Aengus, as they rushed up the beach after it.

When they got to the edge of the trees, they were just in time to see the pig disappearing into a large, fortified castle. Capaillín slowed down and they rode purposefully up to the castle. The walls were high and sheer, offering no footholds for a climber.

'There's only one way in,' Capaillín commented, 'and that's through the main entrance, the way the pig got in.'

When they got to the entrance, they saw that it would not be as easy to get in as they had first thought. The threshold was high and wide, but was guarded by long, sharp, blades that projected from the top and bottom of the doorway. The blades were in perpetual motion, opening and closing like giant steel teeth. Together they watched the rhythmic grinding.

'I've calculated that about every thirty heartbeats there's an opening big enough for me to get through,' Aengus told Capaillín. 'That's how the pig managed to get in.'

'But it's only open for a count of three. You'd never make it on your own, Aengus. You aren't quick enough. We'll have to time it perfectly and I'll jump just as the teeth are coming apart.'

'It's not wide enough for both of us, Capaillín,' Aengus insisted.

'You lie as flat to my back as you can, Aengus, and I'll make myself as small as I can. It's a good thing I'm not the horse you thought I was or we'd never have made it. Count, Aengus, count.'

'Now,' roared Aengus, and Capaillín and he were sailing through the air as if propelled from a catapult.

'We made it! We made it! We made it!' Aengus exulted, leaping off Capaillín's back when her hooves touched down on the inner courtyard.

Aengus led the way through the courtyard and into a large, high room where there was a table laid with all the foods Aengus had ever seen or could ever have imagined.

'Look at that food, Capaillín,' he cried, 'enough for an army.'

Capaillín did not respond, and when Aengus turned around he noticed that the pony was badly cut on her legs and abdomen.

'Capaillín,' he rushed to her. 'Capaillín, you're hurt.'

'It's not too bad, Aengus. Don't worry about me. You're hungry. Go and eat some food and I'll try to find something for my wounds.'

'The food can wait, Capaillín. Let's go to the stables and see what we can find.'

The castle was totally bereft of people and animals, but it was very well appointed and soon they found the stables. Aengus washed Capaillín's wounds in brine, wrapping cloths round the deepest cuts. Then he got her water and food and settled her down for the night.

'Are you all right now, Capaillín?' he asked, stroking her coat.

'I'm fine, Aengus. I'll be all right. Go and look after yourself now. Eat well and have a good night's sleep. We have a long way to go tomorrow.'

'I don't like leaving you out here,' Aengus began, but Capaillín gently butted him on his way, and he was very hungry and very tired so didn't take much persuading.

Aengus returned to the room with the laden table. A fire burned brightly in the big, open grate, and that was almost as welcome to him as the taste of the food. He ate slowly, methodically, savouring every bite and washing it down with a wine that sparkled like dew but warmed like fire. It was almost too good to leave, but he was tired to exhaustion, and on looking into the next room, he discovered a large, soft bed.

'How long is it since I've slept in a bed with a duck down mattress?' he asked himself, 'and where did that pig go?' But there was no one to answer his questions and, indeed, he would not have been well pleased if there had been.

Aengus was in that happy phase between consciousness and sleep when he became aware of a woman in the room. She walked up to the bed, looked at him, shook her head sadly, and went off through the wall.

'I'm dreaming already,' he sighed, and so he was.

The morning light shone in through the narrow windows. It shone so brightly that Aengus knew it was quite late. Still, he did not hurry. Yesterday had been a traumatic day. It would be good to rest for a while. Slowly, he got up, bathed leisurely and found the table groaning with all his favourite breakfast food, including warm, fresh bread and several varieties of honey. Eating

183

contentedly and savouring the peace of his surroundings, Aengus suddenly remembered Capaillín. He was about to rush to the stables when he heard the unmistakable tip-tip-tip-tip of her feet and looked up to see the shaggy head peeping round the doorway.

'I hope you weren't planning to go far today,' came the quietly sarcastic voice, 'because, if you were, you'll have to change your mind. Haven't you noticed that the sun is already high in the sky, Aengus?'

'Sorry, Capaillín,' apologised Aengus. 'I've been so comfortable that I almost forgot about our journey.'

'And about me too,' came the huffy reply.

'I'm sorry, Capaillín. How are your cuts today? Let's treat them now and, if you're well enough, we'll set off.'

They went back to the stables and Aengus washed Capaillín's wounds with salt and water.

'You heal very fast, old friend,' he consoled her, patting her sides.

'I'm not old, Aengus,' she informed him. 'Even allowing for the difference between pony years and human years, I'm only half your age plus seven.'

'And that's a perfect age for a pony, no doubt,' laughed Aengus. 'Come on, then. Let's go. We've both eaten and drunk our fill. There's nothing to stop us going a little further today.'

'Nothing at all, Aengus,' Capaillín a

greed, and they set off. 'Look,' she said, 'there's a gateway we didn't see yesterday. Let's take it. I don't fancy another leap through the metal teeth.'

They walked through the gateway and into a garden that was lush with vegetation. There were tall trees shading tall plants, which, in their turn, gave shelter to younger, smaller shrubs. There were bushes and ferns and lichens twining around branches and boughs. There was fruit, too, all of it in season at the same time, and the flowers were as richly coloured as iridescent rainbows. It was a pleasure simply being in the garden.

'Aengus,' said Capaillín hesitantly after some time. 'Do you see this big, old oak tree?'

'Yes, I do. I was thinking that it would be lovely to climb up into its branches and listen to the birds.'

'Do you notice anything strange about it?'

'Strange, Capaillín? How do you mean strange? It looks lovely to me, a perfect oak tree.'

'It's the third time we've passed it, Aengus.'

'What! Why, you're right, Capaillín. I wondered why everything seemed so familiar here. We've been going round in circles. Look, there's the gate where we came in. We'd better go out again, as we're making no progress in here.'

Away from the sheltering trees, they realised that the sun was already low in the sky.

'We've been wandering in that garden for hours, Aengus,' Capaillín remarked. 'It's too late to set out again now. I think we'd better spend another night here.'

'It's probably just as well, Capaillín,' Aengus agreed. 'It will give your cuts another day to heal. Let me see to your needs and then we'll both have an early night so that we can be up with the sun tomorrow.'

Aengus again bathed Capaillín's cuts, even though they had all but disappeared. Then he made his way into the castle, ate what he needed and lay down to sleep. Once again, when he wasn't quite awake and yet not fully asleep, a beautiful woman came into the room, walked up to the bed, sighed, and went out through the wall.

⬤ ⬤ ⬤

The sun and the lark had barely risen before Aengus. He washed, ate, packed some food and went to the stable for Capaillín. She was already waiting for him.

'I've been looking around, Aengus,' she told him, 'and I've found another exit.'

'Good for you, Capaillín.'

They went out through the gate and found themselves in another garden. This one was much bigger and much more luxuriant than the first garden.

'Is this really a garden?' asked Aengus, as they walked and walked through lanes where the trees arched overhead, canopying them from the sun and where each bend opened into arbours of flowers and long alleyways of trimmed shrubs.

'It is and it isn't,' Capaillín confirmed. 'It's like yesterday's garden. We could walk all day if we liked, but we would still be in the same garden and the only exit leads back to the castle. This is a very strange place indeed. I have a feeling that there is a reason why we are not allowed to leave it. '

Aengus had a thought. 'I wonder ...' he began.

'What do you wonder?' asked Capaillín.

So, as they were walking back to the castle, Aengus told Capaillín about his dream that a young woman had come up to his bed, looked at him, sighed, and walked off through the wall.

'I don't think that was a dream, Aengus,' Capaillín assured him. 'The woman is in trouble of some kind and needs help. Tonight, when she visits you, you must speak to her. You must ask her who she is and what is causing her distress.'

Aengus went to bed early and had almost given up hope that the lady would visit him. Then, just as he was drifting into a light sleep, he was aware that he was not alone in the room. This time, he opened his eyes and watched carefully. The lady approached the bed, moving so quietly and smoothly that there was no sound of motion. Her face was beautiful but infused with such sadness that Aengus instinctively looked away. Then, remembering Capaillín's instructions, he said:

'Who are you, lady?'

She smiled at him and the smile was like a shaft of sunlight on a dark day.

'I'm Bronagh,' she told him, 'lady of this castle.'

'Why are you so sad, Bronagh?' Aengus asked.

'My husband and I were bewitched,' she confided. 'He was transformed into a frog and forced to live in the lake to the south of the castle. By day I live as a black pig and can only regain my real shape for a short time each night.'

'Can anyone help you?' he asked.

'If someone can release my husband from his punishment and return him here to the castle in his natural form, then I too, will be free. But it is hopeless. I must go now, Aengus, but thank you for listening.'

As she moved away, Aengus told her: 'I'll do what I can to help, Bronagh.'

Before disappearing through the wall, the lady looked back at him with a flash of hope in her eyes.

27: Thick Skinned

Aengus slept late the next morning and only woke up when he heard Capaillín calling loudly.

'What?' he asked, half asleep.

'So you're still with us!' Capaillín exclaimed with relief. 'You were in such a deep sleep that I thought you were under a spell of come sort! I've been trying to wake you since the sun rose.'

'Sorry, Capaillín,' he said contritely. 'I didn't get to sleep until after the lady had gone and then my sleep was plagued by dreams of black pigs and flashing blades. I'll be ready as soon as I've washed and eaten.'

Capaillín waited impatiently outside and, eventually, Aengus joined her and told her about Bronagh and her husband.

'It's just as I thought,' sighed Capaillín. 'We were led here for a purpose and, now, we must go to the lake and see if we can help her husband.'

'Will it take very long Capaillín?' Aengus asked anxiously. 'We have lost two days already.'

Capaillín looked at him with eyes that were capable of expressing depths of emotion and he did not like what he saw in them.

'You may go on if you choose, Aengus,' she informed him quietly, 'but I will not leave here until I have tried to help Bronagh and her husband.'

Aengus heard the hurt in her voice and knew she was disappointed in him. 'We'd better go to the lake, then, hadn't we?' he suggested briskly.

'Are you sure, Aengus?' she asked.

'Very sure, Capaillín, very sure.'

This time no obstacles stood in their way and Aengus and Capaillín found themselves outside the gates of the castle without any difficulty. To the south, they could see the lake shimmering in the sunshine and they walked steadily towards it.

'What is Bronagh's husband's name?' asked Capaillín.

'I don't know,' answered Aengus.

'Didn't you ask Bronagh?' Capaillín enquired.

'No, I didn't think of asking her.'

'But there must be thousands of frogs living on the edges of the lake. How are we going to be able to attract Bronagh's husband if we don't know his name?'

Aengus felt a bit stupid that he hadn't foreseen this problem.

'Never mind,' Capaillín said kindly. 'There may be a way round it. I have an idea.'

'I thought you might,' he told her. 'What is it?'

'Well,' she suggested, 'I don't know a great deal about frogs, but I don't think they are likely to be out and about in the bright sunshine of midday. I've usually only seen them at dusk.'

'If you're right,' conceded Aengus, 'why are we going to the lake now?'

'Use your brain, Aengus,' Capaillín upbraided him. 'Bronagh's husband may have been transformed into a frog, but he's still a man. Men and women like being out in the sun, so I'm hoping that he is the only frog we will find.'

When they got to the edge of the lake, Capaillín said: 'I'll go to the right, Aengus, and examine every blade of grass. You take the left and do the same. We'll surely find Bronagh's husband. But don't shout if you see him. We don't want to frighten him. Just stand still and speak very quietly.'

Slowly, methodically, they walked along the side of the lake, their eyes fixed on the ground. They saw grasshoppers and ants, flies, wasps and bees, birds and beetles, but no frogs. Then Aengus noticed that Capaillín was standing perfectly still beside a small rock. Trying hard not to make a noise, Aengus joined her. She had found a frog, all right. It was the biggest frog Aengus had ever seen. It sat on the rock, sunning itself and occasionally uttering a quiet, melancholy 'Rac! Rac!'

Capaillín spoke very gently. 'Don't be afraid, frog. We will not hurt you. We have heard your story from Bronagh and have come to help.'

'Bronagh?' croaked the frog. 'Is she all right?' and he turned to look at Aengus and Capaillín with eyes that were as wet as the lake.

'Yes,' Aengus assured him. 'But she misses you and wants you back. How can we help you?'

'I don't think anyone can help me,' sighed the frog. 'As you know, I am Bronagh's husband, Racaire, and you have seen what has befallen me. But my curse goes back much further than my present situation. I was born doomed, although at the time I didn't know it.'

'Tell us about it, Racaire,' Capaillín soothed. 'We'll help you if we can.'

'It started before I was born,' Racaire began.

My father was a poor fisherman who found it hard to catch enough fish to keep his wife and six daughters alive. Then, one day, while he was fishing in this lake, a beautiful lady rose up and asked him why he was so sad.

'I'm a poor fisherman,' he told her, 'and my wife and children have very little to eat. I work hard but I never seem to catch enough fish.'

'I'll see to it that you catch all the fish you can eat or sell, fisherman,' she told him, 'if you promise to give me your son in marriage.'

Now, my father was poor and hungry and besides, he had no son, so he willingly agreed to the beautiful lady's offer. That day, he took home more fish than he had ever caught before. His family had enough to eat and plenty left over to sell. Day after day, my father caught fish by the boatload and within a short time, he was quite a rich man and a very happy one, because he knew that he could arrange good marriages for each of his daughters.

One day, my mother came to him and told him that she was going to have her seventh child.

'We may be lucky, husband. This time, we may have a son.'

My father was pleased with the news, but convinced that they would have another daughter. He no longer worried that there would be an extra mouth to feed. There was plenty to eat now and another child would only mean more joy in a household that was already joyful. The nine months passed quickly and, to everyone's surprise, my mother gave birth to twin boys.

Everyone rejoiced except my father. He remembered his promise to the lady of the lake. But he had not seen her for years, and he began to hope that maybe he would not have to keep his side of the bargain. Then, one day, when my brother and I were children, we were playing at the side of the lake, close to where my father was fishing. When my father came to bring us home, my brother had disappeared and I was lying asleep, alone.

My mother and sisters wept for months and my father was bowed by the grief, for he believed that the lady had taken my brother to be her husband, even though he was only a small child. In time, of course, the pain lessened. My sisters got married. I grew up and no one thought any more about the lady in the lake. My father was now a rich man and I was selected by the lord of the castle to marry his only child, Bronagh.

For one short summer, Bronagh and I were as happy and carefree as these grasshoppers here. But one day when I was approaching my twenty-first birthday, my father was sitting peacefully by the side of the lake. He no longer needed to work, but old habits die hard and he usually spent part of each day sitting where he used to fish.

'Fisherman,' a voice called out, 'I have come to remind you of your promise. I have come for your son.'

'What!' exclaimed my father. 'Have I been dreaming?'

'You're not dreaming, fisherman,' answered the voice, and my father saw the beautiful lady that he had seen all those years earlier.

'But you have already taken my son,' pleaded my father. 'You took him when he was just an infant.'

'I have never taken a son of yours,' the lady assured him. 'Your promise remains unfulfilled.'

My father arrived at the palace with a heavy heart, but I was young and did not feel unduly worried by his tale.

'I didn't promise to marry her, father,' I consoled him. 'And, anyway, I'm married to Bronagh now. You've lost one son. That's enough.'

'Be careful, son,' my father warned, but I was sure that no one could hurt me.

I continued with my life of pleasure, and soon after, when I was near the lake, I saw a huge frog emerge and slough off its skin before returning to the water. I picked up the skin and it looked almost as big as a man's outer garment. I wondered if it would fit me so I tried it on and it fitted so well that I felt impelled to try it out in the water. With one great leap, I jumped in the lake and swam with the effortless ease of a frog. Up and down the lake I swam, jumping in and out of the water, knowing for the first time in my life the joy of being as much at home in the water as on the land.

As evening approached, I jumped out on to this rock and tried to take off the frog's skin but, no matter how I struggled, I could not shift it, and slowly the terrible truth came home to me. I was a frog.

'Don't be so sad, Racaire,' came a voice close to me and, turning, I saw for the first time the beautiful lady of the lake. 'You are to be my husband.'

'I cannot be your husband,' I told her. 'I've got a wife of my own and I will never give her up.'

'You *will* marry me,' answered the lady in a voice that would not easily be disobeyed. 'Our marriage was arranged before you were born. I kept my side of the bargain and you must keep yours.'

I argued with the lady. I pleaded. But nothing I could say would change her mind.

'Do you refuse to marry me?' she asked.

'I do,' I replied. 'I'm married to Bronagh.'

'Then, if you will not keep the bargain I made with your father, you must stay a frog. And Bronagh will suffer too.'

When he came to the end of his tale, Racaire sighed deeply and looked up at Aengus. 'Well, you've met my poor wife, so you know the fate that has befallen her. The lady has punished both of us because I refused to honour my father's promise. Is there anything you can do to help?'

'If the lady of the lake is so beautiful,' Aengus suggested, 'would it not be possible for you to marry her? Your father did make a promise, after all, so you may be able to get out of your contract with Bronagh.'

'No' said Racaire. 'I want no wife but Bronagh. If I had met the lady before I fell in love with Bronagh, that would be different. But now it's not possible.' He sighed despairingly. 'I knew you couldn't help. I knew there was no hope, but thank you for trying.'

Aengus looked sadly at Racaire and then at Capaillín. She was wearing a very thoughtful expression.

'There is not much hope, Racaire,' she told him, 'but there is a little. Let's look at all the facts. Your father made a promise and that promise must be honoured. *You* cannot honour it, but the promise must be honoured by his son. There is only one possible answer. We must locate his other son, your lost brother, and he must marry the lady of the lake.'

'Gadaire? But my brother is dead,' Racaire insisted. 'He *must* be dead. He probably fell into the water all those years ago.'

'Can you remember anything about the time when you and he were playing?' Capaillín asked. 'Think very carefully. Your life and your wife's future may depend on it.'

'I was only a child,' Racaire said sadly. 'I remember very little. We were playing by the side of the water and we lay down. I fell asleep. I must have done, because I thought I saw a cloud of smoke settling on top of my brother. When I looked again, there was no smoke and no Gadaire. He must have drowned, mustn't he?'

'I don't think so, Racaire. I think he was taken away. If we can find him, we may be able to rescue you and your wife.'

'Find him?' Aengus was astonished. 'How could we find him? He's been missing for eighteen years. If his parents couldn't find him all those years ago, how can we?'

'My parents didn't try to find him,' Racaire confessed. 'Of course, they searched the lake and the woods and asked everyone if they had seen him. But my father was convinced that the lady of the lake had taken him and we all believed him, so they gave up the search. Oh, if you can help us, please do,' he appealed. 'It's hard being away from the woman you love.'

'I know that,' agreed Aengus, 'I am parted from my love, too. We will do our best to help you.'

Aengus and Capaillín walked slowly away from the lake. They were both thinking deeply.

'Racaire's right. It's hopeless, isn't it?' Aengus confided.

'Almost hopeless, Aengus,' she agreed, 'but not completely.'

'Have you got an idea?'

'Yes, but it may not work. We'll have to go back and talk to Racaire again.'

Racaire was still sitting sadly on his rock when they returned.

'You've realised it's hopeless?' he asked sadly.

'No,' answered Capaillín, 'but we must talk to the lady in the lake. Can you bring her here?'

'I don't see what good it will do, but I will go and fetch her.'

Aengus waited expectantly, hoping that Capaillín would tell him what she had in mind, but Capaillín just stared thoughtfully into the lake.

'What do you think we can do, Capaillín?' he asked, but didn't get an answer. Suddenly, almost without rippling the surface,

Racaire reappeared, followed closely by a lady of such beauty that Aengus felt his breath being sucked from his body.

'How could Racaire have resisted her?' he asked in amazement.

'Clearly, more easily than you could have done!' Capaillín replied curtly.

The lady spoke in a voice that was as pleasant to the ear as her face was to the eye. 'You wish to see me?' she enquired.

'Yes, lady, we do,' answered Capaillín. 'Racaire has told us about the arrangement between you and his father.'

'We made a bargain,' the lady insisted. 'I kept my side of it. Racaire failed to keep his.'

'But Racaire didn't make a bargain with you,' Capaillín told her. 'He made a bargain with Bronagh and he is trying to honour that.'

'Racaire's father promised me his son.'

'That's right,' agreed Capaillín. 'But he had two sons: Racaire and his twin brother, Gadaire. If we can find Gadaire and if he promises to marry you, will you release Racaire and Bronagh from their spell?'

'Gladly,' she replied. 'I only want what is rightly mine. If you can find Gadaire and if he is willing to marry me, then I will release Racaire. It gives me little pleasure to have an uncommunicative frog as a companion when I bargained for a healthy, happy husband.'

'Will you help us to find Gadaire?' Capaillín went on. 'He disappeared from the banks of your lake. Someone must have seen what happened.'

'Stay here,' she instructed. 'I will find out what I can.'

As soon as she had gone, Aengus whispered in Capaillín's ear. 'It's useless, Capaillín. Even if the lady gets information and even if

Gadaire is still alive, Racaire will never be able to find him and bring him back. He may be a man on the inside, but he's a frog on the outside and it's not easy for a frog to travel ...'

'Shh, Aengus!' Capaillín warned, 'Racaire will hear you and besides, here comes the lady now.'

The lady broke the surface of the lake. 'I've enquired of the other users of the lake – the fish and the birds – and I have some news. Gadaire is not dead. He was stolen and given to a queen who had no children. But it will not be easy to find him. He is living with his foster parents in a land that is three days' journey beyond the world's end. If you do manage to trace him and bring him to me, I will set Racaire and Bronagh free, but I do not think you'll find him.' And, with that, the lady disappeared without leaving even a ripple on the smooth waters of the lake.

'I am delighted to hear that my brother is still alive,' croaked Racaire, 'but how can anyone bring back someone who lives three days beyond the end of the world?'

'We can try, can't we, Aengus?'

'Us?' asked Aengus. 'Why can't Racaire try?'

'You know very well that he can't be away from water for very long,' Capaillín answered.

'But what about the silver apples? I must find them if I'm ever to find Caillte.' Then, seeing Capaillín's look of disapproval and hearing Racaire's sad croak, he gave in.

'All right. I suppose we should try.'

'If we are to travel to a land that is three day's journey beyond the world's end,' said Capaillín, 'we should set off at once.'

'Good luck, Capaillín. Good luck, Aengus,' Racaire croaked. 'May your quest be blessed with success.'

28: The Road to the End of the World

Aengus and Capaillín set off immediately, and for a long time neither spoke. Aengus walked with his shoulders slumped and his head bowed. When they reached a crossroads, Capaillín asked:

'Why are you so angry, Aengus?'

'We're wasting time. That's why. We'll never be able to find Gadaire. Racaire knew it was a hopeless pursuit. The lady of the lake knew it was impossible. I know it's impossible, but here we are wasting time when we could be looking for the silver apples that will lead me to Caillte.'

'Have you not received help, Aengus?' Capaillín asked. 'Have you not travelled in your mind with Gáire and journeyed through hollow lands with Luch?'

'Well yes, I suppose so,' he answered, 'but I don't know how much help it was. After all, here I am, still wandering and still no nearer Caillte! I've enjoyed good company, but have I actually got help?'

'You don't *have* to come with me, Aengus,' Capaillín told him quietly. 'You can go off on your own and look for Caillte. That road to the left will lead you, eventually, to the garden where the silver apples grow. I'm going to the right because I'm hoping to find Gadaire. I would like you to come with me, but you don't have to.'

Aengus stopped, and Capaillín walked steadily on to the right. He looked to the left. The road was wide and smooth and would lead to the garden. He looked to the right. The road was narrow and rugged and was empty except for the disappearing form of Capaillín. If he chose the left fork, he could go straight to the garden, and not waste his time on Racaire or Bronagh or Gadaire or the lady of the lake. He turned left and walked a short distance. When he looked over his shoulder, Capaillín was almost out of sight. What was it that his teacher used to say? 'A straight line is not always the shortest distance between two points.' Was she right? Aengus turned and looked again, and this time Capaillín had vanished from sight.

'Wait for me, Capaillín,' he yelled at the top of his voice, and ran until he saw that she was waiting for him.

'Wouldn't you rather look for the garden of the silver apples and Caillte?' she asked.

'Yes,' he replied, 'I would. But I did say I would help Racaire, and anyway, maybe I won't be able to find them on my own. Perhaps, when we've found Gadaire, we might get some help ourselves.'

Capaillín looked long and hard at him. 'Perhaps, Aengus,' she agreed softly. 'Perhaps.' And they walked off together.

They had not travelled very far when they heard the shrill sounds of a heated argument. When they got a little closer, they could see a hawk, a mouse and a hedgehog fighting over a large piece of food that they had found in a field close to the road.

'Why are they quarrelling, Capaillín?' Aengus asked. 'There's enough food there for all three of them.'

'Why don't you tell them that?'

So Aengus went over to the noisy trio. 'Excuse me,' he said, 'but your quarrel is foolish. There's enough food for everyone. Let me show you.' And he divided the food into three pieces, each big enough for a good meal.

'You've resolved that well,' said the mouse, appreciatively. 'Because I am smallest, I thought I would end up with nothing. I am grateful to you, so let me do something for you. If you are ever in trouble and think of me, you will have the power to change yourself into a mouse, but don't use my gift foolishly, because it will work only once.'

Aengus smiled to himself, thinking it unlikely that he would ever have the need to turn himself into a mouse, but he thanked the mouse for her kindness and turned to go.

'Not so fast,' the hawk stopped him. 'I, too, have a gift for you. Although I fought for it, that food was too heavy for me to fly off with before, but now I can take my share back to my nest. I can't imagine that you will ever want the abilities of a mouse, but you may, on one occasion, find that you need to fly. If you do, Aengus, think of me and you will be able to soar through the air with the grace and majesty of a hawk.'

Aengus thanked the hawk for his kindness, but, before he could set off, the hedgehog spoke.

'I will not be outdone in generosity,' he informed Aengus. 'I, too, will give you the power to turn yourself into a hedgehog on one occasion when such a transformation might help you.'

Aengus thanked all three for their gifts again and bade them farewell.

'Safe journey,' squeaked the mouse. 'Follow this road to its end and you will find Gadaire.'

'Travel in hope,' called the hawk. 'Gadaire is alive and well.'

'Return in the knowledge,' added the hedgehog, 'that the silver apples will soon be ripe.'

Aengus went back to the road to join Capaillín. There was a spring in his step now and he told Capaillín about the gifts he had been given. 'I'm so glad I came with you and I'm very glad that we met the mouse, the hawk and the hedgehog.'

'There's an old saying, Aengus,' Capaillín reminded him. 'A going foot always gets something, if it is only a thorn. Today, we've been lucky. We've picked up more than a thorn! But we've still got a long way to go, a very long way to go.'

And they had. The road stretched out ahead of them – straight, narrow and seemingly interminable. The moon was high in the sky when Aengus saw a very large house with a barn attached, and suggested that they go there for the night. Aengus knocked on the door, but received no answer. The door was bigger than any door Aengus had ever seen, but it swung open smoothly on well-oiled hinges. There was no one at home.

'The person who lives here must be enormous,' Aengus said, looking around in amazement. 'Look at the size of the door and that chair.'

'I've noticed. Perhaps we should look somewhere else for our night's shelter.'

'It's too late, Capaillín. Besides, the house is empty. Whoever lives here must be away. Come on. I'll settle you down in the barn for the night and we'll leave here early in the morning. With luck, no one will even know that we've been here.'

Aengus led Capaillín into an enormous stall where there was hay to eat and water to drink. 'I'll leave the door of the barn open, Capaillín, just in case we have to leave in a hurry, and I'll leave the door of the house open too. If you hear anything, just call me.'

Aengus walked wearily from the barn. His feet felt so heavy that he was conscious of every step he took and his eyelids were leaden weights on his eyes. He was too tired to look for food and made straight for the huge bed in the corner of the room. Fortunately, the leg of the bed was carved so he was able to get footholds in the wood and climb up. Gratefully, he sank into a mattress that was like soft spring grass.

'I wonder who lives here?' he mused, feeling happily detached from his body. 'I wonder ...' but Aengus was fast asleep before he could finish his next thought.

The sun shone brightly through the open door, falling on Aengus's face and waking him naturally. He had slept deeply and was ready for the day's journey, but he was so very comfortable that he lay where he was, revelling in the fact that he was conscious of neither ache nor pain, but only of a sense of extreme well-being. Without warning, the bed shook violently. Then the entire house was shaking to the rhythm of a loud, regular noise.

Thud! Thud! Thud! he heard. It was like nothing he had ever heard before. It couldn't be thunder; there was no lightning and no rain. It couldn't be drumming; it was too loud and too heavy. It couldn't be ... His next guess was interrupted by the voice of Capaillín calling him urgently.

'Aengus, Aengus! Come out quickly. He's coming home.'

Aengus didn't ask the questions that were coursing through his mind. He moved quickly to the leg of the bed, climbed down as fast as he could and had just stepped out through the open door when an enormous shadow fell over him. He looked up at the sky and saw the sun shining as usual. Everything looked normal, but something was terribly wrong. There was no sound of bird song, no scuffling noises of animals. The shadow over him got darker, and just as he saw what was making it, a voice like thunder rolled in his ears. It was too loud for Aengus to hear what it said but he didn't ask to have it repeated. The voice was coming from the biggest man Aengus had ever seen.

Aengus had heard of giants, of course. Everybody had. He had even seen the mountain of a stone that Fionn MacCumhaill had hurled at a king who had been rude to him. But nothing he had ever heard could have prepared him for the magnitude of this man.

'Quickly, Aengus,' Capaillín advised him. 'Jump on my back and we'll try to get away from him.'

Aengus darted in Capaillín's direction but found that, although his legs were flailing, he was not moving sideways but upwards. He could see the giant's index finger pressed into his stomach and feel his enormous thumb on his spine.

'What have we here?' asked the enormous voice, and Aengus felt his hair and clothes buffeted by the breeze from the giant's mouth.

'I didn't mean any harm,' Aengus told him, shouting at the top of his voice, but the giant appeared not to hear him.

'It looks like a little man,' the voice blared, almost deafening Aengus with its volume, 'but it buzzes like an insect. The best thing to do with insects is to step on them.' And he bent to the ground, still holding Aengus firmly between his finger and thumb.

Aengus was dizzy from the speed of the descent and from the resounding noises, but as his feet touched the ground, he heard Capaillín shouting.

'The mouse, Aengus, the mouse. Think of the mouse.'

What a time to think of a mouse!, Aengus thought in annoyance, and suddenly he was a mouse. He wriggled through the giant's fingers.

'Run up his trouser leg,' Capaillín instructed, and Aengus did exactly that.

Immediately, the giant started running and roaring and laughing and yelling. Aengus needed to dig in all twenty little nails just to hold on to his leg.

'Oh! Oh!' the giant roared, halfway between laughing and crying. 'Stop it, please stop it. I'll give you all that I have. Please. Please.'

Aengus ran down the giant's leg and sat on his shoe. He was picked up, very much more gently this time, and held up to the giant's ear.

'What can I give you?' the giant asked. 'Do you want my gold? My castle? My houses and barns? I promised you everything and I will keep my promise.'

'I don't want everything,' Aengus yelled back. 'I just want to take my pony and to continue my journey.'

The giant gently carried Aengus, the mouse, over to Capaillín and, when Aengus was placed on her back, he reverted to his old shape.

'Are you sure you want nothing?' enquired the giant.

'Nothing,' Aengus assured him.

'Then, since you ask for so little, let me give you three gifts. The first is a green jacket that will give you my strength when it is worn. The second is a good meal for you and your pony.'

'And the third?' Aengus shouted.

'After your meal, I will carry you and your pony for a good part of your journey. That way, we will cover one moon's travel in a day.'

Aengus and Capaillín ate and drank until both of them thought they would never need food or drink again. Aengus draped the green jacket over Capaillín's back. Then Láidir, for that was his name, picked them both up and carried them safely to the edge of the world.

'This is as far as I can take you,' he told them as he lowered them carefully down.

'Thank you, Láidir,' said Capaillín, gently nuzzling his foot.

'Yes, Láidir, we don't know how to thank you,' agreed Aengus.

'Come and visit me, one day, when this journey is finished.'

'I will, Láidir,' Aengus promised.

'We will, Láidir,' said Capaillín.

They both stood still, watching their large friend disappear out of sight, the earth around him quaking at his steps.

'The end of the world, Aengus,' Capaillín commented. 'We have made good progress. In three day's time, we should be at the castle where Gadaire is.'

29: The Longest Mile

From the look of the terrain, their three-day journey would not be an easy one. The road really did not deserve the name of road. It was a narrow, rugged path, winding inexorably upwards. There were no trees to be seen, and what from a distance looked like grass, turned out to be clumps of nettles.

They struggled on, the incline getting steeper all the time.

'Don't worry, Aengus,' Capaillín reassured him. 'All mountains have tops and when we reach the top, the journey will be easier.'

As they continued upwards, Aengus began to think that perhaps this mountain was the exception to the rule. Perhaps this one did not have a summit. Perhaps people just went on climbing and climbing forever.

'It can't be forever,' Capaillín broke in on his thoughts. 'We were told that we'd reach Gadaire's home after travelling for three days, so there must be an end to this.'

She had hardly spoken when the knots in Aengus's calf muscles started to untie themselves.

'Is it my imagination, Capaillín,' he asked, 'or have we stopped climbing?'

'You're right, Aengus, we've reached the top. Look, that path leads around the top of the mountain and down the other side. I think we deserve a rest. Let's just get to the other side and perhaps there'll be something worth looking at.'

Capaillín proved to be right. Walking on the further side of the mountain was like walking from a dark room into sunshine. They looked down on a broad expanse of plain with a large lake at its centre.

'It's like a little sea,' Aengus enthused. 'Look, it has waves. We should spend the night near its shores, Capaillín. It will be warmer than up here and, if we're lucky, there'll be food to eat.'

The journey down the mountain was hazardous, because the path sometimes disappeared altogether and it was particularly hard for Capaillín to find steady footing. Aengus went first in such places, testing out each step for both of them. But, in spite of the difficulties, they travelled cheerfully, because now they had a target to aim for. They would walk to the edge of the lake and then rest.

Eventually, they reached the plain and the grass was high and soft to walk on.

'Aengus,' said Capaillín, as they approached the lake, 'do my eyes deceive me or is someone sitting on a rock near the shore?'

Aengus peered into the distance. He could see the lake very clearly. There was a large rock near the shore, a rock that seemed to be coloured gold and blue on the top. He stared at it closely and it appeared to move.

'I think you're right, Capaillín. I think there is someone on the rock.'

They walked quickly in the direction of the rock and the figure became clearer. It was a little girl with hair like spun sunshine. The glow was so bright that they had to lower their eyes as they approached her. She saw their difficulty and covered her hair with a blue scarf that matched the colour of her eyes.

'Please help me,' she called out to them. 'Help me, please.'

'Can't you swim?' Aengus asked. 'Stay where you are and I'll swim over and help you to the shore.'

Aengus was about to jump into the water when the little girl cried out in alarm.

'No! Don't put your foot in the water or the serpent will get you too.' She began to cry, because she was very young and very sad.

'Let me try,' Capaillín suggested. Then, turning to the child on the rock, she asked, 'What's your name, child?'

The little girl didn't seem to think it was at all strange for a pony to talk, and answered readily. 'Girseach,' she said, and started to cry again.

'And where are your mother and father, Girseach?' asked Capaillín.

'I don't know,' replied the little girl, tearfully. 'I've been sitting on this rock for such a very long time! I can't even remember a time when I wasn't sitting here.'

'Why don't you just come ashore, Girseach?' continued Capaillín.

'I'm afraid to,' answered the child. 'There's a serpent in the water, a giant serpent, and it will eat me if I leave the rock.'

'Don't worry, Girseach,' Capaillín assured her. 'We'll get you off, somehow.'

Aengus and Capaillín looked into the water. It was so clean and clear that they could see fronds growing at the bottom of the lake, waving rhythmically in the tidal motion.

'Can you see a serpent, Capaillín?' Aengus asked. 'You've got such good eyes.'

'I can't, Aengus,' she replied, 'but there's definitely something wrong. I can see shells and rocks and vegetation on the floor of the lake, but I can't see any fish.'

'Neither can I,' Aengus agreed. 'But isn't that a good sign? If there are no fish, it must mean that there is no serpent. After all, the serpent would need fish to live.'

'True, Aengus, true. But it's also possible that there are no fish because the serpent has eaten them all.'

'You're right. I didn't think of that.'

Aengus and Capaillín searched the lake as closely as they could, but saw no sign of a serpent.

'Please help me,' called Girseach again, standing up on the rock with her arms stretched out towards them. 'Don't leave me here on my own any more.'

'I'm going to risk it, Capaillín,' Aengus told her. 'I can't see any serpent.'

'Leave it until the morning, Aengus,' the pony advised. 'The light will be better and we'll have had longer to watch the lake.'

'I don't like leaving that child on her own. She's so upset that she could easily fall off the rock into the water. If anything happened to her while we were asleep, I'd never be able to live with myself.'

Aengus stood on the shoreline closest to the rock and searched the waters again. Seeing nothing, he dived into the lake and swam swiftly towards the rock. The water was cool and invigorating and he was almost within arm's length of the rock when he felt something curl around his legs.

'Watch out, Aengus!' called Capaillín.

'It's the serpent,' squealed the child. 'Quickly, quickly, grab hold of my rock.'

Aengus stretched as far as he could, but it was useless. The serpent was not as big as Girseach had suggested, but it was big enough to drown him. Slowly it wound itself around Aengus. First, his legs were immobilised, then his left arm and then his right. He struggled and tugged, but there was nothing he could do. He felt the air being squeezed out of his lungs as he was pulled under the water. His thoughts were a medley of fear and anger. Images of Caillte and Racaire and Capaillín and the child flashed before his eyes. His head was almost entirely under the water now and he could see the top half of the serpent. Its mouth gaped open as it moved towards Aengus.

'It's going to swallow me, headfirst,' thought Aengus, as he glanced for the last time towards the shore. Capaillín was running about like a mad thing, shouting, 'Hedgehog, Aengus, hedgehog.'

'What on earth is she telling me about a hedgehog?' he wondered in amazement and, just as the serpent's mouth closed over his head, Aengus was transformed into a prickly, spiny, hedgehog.

The serpent thrashed about in the water, trying to dislodge the hedgehog, but Aengus used his quills to pierce the serpent's skin, stitching his gullet together until he was suffocating.

Capaillín watched the struggle from the shore and Girseach looked on from the rock. They saw the thrashing, then the calm and finally, the body of the serpent floated to the surface.

'It's dead,' shouted Girseach.

'And so is Aengus,' cried Capaillín, her voice breaking.

'No, I'm not,' the victorious hedgehog emerged from the mouth of the serpent and rapidly assumed the shape of Aengus. He swam to the rock and brought Girseach to the shore, where Capaillín was waiting for them.

'I'm free!' Girseach cried, hopping and skipping about with joy. She threw her arms around Aengus's neck and then hugged Capaillín. 'Thank you. Thank you.'

Capaillín nuzzled the little girl. 'It's been a long, exciting day,' she told both of them. 'I think we should all get some rest. Who knows what tomorrow has in store for us?'

Aengus used grass to make a bed for Girseach, but she was lonely and cuddled up next to Capaillín.

'Will you be my mother and father?' she asked sleepily.

'For the moment,' Capaillín agreed, 'but we'll try to find you a real mother and father.'

Aengus sighed. Another hopeless task! He could see himself wandering the earth looking for Racaire's brother and Girseach's parents until he was white-haired and stooped, too old to have any desire left for Caillte! Still, she was such a little girl that they could not leave her on her own. And besides, she wouldn't give any trouble. Little girls didn't.

'I can't sleep,' came a tired little voice. 'Tell me a story, please, Aengus.'

Aengus thought for a moment. Should he tell her how Maedhbh led an army against Uladh in order to capture the biggest, strongest, bravest bull that had ever lived? Perhaps not. It was very warlike and far too long. Should he tell her about Gráinne and her lover? Maybe not. It was a bit too grown up for a child. Should he tell her about how Cúchulainn fought the sea? Not a good idea. It might remind her of the serpent and frighten her. Should he ...

Girseach interrupted him impatiently, 'Well, are you going to tell me a story, or not?'

'I can't think of a story, Girseach,' he admitted.

'Will *you* tell me a story, then, Capaillín?' the child asked.

'I'll tell you one tomorrow, Girseach. We're all tired. Try to sleep.'

'Just one little story, Capaillín, please. One story and then I'll go to sleep.'

'All right, Girseach, just the one. Now listen carefully.

There was once a little girl who was so clever that everyone called her Percipience.

'What does percipience mean, Capaillín?'

'Don't interrupt, Girseach, or I won't tell you a story at all.'

'It means that she could observe things and sense things that no one else even noticed,' Aengus told her. 'Now don't interrupt any more, Girseach, or Capaillín won't finish the story.'

'Sorry, Capaillín,' said the child contritely.

Capaillín started again.

There was once a little girl who was so clever that everyone called her Percipience. She lived with her family in a small village in a country far, far away. Percipience was a very friendly child, always willing to help, always very obedient and always eager to learn. Every time she saw people doing something different she asked them what they were doing and why. And she listened attentively to their answers, so that, by the time she was nine years old, she knew more than her parents and more than all the wise people of the village. In fact, the villagers believed that she knew more than anyone else in the whole world.

One day, a visitor arrived in the village and told them how the king of the country had become old and unpredictable. He had built himself a palace with thirteen rooms. He moved into the first room when the moon was full and stayed in it until the next full moon. Then he moved into the second room, and so on until he had spent an entire year sleeping in the thirteen different rooms. But after the year was up, he grew bored with his palace and ordered it to be demolished.

Soon after the palace was knocked down, he decided to build a golden throne, the biggest throne in the world. He sent around the world for the best goldsmiths and craftsmen and they designed a throne that rivalled the sun in splendour. It had a special feature that was not to be found on any other throne: two large golden wheels, so that it could be moved easily and so that the king was always able to sit on his own throne, even when he went visiting.

Over the years, he had married all the beautiful princesses in the land, but he grew weary of them too and of the constant rows about who was the most beautiful princess of them all.

He bought horses that could run as if they had wings on their feet and dogs that could track down the wiliest prey, but always, after a short time, he became fed up with his new possessions. Finally, he issued a decree to the whole world saying that he was bored and that if anyone could tell him a story that would last for a whole year, that person could have half of his kingdom.

When Percipience heard of the decree, she begged her parents to let her go to the king's palace and tell him a story.

'Please, Mother, please Father,' she pleaded, 'let me go to the palace and tell the king a story. I'm sure I could tell him a lovely story which would make him very happy.'

Her parents did not know what to do. They were aware that Percipience was the cleverest child in the village, and maybe even in the whole world, and they would have been very happy to take half of the king's riches, because they were very poor. But they were worried. After all, she was very young and the palace was very big and the king was very unpredictable.

Eventually, however, they agreed to let Percipience go. They gave her the little money they had and as much food as they could spare. Then, sadly, they waved goodbye as Percipience headed off towards the palace.

When she arrived at the gates and demanded to see the king, the palace guards laughed at her. 'What! A little girl of nine who wants to tell the king a story! Go away and stop bothering us.'

One old guard took her aside and said, 'Be very careful, Percipience. Many grown men and women have come to the palace to tell the king a story. Some of the stories have lasted for one hour. Some have lasted for two. One man even told a story that lasted from dawn until dusk, but by dusk the story was finished and the king was very angry. Do you know what the king does with people who tell him stories which are too short?'

'No,' answered Percipience.

'He throws them into his dungeons and, sometimes, he even throws away the key.'

Percipience thought for a while and thanked the old guard for his kindness, but added, 'I still want to tell him a story. I think I can tell him a story that will last for a whole year. Please let me in.'

So the old guard went and told the king about Percipience.

'You stupid oaf,' yelled the king. 'Do you think I want to listen to the prattling of children? Get out and bring in the next storyteller.'

'But there are no storytellers left, sire,' answered the old guard. 'There's only this child, and you have refused to listen to her.'

A day passed and another and still no other storytellers arrived. At last, the king shouted for the old guard.

'Bring that old fool to me,' he instructed.

When the guard arrived in the throne room, the king asked him if Percipience was still outside.

'She is, sire.'

'Does she know that I will punish her if she fails to tell me a story that will last a year?'

'She knows, sire.'

'Bring her in, then, and stay with her. When she has failed I will throw you both in the dungeon.'

The old guard went outside and found Percipience sitting quietly in the shade, thinking. He explained that the king would give her a chance and added, 'I hope your story is a long one, Percipience. If it isn't, I will join you in the dungeons.'

'Don't worry, old friend,' encouraged Percipience. 'I won't fail.'

The little girl followed the old guard into the throne room. She noticed how the guard bowed and she bowed in the same way. The king looked at the child and she was so small and so frail that, for a moment, he felt sorry for her.

'Go away, little girl,' he told her. 'I don't want to hear your story.'

'Why? Are you afraid?' asked Percipience.

'What?' yelled an irate king.

'Are you afraid that my story will last a year and that you will have to give me half of your kingdom?'

The king was very angry. No one had ever accused him of being afraid before.

'All right, little girl,' he hissed between clenched teeth. 'Tell me your story and when you fail, I'll throw you and your family and this fool into my deepest, dankest dungeon and you will never be seen again.'

'But if I succeed?' asked the child.

'If you succeed, you will have not only half my kingdom. You will have it all.'

'Agreed,' said Percipience and settled down to tell her story.

'I hope you are very comfortable, sire,' she told the king, 'because this is a very long story.'

Once upon a time, there was a very rich king who lived in a very large country that was renowned for the high quality of its corn. The land bore corn in abundance. There was more than the people could eat and more than they could sell. The king did not know what to do with all this corn so he sent for his counsellors and asked for their advice.

'Build barns for the corn,' they recommended, 'because there may one day be a famine in the country and we will be able to feed ourselves from the stores.'

'That's a good idea,' agreed the king, and he ordered barns to be built to hold the surplus grain. They built seven barns, each as high as a mountain and as long as a man could pace out in the course of one morning. In fact, they were the biggest barns that had ever been built in the entire history of the world. And each barn was full of grain, so full that the barn needed especially strong walls and doors.

Now, there was a little mouse in this kingdom and she had heard about the possible famine and she was worried that she would not have anything to eat when the hungry time came.

'What will I do?' she wondered, and then she said, 'I know. I'll steal all the king's corn and then, when the famine comes, I'll have plenty to eat.'

So the little mouse found some large caves under the kingdom. They were enormously large caves, big enough to hold all the king's corn. The mouse was very happy and bored a tiny hole into the king's first barn. She picked up one grain of corn in her mouth, carried it to her cave, left it there and went back to the king's barn. She took a second grain of corn in her mouth, carried it back to her cave, placed it beside the first and went back to the king's barn. She took a third grain of corn in her mouth, carried it to her cave, placed it beside the others and went back to the king's barn. She took another grain of corn in her mouth, carried it to her cave, placed it beside the others and went back to the king's barn. She took another grain of corn in her mouth, carried it to her cave, placed it beside the others and went back to the king's barn.

'All right, all right,' interrupted the king, 'when the mouse had taken all the corn away, what happened?'

'Why are you rushing me, sire?' asked Percipience. 'There were seven large barns and she was a very small mouse and she has only taken five grains of corn away.'

So she took a sixth grain of corn in her mouth, carried it to her cave, placed it beside the others and went back to the king's barn. She took another grain of corn in her mouth, carried it to her cave, placed it beside the others and went back to the king's barn. She took another grain of corn in her mouth, carried it to her cave, placed it beside the others and went back to the king's barn ...

Hour after hour, Percipience continued her story: She took another grain of corn in her mouth, carried it to her cave, placed it beside the others and went back to the king's barn ...

Night came, and the king said, 'Stop, I must sleep. I'm exhausted listening to that mouse going to the barn and taking one grain of corn away in her mouth.'

Next morning, the king sent for Percipience.

'All right, Percipience,' he told her. 'I want to hear what happened when the mouse had cleared the barns.'

'Don't be in such a hurry, sire,' answered the little girl. 'Those barns are still full of corn. No one has even noticed that the mouse has taken any corn away. Now, let me continue.'

So the mouse took another grain of corn in her mouth, carried it to her cave, placed it beside the others and went back to the king's barn. She took another grain of corn in her mouth, carried it to her cave, placed it beside the others and went back to the king's barn ...

Day after day, night after night, week after week, month after month, still Percipience went on: The little mouse took another grain of corn in her mouth, carried it to her cave, placed it beside the others and went back to the king's barn.

The king was furious, but no matter how much he yelled, Percipience just sat there, going on with her story, grain by grain.

The little mouse took another grain of corn in her mouth, carried it to her cave, placed it beside the others and went back to the king's barn ...

Finally, the king could not bear to hear one more word from Percipience. He ran screaming from his palace, glad to get away from the interminable story. Percipience was given the kingdom and she, her mother and father and the old guard lived very happily for the rest of their lives.

'That was a great story,' commended Girseach, clapping her hands in appreciation. 'Tell me another.'

'Goodnight, Girseach,' Capaillín and Aengus spoke as one, and Girseach answered, 'Goodnight.'

30: The Winding Road

Aengus woke with a start, not sure whether it was night or morning. He had slept well and was refreshed, but he could see nothing, not even his own hands or feet. A dense fog surrounded him, thicker than he had ever encountered before.

'Capaillín,' he whispered, hoping not to wake Girseach, but there was no reply.

'Capaillín! Girseach!' he called, this time at the top of his voice, but still there was no answer.

Aengus moved slowly on his hands and knees, stretching out his hands to check every piece of ground ahead of him. Finally he found a pathway, and having crawled along it for a short while, he was able to stand up. He called and called for Capaillín and Girseach, but there was neither sight nor sound of his two companions.

Why did they go without me?, he asked himself a thousand times. Why didn't they wait for me? 'Capaillín! Girseach!'

But, no matter how much he shouted, he was answered only by silence. On he went, following the path, still calling, still hoping. Suddenly he heard voices ahead of him. They were men's voices, strangers, but maybe they had seen his friends? He followed the voices and came to a clearing where a group of men stood, squabbling.

They were very small men, shorter even than Luch, and they were dressed in very bright colours.

'Have you seen Capaillín and Girseach?' Aengus asked them.

'Who are you?' asked the little man in red.

'I'm Aengus and I'm looking for my friends.'

'We don't know anything about your friends,' answered the one in yellow, 'but we might have a job for you.'

'I have no time to do a job for you,' answered Aengus, 'I'd like to help, but I'm in a hurry today. I have to find my friends. I have to find the castle where Gadaire lives and take him back to the lady in the lake. I have to give Racaire back to Bronagh; I have to find the garden where the silver apples grow and I have to find Caillte.'

'Oh dear,' laughed the man in red, who seemed to be the leader. 'That's too much for one person! Far too much! You can't be expected to do all that. We'll give you a much easier job. We want you to bury this man who has just died.'

'I wish I could help you,' Aengus assured him. 'Honestly, I'd be glad to help, but I am just too busy at the moment.'

'Did you hear that?' asked the little man in red. 'Did you hear what Aengus said? He said he wouldn't help us even though we were asking him for very little. How long would it take him to dig a grave? No time at all, he's so big. Well, if he won't help us willingly, we'll have to force him to help.'

Aengus tried to escape, but found that his legs wouldn't move. Instead of running, he fell flat on his face and all the little men crowded round, laughing.

'So you were going to run away without helping us? Not very nice, Aengus. Now, we will *make* you do what you wouldn't do willingly.'

Aengus squirmed and twisted, but the little men held him down and placed the corpse on his back.

'Listen carefully,' instructed the little man in red. 'You must take this body to the castle and you must bury him inside its walls. But, if you cannot bury him in the castle, you must take him to the hawthorn circle where the druids perform their ceremonies. If you cannot bury him there either, you must take him to the lake and call out for help. One of these places is where he is meant to be buried, but we do not know which one. And, this is most important – you must succeed in laying him to rest before the fog lifts completely or you will never see your friends again.'

The little men trooped off and Aengus was left with the corpse on his back. He tried to remove it, but the man's hands were around his throat, and his knees were clasped tightly against Aengus's thighs. Aengus tried rolling over. He tried throwing his legs in the air. But nothing that he did would dislodge the body from his back. Finally he stood up. He knew he had no choice but to try to carry out the task.

'The castle must be straight ahead,' thought Aengus, 'there was none in the countryside I left behind.'

He set off, moving as quickly as he could, with the dead weight on his back, and soon he thought the air seemed a little clearer. The fog was lifting so his time was getting short. Just then, he spotted the walls of a castle a short distance ahead.

A gate in the outer wall was open and Aengus walked in, hoping that he would find someone to help him. 'Capaillín! Girseach! Anybody!' Nobody answered. 'I'll have to do it myself,' he said, and searched by the walls until he found a large pick and spade. They were close to some flagstones and Aengus thought that it would be a good idea to bury the man under the flagstones. He used the pick to lever the first flagstone upwards and congratulated himself on his foresight when he found that the ground underneath was soft and easy to dig. He had almost dug down to the right level when he struck something harder than clay but softer than rock. It was another man's body.

'What do you think you're doing?' yelled the body in the grave. 'Can a man not find peace anywhere, these days? Cover me up immediately and go away.'

'I'm sorry,' apologised Aengus. 'I certainly didn't mean to disturb you, but, you see, I have to bury this body and I thought this would be a good spot.'

'It *is* a good spot,' came the indignant answer. 'It's *my* spot. Now cover me up and leave me alone.'

'Would you mind if I put another body in?' asked Aengus, hesitantly.

'Mind? Mind? You want to put someone else in my grave! Is there no respect left in the world? Once I had castles and so much land that I could barely ride from one side of it to the other in the course of a day. Now, all I have left is this little space and you want me to share it with a stranger! Leave me in peace, I tell you.'

Aengus was about to move on to look for the hawthorn grove, when the voice from the grave halted him.

'Are you planning to go without filling me in again?'

'Sorry,' said Aengus. 'I just forgot,' and he quickly put all the clay back into the hole. He was leaving when a muffled voice exclaimed:

'Don't forget the flagstone!'

Aengus fitted it on as neatly as he could with such a heavy weight on his back, put the pick and spade against the castle wall and left by the same gate as he had entered.

'I wonder where the hawthorn grove is.'

'Up the hill in front of you,' answered a voice close to his ear.

Aengus rarely perspired, but the unexpected answer caused the sweat to pour down his face and back.

'Can you really speak?' Aengus asked the man on his back.

'Sometimes,' came the answer, 'but you'd better hurry, Aengus. The fog is rising quickly and I wouldn't like to be you if you disobey the little men. Look at me. I only crossed them over the matter of a dog!'

'What was the matter of the dog?' Aengus asked him as he ran up the hill towards the hawthorn grove, but there was no answer. 'Maybe the conversation has tired him,' thought Aengus, as he found himself entering a ring of hawthorn trees, planted high on the summit of a hill. A druid stood at the centre.

'What do you want?' he asked.

'I want to bury this man here in the hawthorn grove.'

'Is he a druid?'

'I don't know,' answered a dejected Aengus, 'but I was told to bring him here.'

The druid clapped his hands and from every section of the hawthorn grove rose druids – male and female, old and young, adults and children.

'What do you think?' the first druid asked the others. 'It might be different if he had been one of us. We might have been able to squeeze up a bit for him, but in the circumstances, I feel he should be taken away.'

All the druids started chanting 'Take him away,' and Aengus noticed that the fog had almost lifted and he still had not been able to bury his burden.

He raced down the hill as fast as he could and came to a

crossroads. The corpse's left hand pointed straight ahead and Aengus did not argue. The fog was patchy now and through it he could see the outline of the lake. He ran over, calling as he ran:

'Lady of the lake, help me. Help me.'

Against the clearing sky, he could see a boat drawing to the shore, rowed by a serpent wearing a lady's veil. The corpse loosened its grip and fell to the ground. Aengus picked him up and laid him gently in the bottom of the boat.

'You'll see that he gets a decent burial?' he asked the serpent.

She hissed in agreement and rowed the boat to the centre of the lake, disappearing just as the last vestiges of fog lifted.

Aengus found himself lying on the ground with Capaillín touching him gently with her nose. Girseach was there too, laughing at the top of her voice.

'You've been shouting in your sleep, Aengus,' she told him. 'I wanted to wake you, but Capaillín said it would be better to let you finish your dream. Was it a nightmare? Will you tell me about it?'

'Later, Girseach,' he told her, still shaken from the events of the dream – if it was a dream. He looked thoughtfully at the spreading ripples in the centre of the lake.

'It's been terribly foggy,' Capaillín told him. 'I was worried that we mightn't be able to travel today, but the fog seems to have lifted.'

31: Head Light

Aengus sat Girseach on Capaillín's back and set out as soon as he had washed.

'I'm hungry,' insisted Girseach. 'Haven't you got anything for me to eat?'

'What did you eat when you sat on the rock?' Aengus asked.

'I ate the food that was put out for me.'

'Who put it out?'

'I don't know. I never saw anyone putting it there, but I got food to eat every day. Do you think there is some food on the rock now?'

'There may be, Girseach,' Aengus agreed, 'but I'm not swimming out for it. We'll find some food soon, I promise you.'

'I wish I was like Capaillín,' huffed Girseach. 'She's not hungry. She has grass to eat.'

'Well, I don't mind sharing the grass with you,' Capaillín assured her with a smile, and for a while Girseach was quiet.

They had not been walking for very long when they found themselves in a valley that had a wide stream running through it. A man sat beside the water. He looked somehow familiar and yet

Aengus couldn't recall that they had ever met. He had been fishing, and was now grilling the fish he had caught over a small fire.

'Welcome, friends,' he called out when he saw them. 'Come and eat with me.'

Aengus hesitated for a moment. The voice was even more familiar than the man's appearance, but he still could not be sure that they had ever met. Part of Aengus felt that he should be cautious, but Capaillín did not seem to distrust him, and the smell of freshly-cooked fish was more than either he or Girseach could resist. She was already jumping off Capaillín's back to run over and get her share.

Aengus and Girseach ate until they were well satisfied. The fisherman did not eat, but continued to grill fish until neither of them could eat any more.

'If you've finished,' Capaillín told Aengus and Girseach, 'we should be on our way again.'

Aengus helped Girseach up onto Capaillín's back and, as they moved off, he turned to thank the fisherman.

'You must let me give you something for the fish, my friend,' Aengus said.

'I'm only repaying a debt,' the fisherman smiled. 'It's the least I can do, considering the trouble you went to for me last night.' And, before Aengus could utter a gasp of disbelief, the fisherman was gone, and there was nothing there but the grass and the stream.

Aengus stood still for a moment, to try to get his thoughts together. Had his nightmare really happened? The encounter with the fisherman – whom he now recognised as the corpse – seemed to confirm it. Aengus would have liked to tell the story to Capaillín to see what she made of it, but he was afraid that the episode would frighten Girseach, so he said nothing.

'Can I walk?' Girseach asked.

'We can travel more quickly if you're on my back,' Capaillín told her, but Girseach twisted and turned so much that Capaillín agreed to let her walk, on condition that she took Aengus's hand.

'Tell me a story, Aengus,' Girseach asked as soon as she got down from the pony. 'You promised that you'd tell me a story today.'

'I did no such thing,' Aengus told her. 'It was Capaillín who promised to tell you another story. Didn't you, Capaillín?'

'I don't remember,' answered a contented Capaillín, 'but she seems to want you to tell her a story, and I don't want to interfere.'

'I'm sure you don't,' said Aengus, sarcastically. 'Girseach, why don't you look at this lovely scenery? It's much more beautiful than a story.'

'I'm tired looking at scenery,' answered Girseach testily. 'I had nothing to do but look at scenery the whole time I was on the rock. I had nobody to talk to and nobody to tell me stories.'

'All right,' agreed Aengus. 'Just a short story.'

'Not a *very* short one,' Girseach pleaded. 'Tell me one that lasts until we go to sleep tonight.'

'I don't know any story as long as that, unless you want me tell the story that Percipience told the king. Now, do you want to hear a short story or do you not want to hear one at all?'

'All right,' replied the little girl, 'but not too short.'

Once upon a time, there was a powerful king who was married to a beautiful queen. The king was so strong that no one dared to attack him, so everyone in the kingdom lived in peace. And the queen was so kind and generous, sharing all that she had with her subjects, that everyone in the kingdom lived in comfort and happiness.

Well, this king and queen had one son. He was as strong as his father and as kind as his mother. The people hoped that the king and queen would live to a ripe old age, but they knew that when they died, Macanrí would be a great and gentle ruler.

Girseach interrupted the tale. 'Was the son called Macanrí?'

'I've just told you that he was,' Aengus answered.

'No, you didn't,' the little girl replied, indignantly. 'You just started calling him Macanrí and I wasn't sure.'

'Girseach, if you interrupt me again, I won't tell you a story at all.'

'You have to tell it right, Aengus,' insisted Girseach. 'You have to do it right, doesn't he, Capaillín?'

'I'm not interfering,' answered Capaillín, laughing. 'I'm walking along here quietly. I'm totally content and that's the way I mean to stay.'

'Tell me about Macanrí, please, Aengus,' pleaded Girseach, 'but tell me the story right. If you don't explain things, I'll have to ask, and if I ask you questions, you get cross.'

'I'm not cross,' answered Aengus crossly. 'Now listen carefully – and don't interrupt!'

Macanrí was the name of the prince, and he was not only brave and kind, he was also the handsomest man in the kingdom. Everybody loved him and there wasn't a girl in the entire land who wouldn't have been glad to be his wife. But, although Macanrí liked a lot of the girls he knew, he didn't love any of them. So he waited and waited, knowing that, one day, he would meet someone he wanted to marry and share his kingdom.

One day, when Macanrí was in the court, a servant came in to tell the king and queen that there was a beautiful stranger at the door, asking to see them. The king and queen told the servant to invite her in immediately, and Macanrí and the courtiers waited to see what this beautiful stranger was like.

The servant led her in, and when she removed the scarf from her head, everyone gasped. Some people even turned their eyes away, so stunned were they by her beauty. She was fairer than the dawn and more promising than spring.

'My name is Aisling,' she told the king and queen, 'and I have travelled far to see your son, Macanrí. I have heard wonderful stories about him. If they are true, then I would like to marry him.'

Macanrí looked at Aisling and he knew that he would never be able to marry anyone else.

'I'm Macanrí,' he said, and she looked at him for a long time.

'Everything I have heard about you is true, Macanrí,' she told him. 'Come with me to my homeland in Aishee. In my land, Macanrí, no one ever grows old or suffers pain. We live in peace and comfort. Think of your happiest day, and that is a pale reflection of even the poorest day in Aishee. Come with me, Macanrí. My horse is waiting outside. It will take us both to Aishee.'

Macanrí was greatly troubled. On the one hand, he desperately wanted Aisling for his wife, but he knew that his parents would be devastated if he abandoned them. They loved him too and were counting on him to rule the kingdom when they were gone.

'Come, Macanrí, please,' pleaded the lady, as she walked towards the door. 'I will give you everything I have promised and more. I will live with you and love you always.'

Aisling walked to the door and climbed on to the back of her beautiful horse. Macanrí could not bear to see her go. He walked slowly after her.

'Don't go, son,' called the queen, tears streaming down her face.

But Macanrí mounted the horse's back behind Aisling, and put his arms round her waist. For a moment, a bright light shone round the three figures. When the light disappeared, there was no trace of Aisling or Macanrí or the horse. The people of the land gazed sadly at the place where the horse had stood, but they never saw Macanrí again from that day to this.

Aengus stopped at this point because he realised that the story of Aisling and Macanrí was a bit too grown up for a little girl.

Girseach waited expectantly, then asked, 'Is that the whole story?'

'It is,' answered Aengus.

'But there was no proper ending to it. It wasn't as good as Capaillín's. Hers was a real story.'

Girseach was thinking of ways to cajole Capaillín into telling her a story, when they came to a meadow in a low valley, where something even more interesting than a story was unfolding.

The meadow was divided in two by a low wall that ran the length of the valley. The wall was made of some sort of metal, possibly brass, because it shone with a dull glow in the sunshine and it made a metallic clang when anything touched it. There were two large flocks of sheep in the meadow. All of the sheep on the left-hand side of the wall were white, and on the right-hand side of the wall all of the sheep were black. A tall, green man was minding the sheep. He spent his time wandering from one side of the wall to the other, counting sheep. When he had counted the sheep on the right-hand side, he picked up one or two and threw them over the brass wall. As soon as the black sheep fell on the left-hand side of the wall, they turned white. Then, the green man would climb over the wall and count the white sheep, pick up one or two and throw them over the wall. As soon as the white sheep fell on the right-hand side, they turned black.

Aengus, Capaillín and Girseach watched the man counting his sheep and throwing white ones over into the black side and black ones over into the white side. They could make no sense of it.

'Can we walk round the valley instead of going through it?' Girseach asked.

'Why?' asked Aengus and Capaillín together.

'I'm afraid of turning green,' she cried, and they had no choice but to go round the valley, without finding out why the shepherd was counting his sheep and why he threw sheep from one side to the other of the brass wall.

They were still walking when the sun finally set and darkness began to stretch over the land.

'Look,' shouted Girseach. 'There are lights up there on top of the hill.'

Aengus peered into the darkness. 'It's a castle,' he said, 'but it can't be the one we're looking for. We've only been travelling for two days.'

'You're right,' agreed Capaillín. 'However, it would be good to spend the night under a roof, but maybe we'd better wait until morning before trying to reach the castle. It's so dark, we could stumble into a pit.'

'No, we won't,' Girseach boasted. 'Look, now we can see just as well as before.' She pulled the scarf from her head, shook out her hair and the three of them walked safely in its halo to the walls of the castle.

Even though it was late, there were bright lights burning throughout the building, and the doors were all open and attended.

'Come in, come in,' they were welcomed. 'Come in. You've had a long journey, and must be very tired. We'll get someone to look after you all.'

231

Girseach was led away by a nurse who promised her a warm bath, a good meal and as many stories as she could stay awake for. Then, a young ostler came to take Capaillín to the stables. Aengus wasn't happy about being separated from her, but Capaillín whispered that she would be all right. Then he, too, was shown to a room where there was food and a comfortable bed. He knew he should find out who owned the castle and why they were being entertained, but he was so tired.

'Tomorrow,' he thought. 'Tomorrow.' And soon, that's exactly what it was.

'Aengus, Aengus, wake up. You'll miss the wedding.'

Girseach roused Aengus from the deepest sleep he had had since he slept in the giant's bed. 'I've been up for hours and I've even been to see Capaillín in the stables. She's been up for hours, too! I'll stay here and talk to you, Aengus, while you have your breakfast.'

Aengus managed to get rid of Girseach until he was washed and dressed, but he had no sooner started to eat than Girseach reappeared.

'Oh Aengus,' she told him. 'We're invited to the wedding. That's why we got such a welcome last night: everybody thought that we were guests because the king and queen have invited the whole world to the wedding. They have only one daughter and she's getting married this morning. Do you want me to tell you about it?'

Aengus didn't have much choice in the matter, because Girseach was very keen to pass all that she had heard from the nurse, and, anyway he was curious to hear the whole story.

The princess who lived here was called Brodach and she was very, very beautiful. The king and queen didn't have any other children, and so they gave her all she asked for until she became very proud and vain. The king wanted her to get married, but she laughed at every prince who came to ask for her hand. She called the first one 'Fatty' and the second one 'Skinny' and the third one 'Dozy' and the fourth one 'Dopey' and the fifth one 'Shorty' and the sixth one 'Baldy' and the seventh one 'Whiskers'. The king was very cross with her, because she insulted every prince who came. And the princes had all made long journeys, because this castle is a two-day journey beyond the end of the world. Well, the king was furious and he decided that he would put up with Brodach's bad behaviour no longer.

'Brodach,' he told her, 'I've invited princes here from all over the world and you have insulted every single one of them. As a punishment, I'm going to give you in marriage to the first man who comes to the castle gate this morning.'

So they all waited and waited and then they could hear someone approaching the gate. He seemed very cheerful for he was whistling. The castle gate was opened and who should be standing there but a tinker! He was tall and young and seemed very happy, but his clothes were all torn and he carried all that he owned in a handkerchief tied to a stick.

'Any pots or pans for mending?' he called out.

Brodach laughed when she saw the tinker. She knew that her father loved her, and would not want her to live in poverty.

'You'll have to break your word, father,' she laughed.

The king looked at her sadly and sighed. 'I cannot break my word, Brodagh, not even for you. You must go with the tinker.'

Brodach cried and cried and pleaded and pleaded, but her father would not change his mind. At last, she told her lady-in-waiting to pack her clothes and possessions and to get her carriage ready.

'I cannot do what you ask, lady,' replied the lady-in-waiting. 'Your father left strict instructions that you are to leave the castle with only one dress and one pair of shoes. You will never ride in a carriage again, and you must learn to be happy walking the roads with the tinker.'

Off they went, Flann the tinker leading and Brodach following. He walked and walked and soon Brodach was limping because she had never walked so far before and her shoes were made for dancing, not walking. Flann looked back and took pity on her.

'All right, my dear,' he told her. 'We'll spend the night in this little hunting hut. It is owned by a prince, but he won't mind us using it. I store my pots and pans in it, and I often sleep here the night before I go to market.'

Brodach went into the hut and it was small and damp. Flann took some scraps of food from his bundle and told her to prepare his supper. He also took an old shirt out, and asked her to darn it, while the food was cooking.

Brodach tried to light a fire, but she was soon covered with soot.

'I'll cook the food tonight,' Flann told her. 'Now watch how I light the fire and prepare things, because you must cook the meals from now on.'

Brodach watched and tried to learn, but she was crying so much that she could hardly see. Flann shared his food with her, but it was so rough and unappetising that she could not eat it.

'We can't waste it,' Flann told her, so he ate what she left, and lay down to sleep while Brodach tried to mend his shirt.

Brodach had never held a needle in her hand before, and she stuck it into her fingers more often than into the shirt. Soon the shirt was red from the drops of blood that had fallen on it and Brodach had to go out to the river to wash it.

Next morning, Flann gave her some pots and pans to sell at the market. She cried and told him she didn't know how to do such things, but he insisted that she was a tinker now, and must earn her keep. So Brodach took the pots and pans to the market and people laughed at her when she tried to sell them.

'How much do you want for this pot?' a woman asked, but Brodach did not know what to charge so she gave the pot away for too little. Then a huntsman galloped through the market, scattering people and animals and property. He rode through the pots and pans, spoiling them. When Flann came to see how Brodach was getting on, he found her sitting among the ruined pots and pans, with only a few coins to show for all his work.

'You'll never earn any money for us this way,' he told her. 'I'll get you a job in the prince's kitchen. There must be something that you can do there.'

So Brodach was taken to the kitchen and told what to do. She brushed floors and scrubbed them, and carried water and wood. Sometimes, she was allowed to take the scraps of food back to Flann in the hut, and he was always very grateful for the food that she brought.

One evening, before she went home, the cook told Brodach that she could take the scraps, and she stuffed them in her pocket.

'The prince is getting engaged tonight,' the cook told her. 'We're going to take a look at the room where the party is being held. Do you want to come?'

Brodach went with them. The room was decorated with lights and flowers. There was music and dancing and the ladies were dressed in beautiful clothes. At one end of the room stood the prince that she had called 'Whiskers' when he came to ask for her hand. He looked so handsome and kind that she started to cry. The prince heard the crying and saw the servants peeping in through a half-open doorway.

'Come,' he said to Brodach. 'You must pay for your peeping by dancing with me.'

Brodach tried to get away, but he caught her hand and led her to the dance floor. The musicians played a lively tune and the prince swung her around so fast that all the scraps of leftover food fell out of her pockets and on to the floor. Everyone laughed and laughed, and Brodach ran back to the hut in shame.

Flann wasn't there, so she started to prepare his supper. While she was cooking, there was a knock at the door. When she opened it, the prince was standing there. Behind him stood her mother and father. Brodach ran to the corner to hide, but the prince followed her.

'Don't you know me, Brodach?' he asked. And bending down, he took soot from around the fireplace and smeared it on his face.

Brodach could not believe her eyes. 'Flann?' she whispered.

'Yes, I'm the prince,' he told her, 'and I'd still like to marry you. Will you have me now?'

This time, Brodach was only too glad to agree to marry 'Whiskers'.

'And they're getting married here, this morning, Aengus,' Girseach announced. 'Everybody has been invited. Us too. Isn't it wonderful?'

'It is wonderful, Girseach,' he agreed, hoping that soon he and Caillte would be in the same position. 'But we may not have the time. We still have a full day's journey ahead of us.'

'I told Brodach that,' Girseach crowed, 'and she's lending us her carriage. We'll be able to stay for the wedding and ride in style to Gadaire's palace.'

'You seem to have organised everything,' he commended her, as they went down to the feast.

Soon, much too soon for Girseach, it was time for them to go. The carriage was prepared, so that Aengus and Girseach could cover the last day's journey in style.

'I'm sorry you have to walk,' Aengus told Capaillín, as she trotted beside the carriage.

'I'm glad of the exercise, after all that good food,' she assured him, 'and it's so peaceful not to have to tell stories all the time!'

32: How Do You Know My Name?

As the sun began to set, Aengus, Capaillín and Girseach found themselves travelling on a road that grew wider and wider.

'We must be approaching somewhere important,' Capaillín commented. 'This must be where Gadaire lives.'

'Who's Gadaire?' Girseach enquired.

'That's a long story,' Aengus told her.

'Oh *good*!' answered the child, but Aengus did not have time even to begin the tale. There was a sharp bend in the road, and as they rounded it, their eyes fell on the most beautiful palace any of them had ever seen. It was built of pale yellow stone and stood on a hill that rose high above the plain. The wide road snaked gradually up the hill, making the journey to the palace easy. A square stone wall surrounded the palace, with a tower at each corner.

'Oh, can I sleep in one of the towers?' Girseach asked. 'Can I, can I?'

'We'll sleep where we're put,' Aengus told her, but he also found the round towers attractive, so he told her he would ask if she could.

The guards recognised the carriage and so Aengus, Girseach and Capaillín were allowed through the gate and were soon standing at the steps that led to the gateway. A young prince bounded down the steps to meet them. He was so exactly like Racaire that there could be no doubt about his identity.

'Welcome,' he called. 'It's good to see you.'

'Thank you, Gadaire,' answered Aengus.

'How do you know my name?' asked the young man. 'Oh, I suppose Brodach told you. I didn't go to her wedding today because she once refused to marry me. I'm glad she and Flann are happy, but I was hurt when she called me "Stupid".'

'So you're not married then?' Aengus asked.

'No,' answered Gadaire, 'although I'd like to be. But where are my manners? It's late. Why don't we see to the child and your pony and then you can tell me why you've come.'

'I don't want to be seen to,' huffed Girseach. 'I want to hear all about it. And I'm sure Capaillín doesn't want to be seen to, either. Do you, Capaillín?'

For once, Girseach and Capaillín were in total agreement. 'I can see to myself,' the pony answered, 'but I do think it is time you were in bed, Girseach.'

If Gadaire had looked surprised to hear a question addressed to the pony, he looked astonished when she actually answered. He exchanged an amazed glance with Aengus, but made no comment.

'I'll tell you what,' smiled Gadaire. 'Why don't you all have an early night? My parents went to Brodach's wedding, but they will be here tomorrow and then you can tell us all why you've come.'

'Can I sleep in one of the towers?' Girseach asked.

'That's where the guards on watch duty sleep,' Gadaire replied, 'it wouldn't be suitable for you. But there's a lovely little turret room. You could sleep there, if you like. I'll take you to it.'

Girseach turned to Aengus to bid him goodnight. 'Now,' she said firmly, 'you have to promise you won't start telling the story of why we've come until I'm there.'

'I promise, Girseach.'

And, with a happy smile, Girseach went off, hand in hand with Gadaire.

'I'll get you fixed up, Capaillín,' Aengus suggested, 'and then I'll have a good night's sleep. We're so lucky that Gadaire isn't married! Do you think it will be easy to persuade him to come with us?'

'I don't think that will be too hard,' answered Capaillín. 'He looks like a young man who would enjoy an adventure. But will his parents be willing to let him go? That's going to be the difficulty.'

When Aengus had taken Capaillín to the stables and brushed her down, he returned to the front steps where he found Gadaire waiting for him. They talked for a while about horses and travelling. Then Gadaire said:

'I'm dying to know all about you, Aengus, and why you've come here, but I've also given my solemn promise to Girseach that I won't ask any questions before tomorrow, so perhaps I should get you something to eat and then show you to your room.'

Aengus sighed contentedly as he lay on the soft, wide bed. 'I'm getting spoiled,' he told himself. 'This is the second night in a row that I've slept in a bed. I could get used to such comfort.'

Aengus had already bathed and eaten when Gadaire came to his room.

'My parents arrived late last night,' he told Aengus. 'They are eager to meet you and Girseach. I haven't told them about Capaillín,' Gadaire continued, 'because I'm not sure that they'd really understand!'

'Yes. I saw your surprise, and I can tell you that I was equally surprised when I first heard Capaillín speak. In fact, I'm still not sure I understand it, but I have come to accept it,' Aengus reassured him. 'And I would like Capaillín to be able listen at the window when I talk to you and your parents.'

'That should be no trouble at all,' answered Gadaire. 'Perhaps you would go and find her while I bring my parents to the throne room to meet you.'

Aengus didn't get as far as the stables. He met Capaillín walking about with Girseach.

'I've just been telling Capaillín about my room, Aengus. I wish she could see it, but it's up a high, high flight of winding stairs. I'll show it to you, later. Gadaire says I can sleep in it as long as I like, because nobody else uses it.'

Aengus explained to Capaillín that he would be talking to Gadaire's parents alone. 'But you can listen at the window,' he assured her, 'and you can tell me if I leave anything out.'

'Good luck, Aengus. I'll be listening and waiting and resting. Don't forget, we have another long journey ahead of us.'

Aengus and Girseach made their way up the steps, where they were met by Gadaire, and taken to the throne room. Gadaire looked out of the window, saw that Capaillín was at hand, and then introduced Aengus to his parents.

The king and queen were tall and blond and Aengus thought that, somehow, they both looked familiar. 'Who do they remind me of?' he kept asking himself, but the knowledge was like a word on the tip of his tongue, so close and yet so utterly unattainable.

'Our son says you wish to see us,' began the king. 'Perhaps you could tell us the purpose of your visit.'

Aengus looked at the king and queen and then at Gadaire. 'There's no easy way to do this,' he thought, so he blurted it out:

'Your majesties, I've come to take Gadaire back to his real family and to the lady who is waiting to marry him.'

The king and queen were silent and Gadaire was so overcome that he almost fell down. It was the queen who finally broke the silence.

'I suppose we've always known that, one day, we would lose Gadaire,' she said in a quiet, sad voice. 'We never meant to do any harm. The king and I had been married for years, without children, when an old woman arrived and offered us Gadaire. She said he was her own. We didn't believe her, but we didn't ask too many questions. We wanted a child so badly, and here was a little boy, barely able to walk or talk. I loved him the moment I saw him, so the king gave the woman money and sent her off.

"I'll be back for my daughter," she called out, as she left us. We didn't know what she meant, and after a while, we didn't think about it. We were happy, Aengus. We were all happy. I used to think about his real mother and father, but I pushed the thoughts to the back of my mind. I had him, and I would not let him go. But I suffered for my cruelty. The king and I both suffered. Years after Gadaire came, we had a daughter of our own. She was like sunshine and we now thought our joy was complete, but she was taken from us. The old woman came back the night our daughter was born and took her away. Now you have come to take our son too.'

The queen's face was damp with tears and she leant on her husband for support.

Suddenly Aengus knew why he had found her so familiar.

'Girseach,' he called. 'Come here.'

Girseach came shyly from the side of the room where she had been listening. Aengus took her by the hand and stood her in front of the queen.

'Can you remember anything about your daughter?' he asked the queen.

'I remember her hair, Aengus,' the queen replied. 'It was like the golden rays of purest sunshine.'

Aengus gently removed the scarf from Girseach's hair.

'We may be taking your son,' he told the king and queen, 'but I think we are returning your daughter.'

The king and queen fell to their knees, embracing Girseach.

'I've got a mother and father at last, Aengus,' she told him. 'I've got a real mother and father. And I'll be able to stay in the turret room as long as I like.'

There was no thought of time or food in the palace that day. Stories were told and retold and by dusk, it was decided that Aengus and Gadaire would set out the next morning.

'We don't want to lose you, Gadaire,' the king and queen told their son.

'I'll always love you,' he told them, 'and I'll always think of you as my parents, but I must honour the word of my real father, and release my brother from his punishment.'

Before going to bed that night, Aengus sought out Capaillín.

'The past few days have been full of excitement, Capaillín, haven't they? We have achieved a great deal and now I'm sure we'll achieve the rest. We *will* find Caillte.'

Partings are never easy. Everyone stood near the steps of the palace the next morning, in tears or close to tears. The king and queen hugged Gadaire. Girseach hugged Aengus and Capaillín.

'I want to give you a present, Aengus,' Girseach told him, and she plucked three hairs from her head. 'They'll shine in the dark, Aengus,' she reminded him, 'so you'll never be frightened. Have you got a present for me?'

Aengus felt in his pockets, but he could think of nothing that he could give the little girl.

'I'll give you something,' Capaillín told her. 'It's a piece of advice from Aengus and me. Remember Brodach.'

For a moment, Girseach looked at Capaillín reproachfully. Then she smiled and hugged them both.

'There is nothing we can give you that will ever express our gratitude for the return of our daughter,' the king told Aengus, 'but I can, at least, make your journey back to Gadaire's home an easy one. My boat is ready. It will take you, Gadaire and Capaillín back in comfort and in safety.'

He led the way down to the inlet behind the castle. The boat was ready and its sail was already straining in the wind.

'May the Powers-that-be keep you safe on your journey,' prayed the queen, 'until we meet again.'

'Until we meet again,' they all answered, as the boat took them swiftly away from the shore and from the group of people who got smaller and smaller until they could not be seen.

33: Fulfilling a Promise

The voyage by boat was much quicker and easier than it had been by foot. The captain seemed to know every inlet and every current and he sang to his boat, as they travelled smoothly and safely.

> *Sweeper of waves, steed of the sea,*
> *Sail us with speed, bird of the deep.*
> *Haven in storm, port on the brine,*
> *Safeguard our lives, awake or asleep.*

Aengus and Capaillín spent much of their time talking to Gadaire and telling what they knew of his brother and about the lady of the lake.

'But what will happen if I don't like her?' Gadaire asked a thousand times.

'She's very beautiful, Gadaire,' Aengus assured him. 'Most men would think themselves fortunate to have such a wife.'

'Would you marry her, Aengus?' Gadaire asked.

'I'm like your brother,' Aengus told him. 'I had already met the only woman I can ever love before I saw the lady of the lake. But if

I hadn't met Caillte first, I would have tried to win the lady of the lake from you.'

Such comments, in part, reassured Gadaire, but he was eager to see the lady with his own eyes, and to greet the twin brother he never knew he had.

The winds and tides were kind, and soon the boat had landed.

'This is as far as I can take you,' the captain announced. 'The lake is inland from here. If you are good walkers, you should be there before noon.'

'Give my love to my parents,' Gadaire urged the captain, 'and to my little sister.'

'And ours too,' Aengus added. 'Tell Girseach that I'll bring my wife to see her one day.'

Aengus, Capaillín and Gadaire turned their backs to the sea and headed inland towards the lake and Gadaire's future. The journey took them a little longer than the captain had predicted, but not too long after noon they were approaching the lake.

'Let's find Racaire first,' Capaillín suggested. 'He's probably still sitting on the rock where we found him before.'

And Capaillín was right. As they approached the rock, they could hear the mournful croaking: 'Rac! Rac! Rac!'

'There he is,' Aengus told Gadaire. 'That's your brother, Racaire.'

'It's hard to think that I have a frog for a brother,' whispered Gadaire, but he tried to hide his feelings as he approached the rock.

'Racaire,' he called. 'Racaire, it's me, your brother. I've come to help you.'

Racaire leapt into the air, turning somersaults of joy.

'Gadaire, Gadaire. Is it really you? Of course it is. It's like looking in a mirror when we look at each other, isn't it?'

'It is,' lied Gadaire, for he was a kind young man, and didn't want to hurt his brother's feelings.

'I'll get the lady of the lake,' Racaire announced, jumping into the lake. Then he leapt back on the rock. 'Gadaire,' he said, 'I'd love to be a man again, living with Bronagh, but you have your own happiness to think of. Don't sacrifice yourself for us. If you feel that you cannot marry the lady, you must walk away. I'll understand.'

'Thank you, Racaire,' Gadaire replied, 'but I'd like to see the lady in question before making up my mind.'

Racaire once again leapt into the water, and when he re-surfaced, the lady of the lake followed. She looked at Gadaire and he stared at her, neither of them, for the moment, exchanging a word.

'I've waited for you all my life,' Gadaire told her. 'You're the woman I have dreamt of and longed for. Will you accept me as your husband?'

'And I have waited for you, Gadaire,' she agreed. 'I will take you with me to a land under the lake where time stands still and where we will never grow old. You will be able to visit your family once a year, and you will always be here if they need you. Come, Gadaire.'

Gadaire stepped into the lake and was quickly at her side.

'Before we go, Gadaire, I have some duties to perform. Racaire, you are free.'

Racaire sloughed his skin and, in the place of the frog, stood another Gadaire.

'Now it really is like looking in a mirror, Racaire,' Gadaire told him. 'I look forward to visiting you and my other family next year.'

The lady of the lake then turned to Aengus. 'It is hard to express the depth of my gratitude to you, Aengus', she said. 'You and Capaillín set out on a long and hazardous journey for the sole purpose of helping people you hardly knew. And your journey has been a success. I cannot, myself, give you directions to the garden where the silver apples grow, but I can direct you to Eaglach, who knows the location of every garden in the world. You must travel to the top of the mountain you see to the north. Eaglach will be there. If he refuses to help you, give him this ring.'

The lady handed Aengus a ring containing a magnificent green stone. 'Eaglach gave this to me once when I saved his life. He will recognise it and help you.'

Aengus tried to thank the lady, but she stopped him. 'I have another gift for you and Capaillín,' she told him. 'For the rest of your lives, you will have the power to walk in or under fresh water without fear of drowning.'

'My last gift is to you, Racaire. Bronagh is now released from her punishment and is waiting for you in the castle.'

She took Gadaire by the hand and, with one last wave, they disappeared beneath the surface of the lake. Racaire leapt high in the air with delight.

'I learnt to do that when I was a frog,' he said, triumphantly. Then they all headed back to Bronagh.

Perhaps it was because Racaire was not tired from journeying, or perhaps it was because he was able to stand upright and walk on two legs again, but he easily outstripped Aengus and Capaillín on their journey to the castle. By the time they arrived he was already standing at the entrance with his arm around a smiling Bronagh. The gates were wide open and welcoming, and the blades which had cut Capaillín when they followed the black pig were drawn back and harmless. There was music coming from the castle and the sound of laughter as busy people went about their work.

'Tonight, we are having a feast,' Bronagh told them. 'We have so much to celebrate, and we owe it all to you both. Capaillín, Aengus, you will be the guests of honour.'

Gently but firmly Capaillín declined the invitation. 'Thank you for the kind thought,' she told them. 'I'm not very interested in parties, but I'll be glad to have an extra supply of oats, if you have them, and a quiet night. One task is behind us, but we have another yet to complete and must be on our way again early in the morning.'

Aengus was happy to accept the invitation, even though he felt a little envious of the unadulterated joy that he could see on the faces of Bronagh and Racaire. Aengus danced with Bronagh and with Racaire's sisters, and listened with joy to the songs of the visiting poet. Yet, he felt apart from the merrymaking, and the feast was still in its infancy when he slipped away. He went to the stables to see that Capaillín had all she needed, and then returned to the room where he had first seen Bronagh.

'I hope that I don't have any strange visitors tonight,' he murmured, as he stretched himself out on the comfortable bed. And he didn't.

Mornings came a little more slowly now that the sun was already moving south, but Aengus found that Bronagh and Racaire were waiting for him when he got up.

'You can't have had much sleep,' he commented.

'There'll be more than enough time to sleep, Aengus,' Racaire assured him. 'Besides, I'm almost afraid to sleep in case I wake up and find that this happiness is only a dream!'

Aengus shook their hands and wished them many years of dreaming. Bronagh gave him a wicker basket.

'Before you go, Aengus, we'd like you to take this basket. We've filled it with food, and, no matter how much you eat, there will always be more food in it when you open it again.'

Aengus gratefully took the basket and went to collect Capaillín.

'Next time I call here, I'll have Caillte with me,' he assured them, and all of them hoped that this would be true.

34: Seeking the Garden

'We're on our own again, Capaillín,' Aengus commented as they walked towards the mountain. 'We've been with people for such a long time now that it is seems strangely quiet without them.'

'Perhaps it's as well that we are alone, Aengus. I have a feeling that our journey may be a hard one.'

It was certainly a steep one. Soon they were on the side of a mountain that rose almost vertically from the plain, and which was covered with cloud at the top. The path did not wind much, and the gradient became steeper the higher they climbed. Aengus though of Luch and wished he had studied his mountain walk a bit more closely. But tired and footsore though they were, they eventually reached the top.

Aengus straightened and realised how cramped his back muscles were. Then he forgot about backs and cramps and muscles. When he looked up, he could see a crisp blue sky, but when he looked down, he could see clouds below them.

'This is what it is like to fly, Capaillín. It's a long time since I have been so high that I could look down on clouds.'

'Don't exert yourself too much, Aengus,' advised Capaillín. 'The air is thin up here and everything we do takes more of an effort. Don't you find it harder to breathe?'

'I hadn't noticed it,' he told her, 'but I do feel a little light-headed, like a child that has rolled down a steep, grassy hill. Still, there's no time for these concerns. We'd better find Eaglach.'

They didn't have to search far, because Eaglach found them. First, Aengus heard the beating of wings, and then he looked up into the eyes of a magnificent eagle. Eaglach circled above them, coming closer and closer with each circuit. Aengus shouted, but his voice was carried away.

'Hold up the ring,' Capaillín advised.

Aengus did so and the eagle came to rest on a rock just above them.

'Who are you and why have you come uninvited to my home?'

'We've come because we need your help, Eaglach. The lady of the lake told us that you would know how to get to the garden where the silver apples grow. We have brought you this ring.'

'The lady of the lake once helped me,' Eaglach confirmed, 'and now she has given me the opportunity to return the kindness. I will tell you how to get to the garden, Aengus, if you still want instructions after I have explained the dangers that await you there. Many people have sought the silver apples. Some have even found them. But nobody has ever been able to find them and keep them. All have suffered terribly in the effort. In the end, if they were lucky to escape with their lives, they had still not won the prize. It is true that each silver apple that grows there will grant you one wish, but will you be alive to enjoy it? My advice is, go home, and forget about the apples. Will you take my advice?'

'I can't, Eaglach,' Aengus told him. 'I must find the apples because I must find Caillte.'

'Are you not afraid of what you may lose?'

'Whatever I lose will be worth it, if I can find Caillte.'

'Very well, Aengus,' sighed Eaglach. 'Since I cannot dissuade you, I'll help you. When you get to the bottom of my mountain, take the path to the west. Between a wood and a river, you will see a large metal door in the ground. Open the door and you will find steps leading to an underground room. In the middle of the floor, there is a large iron ball. Take it and throw it in front of you. It will lead you to the garden where the silver apples are, even now, ripening.'

Aengus gave the ring to Eaglach, thanked him for his kindness and, slowly, he and Capaillín began the difficult descent. When they reached the bottom, they were both exhausted. Aengus ate a little from Bronagh's basket. Capaillín nibbled some of the rich grass of the plain. But they were both asleep before they had even had time to discuss the proceedings of the day or to bid each other goodnight.

In spite of sleeping in the open air and in spite of the bright light, morning was well advanced before Aengus woke up.

'I had a wonderful sleep, Capaillín. I don't think I moved once.'

'Are you well rested now?'

'I am, Capaillín, and while we have our strength I think we should try to travel as far as we can. Remind me of Eaglach's instructions.'

'First he told us to take the path to the west. Here it is, Aengus. While we're on this path, we must be on the lookout for a wood and a river. Let's go.'

The walk along the path was pleasant and they were fanned by a cool, westerly breeze.

'Look Capaillín, there's a wood on our left.'

'I see it, Aengus, and a stream to our right.'

'It's not a very big stream, is it, Capaillín? Do you think that's the one Eaglach meant?'

'We'll soon find out. There should be a large metal door between them.'

Taking a centre line between the wood and the stream, the pair began to search the ground in front of them, but discovered no door.

'It must be the wrong place, Capaillín. Eaglach mentioned a river, and this one is little more than a stream. We'll have to go on.'

'We could have missed it, Aengus. Let's rest for a little and try again. Next time, take a stick with you and poke the ground ahead of you. That way, you might feel the door.'

As they were resting, Capaillín laughed quietly to herself. 'Speaking of poking the ground with a stick, did you ever hear the story of the queen and the hole of corn?'

'No.'

Apparently, a queen once went to an old woman to ask for advice. She knew the woman was one of the wisest in the land. The queen was known to be mean-spirited, so before she asked for help, she decided to find out what the old woman wanted in return.

'Oh, very little,' answered the wise old woman. 'I just want you to fill a hole with corn for me.'

'A hole?' asked the queen. 'What size of hole?'

'Oh, just a hole that I will bore with this stick of mine.'

It was just an ordinary stick and the ground was very hard, so the queen thought it would be a very easy request to fulfil.

'I agree,' said the queen, and asked for advice. She got excellent counsel from the old woman and was amused when she thought how little it would cost her.

'I'd like to make the hole in the presence of the court,' suggested the old woman.

'I don't see any need for that,' countered the queen, 'but, so that all may see that the queen does not break her word, I'll agree to your request.'

The queen sent for her courtiers and they all gathered outside the old woman's house. They were full of anticipation because the old woman was known for her cunning as well as her wisdom.

'Take your stick and make your hole,' instructed the queen, 'and I will fill the hole you make with corn.'

'Oh noble and generous queen,' laughed the old woman and climbed on to the roof of her house. With her stick, she made a hole in the roof, and so the queen had to fill her entire house with corn.

'I heard of an old woman like that,' Aengus reminisced. 'Who knows? Maybe it was the same old woman.'

The story begins much as yours did, except that it was a king who was involved. The old woman was asked by the king what payment she wanted for her advice.

'Wool,' she replied. 'Only wool.'

'How much wool?' enquired the king.

'Not much sire. I'm an old woman and my needs are small. I just want as much wool as will fill the cavity of my arm when I put my fingers on my waist.'

The king looked at the old woman. She had very short arms and a very thick waist, so he was sure that the cavity of her arm would hold very little. When he came to pay his debt, however, the old woman went and stood in her doorway with her fingers on her waist. They pushed the wool through the cavity of her arm until the entire house was full of wool. And, only then, was the cavity of her arm full.

Their stories exchanged, the pair set to their search again. Aengus used his stick to prod the ground but it was Capaillín's hoof that struck metal.

'You've hit something.'

'I have, and I think it's what we've been looking for.'

The door was covered with green moss and overgrown with weeds, and it took a lot of time and effort to uncover it. It was as wide as Aengus was tall, and one and a half times as high. It was quite rusty, as if it had not been opened for a long time. A large ring hung at its centre.

Aengus tried pulling the ring but nothing happened. He yanked and heaved with all his strength, but there wasn't the slightest movement from the door. He found a large branch and tried to lever it open, but he might as well have tried to open a treasure chest with a kiss.

'It's no good, Capaillín. I've almost broken my back and I haven't been able to make it budge.'

They were about to go looking for help when Aengus asked: 'Capaillín, where's the green jacket that the giant gave me?'

'It's with your other clothes in that bundle, I think.'

Aengus opened the bundle, put on the green jacket, thought of his giant friend and grasped the handle. The door opened as easily as a ripe peapod. As Eaglach had described, there were steps leading down to a large underground chamber.

'Stay here, Capaillín. I'll go down and look for the iron ball.'

'Be careful, Aengus,' she warned, but there was no need to worry.

Before Capaillín had got herself into a good position to see what was going on, Aengus was back up the steps, carrying the ball.

'Shall we throw it at once, Capaillín?' he asked.

'Yes, but close the door first. Who knows what else is in that room and how it may benefit other people in the future.'

Aengus gently lowered the door back into place. They covered it with moss and loose grass and then Aengus was ready to throw the ball.

'I think you should take off the green jacket, Aengus,' Capaillín advised. 'If you throw the ball while you are wearing it, we'll never be able to follow it.'

Aengus wrapped the green jacket up with his other clothes, then he threw the iron ball into the air and they watched intently as it fell, a short distance in front of them.

'That wasn't very far,' Aengus complained, but as he walked towards the ball it rolled ahead of them, leading them on.

And so they continued, the ball rolling just far enough away for them still to see it, then waiting until they were very close before rolling away again. On and on it led, leaving no time to rest or eat. It climbed hills. It ran through shallow streams and around woods, moving at a speed to suit the terrain until it arrived at a large lake, where it came to a stop.

Aengus sighed with relief. 'I thought it was going to go on forever,' he said. 'After the mountain climbing yesterday and today's long walk, I'm ready for a good meal and a long sleep.'

'I, too, will be glad of a rest,' Capaillín agreed. 'I dread to think where the ball will lead us tomorrow.'

35: Paying for Paradise

Aengus was woken by a rumbling noise. It was very early, the sun only beginning to streak the sky, but the ball was rolling backwards and forwards, obviously keen to be on the road again.

'It will wait,' Capaillín advised. 'You should have a very good breakfast first. It seems to me that this is a very big, very deep lake and we will need all our strength to get across.'

Aengus opened the wicker basket, blessing Bronagh in his mind for the gift of constant food. He ate and drank while Capaillín did the same. Just as soon as Aengus had closed the basket and fastened it to Capaillín's back, the iron ball rolled away and into the lake.

'I was afraid of that,' said Capaillín, 'but, fortunately, we have the lady's second gift. She promised us we'd be able to travel unhurt through fresh water. It is a freshwater lake?'

Aengus cupped his hands and tasted the water. It was indeed fresh water, clean and wholesome, though he didn't know what they would have done if the water had been salty. They plunged in and the water immediately rose over their heads.

Soon they were walking on the bed of the lake. The ball stayed close to Aengus's right foot. It never moved more than a pace in front of him so that he could stretch out his foot and feel it. Aengus tried to talk to Capaillín, but it was useless. All she could see were the bubbles and, although he knew she could read minds, he wasn't too certain how skilled she was at interpreting bursts of bubbles.

They followed the ball for a long while, until it stopped at the mouth of a large cave. Aengus and Capaillín went inside, glad to discover that there was air and not water in the cave, so that they could talk, even though they could scarcely see because it was very dark.

'I wish I could see clearly,' sighed a voice, making them both jump in surprise. The figure of an old man emerged out of the shadows. 'I've got all that I want down here, peace and quiet, friendship and companionship, food and drink, jewels and pearls, medicines and remedies. I've got everything except light. I don't suppose you can give me light, can you?'

'You're in luck,' answered Aengus, 'because we just might be able to help you. Where's my bundle of clothes, Capaillín?'

'On my back.'

'I can't see your back, Capaillín.'

'Stay where you are, Aengus. Talk to me, and I'll follow your voice.'

Aengus felt the shaggy coat of his friend rubbing against his arm. He fumbled inside the bundle, finally locating the pouch he was looking for. As he opened it, light flooded the cave.

'These hairs will give you all the light you could want,' he told the delighted caveman, holding up the strands that Girseach had given them. Since we do not intend to live underwater, we won't need them.'

'Tell me what you want in exchange,' offered the old man.

'We don't want anything,' Aengus assured him. 'We are going to the garden where the silver apples grow, but we have a guide to lead us there and food to eat, so we really don't need anything else.'

'There is one thing that you may need,' answered the old man, going to a recess in the cave and taking out a bottle containing a colourless liquid. 'The medicine in this bottle will not bring the dead back to the world of the living, but it will do everything else. Use it sparingly, because you will never be able to replace it. Use it on any wound or any pain and the discomfort will disappear faster than you have made my darkness go.'

Aengus thanked the old man, put the bottle in his bundle and started again to follow the ball. 'It seems even darker, now,' Aengus thought as they followed the rolling sphere. 'Maybe we should have kept one of those hairs for ourselves!' But the ball continued to move, and, in time, they could see more clearly. It was never as bright as above the water, but they could distinguish fish and fronds and rocks.

Suddenly, Capaillín struck him across the face with her tail. He was so shocked that he opened his mouth to complain, and it was instantly filled with water. Capaillín was standing rigid, her ears pointing upright. Aengus peered hard and saw something that he would never forget. The ball was rolling past a sea snake that looked as if it could swallow himself and Capaillín whole and probably still not be full.

There was no way to avoid the monster if they wanted to stay with the ball. Aengus remembered the wicker basket. He picked it up and walked as close as he dared to the serpent. Just as her vast jaws opened to crush him, he opened the basket and hurled as much food into her mouth as he could. Again and again he tipped the basket into her gaping maw and she swallowed all that he threw at her in single gulps. Finally, the serpent swept her tongue across her mouth, and sank to the floor of the lake, her body swollen and distorted with the amount of food she had consumed.

Aengus and Capaillín went past the serpent so quickly that they had to wait for the ball to catch up with them. Then, quite suddenly, the water seemed to glow gold, and soon they found their heads in fresh air and their feet on the banks on the far side of the lake.

They were so pleased to reach the surface that, for a while, they simply revelled in the pleasure of breathing air and feeling the sun on their skins.

There were still a few hours of daylight left, so they, and the ball, decided to go on.

They stopped when it became so dark that they could hardly see their guide. Ahead of them loomed a large, conical mountain.

'I'm glad we don't have to face that tonight,' Aengus told Capaillín, as they prepared for sleep. 'It looks almost as steep as Eaglach's mountain.'

'As steep but not as high, so we shouldn't have too many problems tomorrow. At any rate, it's in the open air!'

Aengus relaxed, happy in the knowledge that each step they took was a step nearer the garden, a step closer to Caillte. He filled his mind with thoughts of Caillte and of their life together until he eased into oblivion.

The rumble that woke him was too loud to be the impatient rolling of the ball. Aengus opened his eyes but could scarcely see. For a moment of panic, he thought he was reliving his nightmare, but no, Capaillín was with him. They were enveloped in clouds of thick smoke, the fumes catching in their throats and lungs.

Aengus succumbed to a fit of coughing.

'What is it, Capaillín?' he gasped. 'Is something on fire?'

'It's the mountain, Aengus. I think it's going to erupt. I heard some rumbling last night but thought it was distant thunder. Then, at first light, this poisonous smoke started to billow out of the mountain top. I don't think we're in immediate danger, but we'd better go back to the lakeshore. We'll be safer there.'

Aengus agreed. 'I'll pick up the ball and keep it with us until the mountain settles down.' He went to get the ball but it rolled in front of him, always just out of reach. 'I can't get it, Capaillín. It won't let us turn back.'

By this time, the ball had rolled a little way up the mountain path, and was heading further upwards.

'Maybe this is where you and I should part, Capaillín. I have to follow the ball, but you don't. I can't risk your life any more. I'll go on alone.'

'Don't talk nonsense, Aengus,' Capaillín scolded. 'I feel that the garden is close, and you may need me there. Remember what Eaglach told us of its perils. I won't leave you until you have the silver apples. My job will not be finished until then. Now, let's not waste any more time. The sooner we get over this mountain, the better.'

They followed the ball up the mountain. The smoke smelled of sulphur and it invaded every pore, hurting their eyes and throats and chests. Aengus took a cloth from his bundle and wrapped it around Capaillín's nose. Then he did the same for himself. They walked as fast as they could, keeping a watchful eye on the peak, where an occasional flame shot through the billowing smoke.

Suddenly, they were on a decline.

'We're going down, Capaillín,' Aengus exulted. 'We're going to be all right.'

Capaillín didn't have time to reply. There was huge roar and the entire mountain shook. It spewed fire and smoke and rock, not only from the peak but also from a fissure in its side, a little bit below them.

'Get on my back, Aengus,' Capaillín shouted above the din. 'Get on my back and we'll make a run for it.'

'We won't be able to see the ball,' said Aengus.

'Forget about the ball.'

Aengus didn't argue. His skin was scorching and his eyes felt as though someone had branded them with a red-hot poker. He leapt on Capaillín's back and she galloped off. He could feel her hooves slithering on the loose stones as they moved closer and closer to the gaping hole in the side of the mountain. The eruption was not continuous. It came in spurts as if the mountain was clearing its throat several times before launching into full song.

'We're going to be all right,' he kept thinking, as they skidded along the path. They were just under the fissure when the mountain shook again. Aengus bent low over Capaillín's neck, clinging to the pony as the gash in the mountain became an open mouth, vomiting burning rocks and steaming gases onto them. A glowing rock hit Aengus's back, burning through his clothes and flesh. He wanted to throw himself on the ground, writhing, but Capaillín was shouting.

'Hold tight. Hold tight. We're nearly out of it.'

Rock after burning rock rained on Aengus. He was no longer conscious of breathing or holding on. He was a single pain, shrieking for respite. The pain did not abate, but the smoke began to clear as Capaillín galloped towards a clearing.

'We're safe, Aengus,' she told him, as she stumbled to a stop. 'We're out of reach of the mountain. And look, Aengus, the ball is here with us.'

Aengus knew he should be glad that they had not lost the ball, but he was trembling uncontrollably and could think of nothing other than his charred flesh.

Capaillín was breathing in great ragged gulps, her sweat-soaked flanks heaving. She looked pityingly at Aengus. 'Don't forget the medicine the old man gave you, Aengus. But use it sparingly.'

Aengus fumbled with the bundle. His hands were so swollen that he could barely move the fingers. 'I can't open it, Capaillín. I can't bend my fingers.'

'Put one end in my mouth,' she advised, 'and we'll pull.'

They pulled, and the medicine fell to the ground. Aengus picked it up, opened it with his teeth and drank a little. His lips and tongue and throat felt liquid healing roll over them. He held the medicine bottle in his swollen left hand and poured a few drops on his right hand. The pain melted away and he looked in joy and amazement at a hand that had returned to its normal size and could open and close at will.

'It's working, Capaillín,' he told her, and then saw that the pony was lying on the ground, twitching.

'Capaillín,' he cried, 'I didn't think. I'm sorry.'

He grabbed a tunic that had fallen from the bundle and tore it. He soaked it in the medicine and started to rub Capaillín's legs and hooves. They were so blackened by the fire that Aengus didn't know whether he was rubbing skin or bone.

'Don't waste it all on me, Aengus,' Capaillín told him, but Aengus found that he was healing his own hands and arms as he rubbed the medicine on Capaillín.

When she was treated, Aengus gave her the cloth in her mouth.

'Can you rub my back, Capaillín?' he asked. 'It's still scorched.'

Capaillín gently healed his back, moving from the neck downwards. Soon they were both well again, singed but with no wounds and in no pain.

'Is there any medicine left, Aengus?' she asked.

'No, Capaillín, it's all gone. If I had saved any of it, we would be too hurt to continue.'

For a while, they sat in companionable silence, resting and revelling in the absence of pain.

'I think we should move,' Capaillín advised. 'The volcano is still rumbling and we're too close to it for comfort. Let's follow the ball again for a short while.'

Almost as if it could hear what she said, the ball began to roll slowly ahead of them. They walked together behind it, taking pleasure in things they had taken for granted before, things like steady ground and unscorched bodies. They were just about to stop for the day when Aengus looked up and saw in the distance a high, circular, stone wall. Even from far away and in the fading light, it was possible to see the trees that grew within the walls.

'It's the garden. It must be,' he exulted.

'I believe it is, Aengus,' agreed Capaillín. 'Our journey is almost over. Tomorrow we will reach our goal.'

36: Lost and Found

For once, Aengus was awake before Capaillín. He sat and stared at the spot where the garden was just beginning to emerge in the dawning light.

Capaillín stirred. 'You're up early,' she commented.

'I know,' Aengus answered. 'I was too excited to sleep on. I was afraid that, somehow, we'd find another obstacle in our way, but it seems that the dream we have followed for so long is finally within our grasp.'

While they could see it more and more clearly, as they journeyed they realised that the garden was further away than they had first imagined. By noon, however, they were sitting on a little hill overlooking the garden where the silver apples grew. They sat in silence for a while, looking at the garden and watching the apples sparkling in the sunlight.

'We've made it, Capaillín,' Aengus told her. 'All we have to do now is get into the garden, pick some silver apples, and make all our wishes come true!'

'It may not be as easy as you think, Aengus,' Capaillín cautioned. 'Remember Eaglach's warning. Many people have looked for this garden and some people have actually found it and seen the apples, but no one has ever been able to pick the apples and take them away.'

Nothing she could say could dampen his spirits. He was already planning what to do with the many apples he would take from the garden.

'First, of course, we'll use one apple to find Caillte. Then we'll arrange a party. We'll see Gáire again and Diuran and even Maeldun, and we'll invite Luch and Racaire and Maedhbhín and Girseach, of course.'

He broke off, because Capaillín was looking at him with her big, sad brown eyes. 'Oh, Capaillín,' he apologised. 'Here am I going on about what I'll do and I haven't asked you what you want to do with your wishes. You will share the apples. That's only right. What will you wish for, Capaillín?'

'Let's get the apples before we decide what to wish for,' Capaillín advised. 'I don't think it's going to be that easy.'

They walked down the hill towards the wall, still following the rolling ball. When they were close to the wall, Aengus joked. 'I don't know why the ball is still rolling. We don't need it any more. We can see where the garden is.'

Before the ball had reached the wall, it suddenly disappeared, almost as if it had been sucked into the ground.

'Did you see that, Capaillín? What happened?'

'There's a quagmire around the wall, Aengus. Get a stick and some stones and we'll find out how wide it is and how dangerous.'

Slowly, they walked around the wall, testing the ground near it. The swamp was cunningly concealed. It looked so much like the rest of the ground that they would never have seen it, if it hadn't been for the ball. They tested the earth as they walked round and round, finding more and more areas of treacherous ground. By evening time they knew just how difficult it would be to get into the garden.

'It's impossible, Capaillín, utterly impossible,' Aengus said despairingly. 'We've come all this way and found the garden, but it's impenetrable. The walls are absolutely sheer. There isn't one foothold in the entire structure and it's twice the height of a man, so there's no way of jumping on to it or over it. And, as if that wasn't bad enough, there's this deep quagmire round the wall. If I stand on it, I'll be sucked in. It's just hopeless.'

He slumped to the ground, his head in his hands.

Capaillín had never seen him so dejected.

'There's a solution to every problem, Aengus,' she said. 'We just haven't thought of it yet. You could fly in. After all, you still haven't used the gift the hawk gave you.'

Aengus lifted his head. 'You're right. I *could* fly in, but how would I get out? The hawk only gave me the power to fly once. The wall is just as high on the other side and there may be a quagmire there, too.'

For a while, they sat in silence. Aengus was too depressed to speak. It seemed to him that they had done so much and yet they were to be thwarted at the last moment.

Capaillín was putting her silence to better use. She was thinking, and suddenly she lifted her head, her ears pinned back.

'I have an idea,' she announced. I've considered every possibility and we have only one chance. We'll wait until noon tomorrow, when the heat of the sun is full on the earth and the quagmire will be at its firmest. You will stand on my back while I gallop around the walls outside the quagmire. When I've gained enough speed, I'll leap into the air as close to the wall as I can.

You'll have to leap even higher to get to the top of the wall.'

'But you'll sink in the quagmire if we do that.'

'I've thought about that too, Aengus. I was sent to help you. If I don't help you this last time and you fail, I will have failed too. Let me do this for you.'

'No,' insisted Aengus. 'No. I'm not going to sacrifice you. There must be some other way.'

'Think of one then, Aengus,' Capaillín advised. 'You have all night to put your mind to it.'

When Aengus lay down his mind was set. He would explore every recess of his brain, channel every reserve of intellect into finding a plan that would achieve his aim without endangering Capaillín. He reviewed their past adventures for clues; he listed all the gifts and powers he had been given for any that he might not yet have used. He thought of bridging the quagmire, of vaulting the wall, but for every possibility there was an insurmountable obstacle. Finally, his mind exhausted, he fell into a deep sleep.

In the morning he went to Capaillín and confessed: 'I can think of no plan that has any hope of success. I am ready to give up.'

'No. You can't give up, Aengus,' Capaillín told him. 'If you do, you'll never find Caillte, never, not in this life or in any other.'

'I know that, but I can't let you give your life for me.'

'It's my life and my decision, Aengus. We would have been parting anyway. This way, we part a little earlier, but you will have a chance to get into the garden and realise your dreams.'

'Even if I go along with your plan, I'd never be able to stand on your back.'

'We have a few hours to practise, Aengus. Why don't we

practise anyway, and if you decide not to use my idea after all, then we'll just have used up some time that was of little value.'

There was nothing else to do, so Aengus agreed. He stood on the pony's back while Capaillín walked slowly. But as soon as she began to trot, he fell off.

'Place your feet as wide apart as you can, Aengus,' Capaillín instructed. 'That way you will have more balance. Stand near my rump where I'm broadest.'

Hour after hour they practised and, although Aengus no longer fell off, not even when she galloped, he still could not bring himself to go through with Capaillín's plan.

'I can't let you do it,' he told her. 'I just can't.'

'All right, Aengus,' Capaillín agreed. 'Let's just try it one more time. You're getting very good at it.'

Aengus's pride was wounded. 'I'm *better* than very good. All right, one last time and then we go home.'

Aengus got on Capaillín's back, putting his feet as wide apart as he could, and digging his toes into her shaggy coat.

'Are you ready, Aengus?'

'Ready.'

Capaillín moved very gently at first until Aengus felt secure, then she increased her speed and headed straight for the wall.

'Jump, Aengus,' she shouted, as she leapt through the air, and Aengus found his hands clinging to the top of the garden wall.

His muscles ached and his arms felt as though they were being wrenched from their sockets, but he held on and eventually swung himself on to the top of the wall.

'I've made it, Capaillín,' he shouted, but there was no Capaillín, only a sucking sound from the quagmire below.

Aengus sat on the wall, barely able to understand what had

happened. He could see the trees, all of them bearing the silver apples and the promise of his destiny fulfilled, and yet he could only think of Capaillín. What should I do, Capaillín? he wondered, and immediately knew what Capaillín would have said.

'Get on with the job, Aengus. There's nothing else to do!'

Aengus looked down. There was no way of telling whether or not there was a quagmire on the garden side of the wall. He would simply have to drop down and hope.

He lowered himself until he was hanging from the wall by his fingers, then let himself fall. The ground was soft, but not too soft. It certainly wasn't a deadly swamp. He walked quietly up and down under the apple trees. He could see no snakes, no man-eating insects, nothing to harm him in any way. There was only the rich smell of ripening apples and the unearthly glow of the silvered orchard as it shone in the midday sun.

He climbed the tree nearest the wall and selected a branch laden with seven large silver apples. 'These should be enough,' he mused, and decided to use the hawk's gift to get over the wall.

Aengus turned his thoughts to the hawk and felt himself change. His body shrank and his arms stretched and feathered into powerful wings, eager to fly. Aengus wrapped his talons around the branch and tried to take to the air, but it was too heavy for him. He took one apple off, then two, but he still couldn't get airborne. Even with five apples removed, the branch was too heavy. He picked up one apple in his claws. Yes, he could fly with that. He soared over the wall, skimmed past the dreaded quagmire and came to rest on the hill where he and Capaillín had sat to discuss getting into the garden. As soon as his talons touched the earth he returned to his own shape.

Aengus sat for hours with the silver apple in his hand, the prize for which he had struggled and sacrificed. He had only one apple, instead of the many he had hoped for, so he would have to abandon his hopes of travelling with Maeldun or searching the hollow lands with Luch. He would have liked to spend some time in the school for poets. He had only one wish and his wish would be for Caillte.

'Caillte,' he whispered, 'Caillte. I've followed you over land and sea. I've risked my life for you. I've been willing to give up my powers and win you as a man. You're so close that I can almost touch you. One wish and you are mine forever. Oh Caillte, Caillte, so close and so impossible. I cannot use my wish for you, Caillte.'

Aengus stood up, cleared his throat and said:

'My one and only silver apple, my one and only wish is that Capaillín should not be dead. Give life back to Capaillín.'

For a moment, the apple glowed in his hand, then gradually evaporated. The air in front of Aengus thickened and slowly formed into the well-loved shape of a thirteen-hand pony – not a horse, but a pony. The coat was still as shaggy as Aengus remembered and the eyes just as deep and trusting. The form shimmered, shining, shifting, then transforming. Aengus watched in amazement as the outlines of the pony blurred and another shape emerged. There stood Caillte, as beautiful as he remembered, still barefoot, still with apple blossom in her hair.

'Follow me, Aengus,' the beloved voice invited, and Caillte held out her hand. Aengus clasped it in his own and followed.